UNDER THE AFRICAN SUN

Whilst on her Gap year, Patsy Whittaker travels to Cape Town to visit her elderly great-aunt Grace. After a break-in at the shop Grace runs, Patsy convinces her mother Maureen to finally return to South Africa to help out. Whilst there, both mother and daughter find reasons to stay on longer than intended — but Daniel Clayton needs to convince Maureen she really is the one for him, and Patsy suspects that her new man isn't all he seems to be . . .

GINNY SWART

UNDER THE AFRICAN SUN

Complete and Unabridged

LINFORD
Leicester

First published in Great Britain in 2008

First Linford Edition
published 2009

British Library CIP Data

Swart, Ginny.
  Under the African sun - -
  (Linford romance library)
  1. Gap years- -South Africa- -Cape Town
  - -Fiction. 2. Romantic suspense novels.
  3. Large type books.
  I. Title II. Series
  823.9'2–dc22

  ISBN 978–1–84782–834–7

Published by
F. A. Thorpe (Publishing)
Anstey, Leicestershire

Set by Words & Graphics Ltd.
Anstey, Leicestershire
Printed and bound in Great Britain by
T. J. International Ltd., Padstow, Cornwall

This book is printed on acid-free paper

1

A Certain Charm

Hi, Mum and Jack, I've reached Cape Town!

I know I told you I was going to fly from Kuala Lumpur straight to Johannesburg, but then I found it was cheaper to fly here and take a coach in a couple of weeks. That way, I get to see more of South Africa before flying home from Johannesburg in about a month.

I've been to so many places and done so much in the past nine months that I'm glad I've been keeping a diary every night. When I get back I will bore you both with all my adventures in great detail!

I arrived in Cape Town two days ago and I'm staying at a backpackers' lodge near the centre of the city. It's very clean and has a good laundry — something I've stopped taking for granted after that little stay in Hong Kong!

I'm starting to run out of money so hopefully I'll be able to get some work as a waitress, which would help stretch my last remaining cash. I've heard the tips are good.

Just wandering around this city is lovely. Lots of coffee shops and little eateries, and, of course, Table Mountain looks down on everything. Wherever you go in this city, this enormous flat mountain forms a backdrop. You can travel to the top in a cable car, but people who are really fit walk up it quite easily in a couple of hours. At the moment it is covered in thick white cloud. The locals call it the tablecloth, but the cloud means it's blowing a gale.

If the wind carries on tomorrow, I'll probably go and visit Auntie Grace. I'm really looking forward to meeting your one and only living *relative, Mum! Simonstown is the last stop on the railway line. I will give her a call tonight.*

Lots of love,

Patsy.

P.S. Jack, how's school going? Your exams must be coming up pretty soon. Do you have any plans yet about what to do when you leave?

Maureen Henderson smiled and pressed the print button to make a copy of Patsy's e-mail for her son Jack to read when he came home from school. To think that Patsy was actually in Cape Town! For the first time in years Maureen felt tears of homesickness prick her eyelids.

After twenty years away, she should have got over the longing for her old home. This was home now, two up, two down in Meeker Street, Whitham, with a tiny patch of grass in front and a bird-feeder for the sparrows at the back. Not the rambling old Victorian house on the mountain, set in a huge

3

stretch of lawn under the oak tree with the stately sacred ibis strolling around, pulling out earthworms.

She sat down and read Patsy's e-mail again from the beginning. All those exclamation marks — they were almost a signature of her globe-trotting daughter. Patsy was so full of life and fun, and her ready smile and cheerful personality made people smile when they were with her.

Maureen missed her daughter dreadfully and couldn't wait for the final month of Patsy's trip to pass. She'd painted her old room and made new curtains to welcome her home.

At first, when Warren had given Patsy a round-the-world ticket as a reward for her excellent GCSE results, Maureen had been furious with her ex-husband.

'How could you do this without consulting me? She's too young, too inexperienced. That's typical of you, Warren, to be so irresponsible and give her a completely unsuitable gift!'

'Not at all,' Warren had said. 'Our Patsy's the most sensible, level-headed girl I know. They didn't make her head girl at school for nothing, you know! And those months as an exchange student in France did her the world of good, too. I reckon she can handle anything that comes her way.'

'I still think she should do the two years' catering management course as she planned, and then travel,' Maureen had said stubbornly. 'She'd be nearly twenty-one then, and she'd get far more out of the trip.'

'But she'll probably want to start work as soon as she's trained,' Warren had argued. 'That college pamphlet she brought back said most of their students were offered good jobs the minute they graduated.'

'Well, that's a good thing, isn't it? She'll be fortunate,' Maureen had replied.

Warren had shaken his head.

'But then she'll go off to some hotel and never get her nose out of the kitchen for the next few years. No, I think this travelling experience during a gap year will be excellent for her,' he'd said firmly.

'I totally agree!' Patsy had burst into the kitchen and kissed her father on the cheek. 'Dad, ever since you gave me this ticket I've been finding ways of travelling on the cheap. There are loads of jobs I can do just about everywhere. My first stop will be Italy! Some of the girls I know are going grape-picking in Tuscany and they've invited me to go along. We're all going to sleep in a caravan.'

'But you can't speak Italian!' Maureen protested.

'It's only for a week or two,' Patsy had said patiently. 'And, after that, I can earn money with casual jobs wherever I go. I'll be fine, you'll see.'

And, of course, she had been.

Everywhere she went, she had met someone who recommended the next exciting place to visit. After three weeks in the Italian vineyards, she'd worked as a tractor driver on a collective farm in Israel.

* * *

After that, she'd flown to Australia and worked as a char before travelling to Hong Kong where she had taught English to five-year-old Chinese children. Then she'd spent two weeks in Malaysia before reaching South Africa. Right through all her travels she'd kept up an entertaining flow of bubbly e-mails to her mother and Jack.

Jack. Maureen sighed as she thought of her son. Were all teenage boys so difficult?

Maureen worried about him constantly. He was so like his father. She and Warren had separated six years previously because, although he was a lovely man, he simply hadn't been able to handle the responsibilities of being a husband or a parent.

Like Warren, Jack was tall and good-looking, full of jokes and able to charm everyone he met, especially girls. But he seemed to have absolutely no thought for his future beyond what he and his mates would do at the weekend.

Also like Warren, Jack had wild enthusiasms for various projects which he would drop if things got difficult, or if he found some new interest. These days the only thing he seemed interested in was those wretched computer games, and Warren was no help. He bought all the new ones for his son, telling him to have fun.

With his exams just three months away and Jack looking for any excuse not to open his schoolbooks, Maureen seethed when she thought about the pile of disks next to the computer. Sometimes she wished they didn't have one — but then, how would she keep in touch with Patsy?

'Hi, Mum.' Jack barged in noisily, flung his satchel on a chair and planted a smacking kiss on her cheek before diving for the fridge. 'I'm starving. Do you have any plans for this leftover potato salad? I gotta hurry, Andy's coming round and we're going over to Duggie's . . . '

He left the room, spooning up potato salad from the bowl as he went.

Maureen's heart sank when she heard Duggie's name. The first time she'd met him she'd known he was trouble, and she didn't like the idea of Jack becoming friends with him and the rest of his gang.

She heard her son crashing around in his room and followed him up the stairs.

'Jack, wait,' she said. 'Before you go off to Duggie's, I think you need to sit down and do some homework. Didn't you tell me you had a science project to finish? And I promised Miss Hodgson that I'd make sure that you did an hour of maths every evening. So you can't go out this afternoon.'

'Mum! Don't be like that!' Jack turned on his easy charm. 'I'm nearly done with that science thing. It's only four o'clock, I've loads of time to do maths. I've been working the whole day as it is. You wouldn't want your little lad to have brain fatigue, would you?' He put his arm around her and grinned cajolingly.

'Never mind your blarney,' Maureen said firmly. 'Phone Andy and tell him you've too much work to do and you're staying in. For a change,' she added pointedly.

'I can't phone him, Mum, he's lost his mobile. And he's probably on his way by now.'

As if to confirm this, the doorbell rang loudly.

Jack smiled.

'See? He's here already. I can't chase him away, can I? I promise, Mum, I won't stay at Duggie's longer than half an hour.'

'Back by five, then?' Maureen asked in resignation.

'Sure thing.' He scooped up some computer disks and thundered down the stairs and out of the front door.

'There's an e-mail from Patsy,' she

called after him.

'I'll read it later. 'Bye, Mum.'

She knew he wouldn't be back before dark. And then they'd have another argument about his schoolwork. It was hopeless to ask Warren to have a word with him, because Jack didn't listen to either of them.

★   ★   ★

On the phone, Great-aunt Grace had sounded as excited as a child.

'Mo's girl! I can't believe it!' she'd said. 'Your mother told me you were off seeing the world and I did so hope you'd call at Cape Town at some point. I can't wait to meet you!'

Mo? Patsy couldn't recall anyone ever calling her mum that before.

'And you're coming to see me tomorrow? Wonderful! Let me tell you how to get here . . . '

Her directions sounded easy enough; catch the train to Simonstown, turn left outside the station and walk along the main road until you come to a shop called Whittaker's.

Her great-aunt was Grace Whittaker. Patsy remembered her mother's maiden name had been Whittaker, and she'd mentioned that her aunt had run a shop while she was growing up, but surely Grace wasn't still behind the counter at her age?

She wished she'd listened more closely when her mother had read aloud the letters from her aunt, written in a spidery, elegant hand.

At Last

The next afternoon Patsy sat by the train window, unable to take her eyes from the gorgeous view of the sea only twenty yards away. The carriage was old and the leather seats were patched, but she was travelling alongside the sparkling blue water of the Indian Ocean, with just an edging of rocks between the railway line and the pounding waves. Every now and then an explosion of white foam would burst up and almost wet the carriages.

On the other side, mountains reared up behind a line of solid family homes. As they passed, she was struck by the very English names on the polished brass plates and decided that *Dun Roamin, St Mawr* and *Pengelly* must have belonged to people who were very homesick.

The man on the seat opposite lowered his newspaper and grinned at Patsy.

'Are you visiting from England?' he asked her politely.

'Yes,' Patsy replied. 'Oh, dear! Is it that obvious?'

After Australia she was beautifully tanned and brown, but he pointed in amusement to her Manchester United T-shirt.

'Visitors can't stop looking at the view,' he explained. 'You can always tell us locals — we're all reading!'

So they were. How could anyone not

look at the wide curve of the bay?

They rattled past the white sands of a beach dotted with children playing.

'Fish Hoek,' her companion said. 'It's the best beach for swimming in the Peninsula, in my opinion. There's hardly any waves and the water's usually warm. It means Fish Corner, but people come to watch the whales these days. You'll see plenty of whales in September and October. They come into the bay to have their calves.'

What a pity I won't still be here then, Patsy thought. I'd love to see a whale. Then she suddenly remembered her mother telling her that she'd gone to school in Fish Hoek, biking every day along the sea road from Simonstown. They must be getting quite close!

With a hiss of brakes the train drew to a stop and Patsy stepped out, suddenly excited at the thought of meeting her unknown great-aunt. Once she was out of the station, she turned left as directed, and walked past a handsome white house with gates that read *Admiralty House,* and then the high stone walls of what appeared to be naval dockyards running right down one side of the street.

Opposite, a long line of charming double-storey buildings and hotels, some with verandas, straggled along the busy road.

She spotted Whittaker's General Dealers right away, sandwiched between two smartly painted buildings.

From the outside, the shop appeared badly in need of maintenance. The name above the door was faded and chipped, and the windows on either side displayed garden tools and dusty plastic bowls that looked as though they had been there for years. Above the glass windows, a veranda decorated with wrought-iron work sagged down alarmingly.

She crossed the road, hesitated, then pushed open the door and entered the gloomy shop.

A bell tinkled and a figure in an apron appeared from behind a curtain near the long wooden counter.

'Great-aunt Grace?' Patsy asked uncertainly.

'Patsy! Welcome, my dear, welcome. How very nice to meet you at last.'

She flew out from behind the counter and embraced Patsy in a warm, all-enveloping hug.

'And I think you'd better call me Auntie Grace. My full title makes me feel far too old and doddery!'

Unmistakable

Grace Whittaker was not at all what Patsy had expected. She was short and plump, with her grey hair piled high into a small, wispy bun on the back of her head. Her face was brown and wrinkled from years under the African sun, and she had intelligent, twinkling blue eyes. She radiated energy and enthusiasm and wasn't at all like the frail, elderly woman that Patsy had imagined.

Patsy couldn't help staring. Apart from her grey hair, Aunt Grace looked exactly how she imagined her own mother would look when she was seventy. Maureen was younger and slimmer, of course, but the family likeness was unmistakable.

Before she could speak, her great-aunt spoke happily.

'You're the picture of your mother at the same age. But I expect plenty of people have told you that.'

'Nobody ever has.' Patsy smiled. 'Mum doesn't have any pictures of herself when she was younger. But I'm pleased to hear it, anyway.'

Grace returned her smile.

'She was a lovely girl, like you, but not as tall, and her hair was darker than yours. Now, how about a nice cup of tea? You do drink tea, don't you? I remember your mother was a regular teapot!'

'Yes, thanks, I'd love some.'

Patsy wasn't sure if Aunt Grace intended to make tea at the back of the shop, or if they would go to a café somewhere close by, but her great-aunt grinned conspiratorially.

'In that case, let's shut up shop and go home, shall we? I don't get to meet my one and only great-niece every day. I'll just fetch my bag, and my keys.'

While her aunt disappeared behind the curtain, Patsy took a good look around.

The shop was an Aladdin's cave of everything under the sun, and there was a smell of spices, leather and exotic fruit. A haphazard assortment of sweets, glossy magazines, porridge oats, tins of paint, nail varnish, cooking oil and shoelaces filled the shelves.

Cartons of bananas, mangoes and pineapples and a rack filled with brilliant Indian saris jostled for space on the floor next to a bright red tricycle and some builders' wheelbarrows and spades. Netting sacks of onions and brown bags of potatoes were piled higgledy-piggledy next to the door with enormous white pumpkins piled in a heap.

'We Keep Everything!'

Hanging from the ceiling on thick wire hooks were big oval tin baths, metal buckets, coils of rope and pairs of heavy brown boots. Bright orange sou'westers and wellington boots were piled in a corner and cartons with strange metal fittings stood open on the counter. Closer inspection revealed them to be stainless steel yacht fittings, next to what looked like a pile of dried kindling. Patsy was examining these when her aunt returned, beaming.

'Whittaker's General Dealers — we keep everything!' she announced. 'That used to be my mother's motto. She always used to tell our customers that if we haven't got it, we can get it! We had an excellent reputation.'

'That's wonderful,' Patsy murmured, privately wondering how anyone found anything in the jumble. 'What's this, Auntie Grace? Firewood?' She gestured towards the counter.

'Good heavens, no, that's *biltong*!'

Her aunt took a small pocket knife from her bag and sliced off a small piece. 'Dried beef. It's delicious, try some.'

Patsy took it gingerly and chewed. It tasted salty and rather nice.

'One of my best lines. People can't resist *biltong*, especially sailors,' Grace said. 'Oh, bother, there's the phone. I won't be a minute.'

Family History

Patsy waited and couldn't help overhearing her aunt's end of the conversation.

'Yes? No, I'm not . . . indeed . . . well, your opinion of progress and mine are two very different things, I'm afraid . . . ' There was a long pause. 'I have absolutely no intention of changing my mind, so please stop pestering me, Mr Hugo!'

She slammed down the phone and turned to Patsy, her voice shaking slightly.

'That young man had the nerve to tell me I can't stand in the way of progress! Well, Richard Hugo doesn't know what he's dealing with! Come on, my dear, let's go home and have that tea.'

Patsy leaned back on the old cane chair and gazed out at the spectacular view of the bay. The shoreline seemed to curve for miles in either direction, edged by massive blue mountains that ran down to the sea. Far out she could just see a small dark island on the horizon, and skimming across the water closer in, a line of white sails.

It was strange to think that this had been her mother's home for the first eighteen years of her life, and it made her realise just how little she knew about her mother's childhood.

'Beautiful, isn't it?' Aunt Grace said with satisfaction, bringing out a small tray with tea things. 'I never get tired of looking at the sea. It's Wednesday, so it's the yacht club regatta and we'll have a good view of the finish line from here.'

The house was high on the hill, a stiff walk up from the shop, which Aunt

Grace took in her stride. An enormous, rambling Victorian, the house had stained-glass panels set in the front door and deep sash windows. A wide *stoep* ran around three sides, shaded by a tangle of jasmine and wisteria, which scented the air and was alive with the buzzing of bees. In the garden below an old swing moved gently in the breeze.

'It's odd to think my mum looked at this same view when she was a child,' Patsy said dreamily. 'Was that her swing? I wish she'd told me more about living here. It must have been a wonderful place to grow up, right on the sea like this.'

'It was indeed,' Aunt Grace said. 'This old house used to be full of life. Full of her school friends laughing and playing the piano . . . we had a lot of fun.' She paused, remembering. 'This house has been our family home ever since my father's day. That would be your great-great-grandfather. He bought it in 1940, just before he went off to war. I was four then and my little brother,

Ron, was born here.'

'Ron was my grandfather, wasn't he? My mum's father? So you've lived sixty-seven years in the same house? That's amazing.'

Patsy thought of the narrow little terraced house that was her home in Whitham, and wondered how her mother had adjusted to such a different life from the one she'd known here.

'Ron never knew our father. He was born while he was at sea and he never came back. His ship went down with all hands somewhere off Jutland.'

Aunt Grace gave a deep sigh before continuing.

'Things changed for us after that. My mother used my father's insurance to buy the shop and open Whittaker's. Although she knew nothing about running a shop, it was the only way she could provide for me and Ron. And then when she died, I took over and kept it going.'

'How old were you then, Aunt Grace?'

'Twenty. And your grandfather was

only fourteen. He was still at school, of course, but he helped behind the counter every afternoon and at the weekends.'

Patsy did a quick sum. Her great-aunt had been working in the shop for more than fifty years.

'Mum never told me,' she said slowly. 'She just said that you ran a shop and she used to help out sometimes. I know that my grandparents died when Mum was very young.'

Aunt Grace nodded, smiling sadly.

'They were very young themselves,' she told her. 'My brother and his wife, Jean, were only thirty and your poor mother just seven. It was a real tragedy — the brakes on their car failed. It was just a blessing that little Mo was with me, on the beach.'

'You raised my mum, didn't you, Aunt Grace?'

'Yes, I did. With Rugaya's help, of course.'

Patsy frowned.

'Rugaya?' she asked.

'Rugaya Daniels. She was our Muslim maid, a wonderful woman and a pillar of strength,' Grace explained. 'I don't know how we would have managed without our dear Rugaya. She loved your mother like one of her own.'

'Does she still work for you, then?' Patsy was curious.

Aunt Grace smiled.

'Goodness me, no. Rugaya must be nearly seventy. She retired a long time ago. These days I have a char who comes in once a week and does a quick whisk around. That's quite enough for me.'

Patsy smiled. Clearly other people could retire at seventy, but her great-aunt obviously had no intention of doing that herself!

'So, dear, you said you're staying at a backpackers' hostel in town?' Aunt Grace asked hesitantly. 'What would you say if I asked you to stay here with me for a week or two? You can do all the sightseeing you need from here just as easily, and I'd be delighted to have your company.'

'Really? I'd say it was a wonderful

idea!' Patsy exclaimed. 'That's if you're sure I won't be a nuisance?'

'I can't think of anything I'd like more,' her aunt said. 'Let me show you the rest of the house. You can sleep in your mother's old room. It's exactly as she left it when she went off to England. She only took what she could fit into her rucksack, and left everything else behind. She was so sure she would only be gone for six months.'

Patsy followed her aunt into the dim interior of the house. She felt as if she was stepping back into the unread pages of her mother's life.

Guilt

Maureen was turning out a cupboard when she came across an old photograph of herself and Aunt Grace standing in front of Whittaker's. She remembered one of the British sailors from a boat in the harbour taking the shot, then bringing it into the shop a few days later.

I must have been about ten, she thought, smiling at her long dark plaits and remembering the fights she'd had with Rugaya, who'd insisted she brushed a hundred times before she plaited her hair every morning.

'Stand still, Miss Mo! There are still some knots here. I don't know what you do — is this toffee in your hair? I think your auntie must have your hair cut and make my life easier.'

Rugaya in her crisp white apron and her solid, no-nonsense approach had been a part of Maureen's life as long as she could remember. Poor Rugaya, such a stickler for cleanliness and doing things just right. I must have given her a terrible time, she thought. And Aunt Grace looks so young and pretty here. I wonder why she never married? She must have had plenty of offers. She must have been too busy in the shop, I suppose.

For the first time the thought struck

her — it must have been because of me. Auntie Grace was too busy looking after her brother's child to think of having a life of her own.

How could I have been so self-centred and thoughtless, Maureen wondered in shock. I took Aunt Grace for granted, knowing she'd always be there for me. I don't think I ever said thank you to her in all the time I lived with her!

Maureen felt a huge wave of remorse. For the past twenty years she'd been so taken up with her own life and problems that she'd not given Aunt Grace much thought.

Of course, in the beginning, she'd written often with news of her travels and the fun she was having in England. But slowly this had dwindled to letters at birthdays and Christmas, briefly keeping her up-to-date with family news. She'd never discussed her worries about Jack, though, and six years before, she'd only mentioned her divorce from Warren very casually. Aunt Grace had always made it quite clear that she thought Maureen had married him too soon after meeting him.

'I'm sure he's a very nice young man, my dear, but you're still very young,' she had told her. 'Why not take some time to get to know him better? Three months really isn't long enough to get to know someone properly. You know what they say: 'Marry in haste and repent at leisure'.'

Maureen, nineteen and madly in love with the most handsome man she'd ever met, didn't care a hoot what 'they' said. She replied by sending Aunt Grace a postcard from the Isle of Man, where she and Warren went for their three-day honeymoon.

That had been the last holiday they'd ever had together.

Well, there's no sense in brooding over history, she thought briskly. I'll write to Aunt Grace tonight, something I should have done weeks ago. A nice, long, chatty letter.

She heard Jack coming home so she quickly finished tidying her drawers and went downstairs to make his tea.

'Hi, Mum.'

He was standing with the fridge door open, drinking milk straight from the bottle.

'Jack! How many times have I told you to use a glass?'

Irritated, she offered him one, but he wiped his mouth and shook his head.

'Sorry. I was just a bit thirsty — I'm going to the café with Duggie and the guys, anyway,' he told her.

Maureen frowned.

'Duggie? How can you think of going out, when you've got exams so close?'

'Don't nag, Mum. Exams are weeks away.' Jack's face closed mutinously. 'You never used to carry on like this with Patsy.'

'I didn't need to. Your sister always made sure she did all her schoolwork before she did anything else!'

'Oh, Patsy's always been perfect, hasn't she?' Jack snapped.

He slammed the door as he left the room.

A minute later she heard the throaty roar of a motorbike idling outside and Jack shouting something from his window upstairs.

'Coming! Hang on a minute!'

Duggie and his awful motorbike. When Jack reached the bottom of the stairs, she stepped in front of him.

'No, Jack,' she said, 'you simply can't go off with Duggie like this. That bike's dangerous, I've seen how he roars through town. And, anyway, you have too much homework to go anywhere right now.'

'Mum! Get off my case! I haven't any homework, I finished it all at school,' he insisted, but Maureen knew better.

'I seriously doubt that, but if that's the case you can spend some time revising your maths instead.'

'No way!' Jack pushed past her roughly, making her step back and lose her balance, forcing her to clutch the umbrella stand for support.

'Sorry, Mum,' Jack mumbled. 'I gotta go. Duggie's waiting.' He fled down the path. By the time Maureen regained her balance and looked out, the bike was gone in a cloud of noxious blue smoke.

Where have I gone wrong with that boy, she thought miserably. Or rather, where have *we* gone wrong. Even if we're divorced, Warren's just as much to blame as I am.

★   ★   ★

That evening Jack came back earlier than she expected and he seemed strangely subdued.

'Sorry, Mum,' he whispered, hugging her. 'I didn't mean to push you.'

'Oh, Jack.' Maureen leaned against him and allowed herself to be hugged. She couldn't stay angry with her son for long. 'I worry about you. If only you'd apply yourself, just for the next month or two . . .'

'I will, I promise. Hey, what's this you have here?' He gestured towards the coffee table.

'An e-mail from Patsy. It came just

now and I've printed it off. Shall I read it out loud? I haven't had a chance to look at it myself yet.'

'Sure. Go ahead.' He settled his lanky frame across an armchair. Maureen was almost certain he hadn't read the last e-mail from his sister. Jack hated reading anything.

From: Patsy Henderson
To: MaureenH@atlantis.co.uk
Sent: March 21
Subject: In Simonstown
   Hi, Mum and Jack.
   I have loads to tell you! I've moved in with Aunt Grace and I'm actually staying in your old bedroom, Mum! It's so beautiful here, how could you ever leave? I just love this house. It must have been fabulous living here. It's so big, with those high ceilings and big chandeliers for lights.
   Aunt Grace seems to have three generations of furniture here, too — lovely antique wardrobes and a dining-room table that seats ten

people, with gorgeous carved chairs.
There's even a grandfather clock that
strikes the hour.

Maureen smiled as she remembered the clock with its deep sonorous chime and the round brass weights that ticked slowly back and forth.

'Rugaya used to polish those weights until they shone and she'd wind the clock every week on a Saturday night before she went back to her own family,' she said. 'I'd forgotten that clock.'

'Who's Rugaya?' Jack asked.

'She was our maid. No, she was more than a maid, more like a housekeeper, really. I loved her to bits.'

'Mum! You had a maid! Were you rich?' he asked with a surprised tone.

'Not at all,' she said. 'In fact, quite the opposite. But my aunt Grace needed someone to look after me while she worked.'

Patsy's e-mail continued:

I love walking through the house and imagining you living here. Did you know your old swing is still hanging from the gum tree? The whole place needs a lot of work, though. The kitchen sink and the bath are so old they could be collector's items! Everything needs painting and the windows don't open very easily and great chunks of plaster have fallen off at odd places. I don't think Aunt Grace can afford to do much about it, though — she doesn't even own a TV!

'Oh, dear,' Maureen said. 'I remember it as such a grand old place. It's at least a hundred and fifty years old. What a shame she can't keep it up.'

'No TV?' Jack exclaimed in horror. 'She's living in the dark ages.'

'I'm sure she still plays her records,' Maureen said, remembering the polished walnut cabinet with the built-in record player and the pile of long-playing records. 'Aunt Grace loved jazz.

We used to dance to Dizzie Gillespie. Do you know the piece 'Night In Tunisia'? I must find it for you.'

'Don't bother, Mum, it doesn't sound like my kind of stuff.'

Maureen grinned and continued reading.

But here's the best bit, Mum! Your room is exactly as you left it. All your books and records and clothes. Even your old school books and a whole lot of posters. I didn't know you were a Bob Marley fan! And you've got a Michael Jackson 'Thriller' poster dated 1982! I bet I could bring it home and you could sell it for a fortune to some Jackson collector. Shall I do that?

Jack sat up straight.

'Yes! Tell her to do that, Mum. I wouldn't mind it on my wall.'

'Dream on, lad,' Maureen said. 'I queued for hours to buy that poster and it cost me all my wages.'

'Wages?'

'I helped Aunt Grace in the shop after school in the afternoons and on Saturdays, so she paid me. Not much, but enough for pocket money, and I saved the rest for my air fare over here.'

Aunt Grace said I should go off every morning and do a bit of sightseeing, but I've actually been helping out in the shop.

I didn't know she still ran it and I'm sure nothing has changed since you were helping her, Mum. By the way she says you were very good at adding up change and the best assistant she has ever had!

A Friendly Lot

Maureen remembered the thrill of standing on the small wooden ladder behind the counter stacking the shelves for her aunt. Aunt Grace would be using an old metal scoop to fill packets of flour, oats and sugar from enormous hessian sacks, and it had been Maureen's job to write the contents and price on the packet in her best handwriting. She remembered how disappointed she'd been when Aunt Grace had switched to ready-packaged dry goods and her services were no longer needed on the ladder.

She has one of those old tills where you have to wind the handle to make the money drawer pop out, and she does all her adding up on bits of paper! She doesn't seem to have an assistant at all these days. If she wants to leave for any reason, she locks up and goes away for an hour or two.

The shop is very quiet; we have hardly any customers, except for the magazines and cigarettes. African labourers come in and buy pumpkins and big sacks of potatoes, and yesterday a builder came in and bought a wheelbarrow. There is such a crazy mixture of stuff here, you wouldn't believe it.

'Oh, yes, I would,' Maureen remarked, looking at Jack. 'A general dealer means just that. Something of everything. It sounds just as I remember it. When I was little I thought it was the most exciting place in the world and we were always busy. I can't believe trade has fallen off so much. Poor Aunt Grace.'

Some of the stock looks really old and dusty and I don't know how she makes ends meet. On Monday we only took about a hundred rand the whole day and then she gave five away to a beggar who walked in and said he was hungry. I think he knew she has a soft heart!

I'm having a great time, though. You always said South Africans were a friendly lot, and they certainly are. Last week a boy called Steve came in while I was serving behind the counter and we got chatting. He invited me for a drink at the Yacht Club. It turns out he's got a dinghy that he keeps at the club next to the

Navy base. I've been invited for a sail across to Seal Island on a 30-foot catamaran on Sunday — I can't wait!

I hope you won't mind too much, Mum, but I've changed my mind about coming home so soon. It's really great here and I'd like to stay longer.

Maureen's heart plummeted. She'd been counting the days until Patsy's return and had so looked forward to having her back. She missed their lively chats and the easy, uncomplicated friendship she enjoyed with her daughter. She had also hoped she'd be a good influence on Jack and his attitude to his schoolwork.

I suppose I can't blame her, she thought sadly. *She's having such a good time and it will be a very long time before she visits again. If ever.*

'The lucky thing,' Jack grumbled enviously. 'It's not fair. Patsy's having all the fun and meeting interesting people and I'm wasting my time in school. I'd give anything to go sailing. Maybe next year I could get a job crewing on an enormous yacht going to the West Indies or somewhere.'

'Once you've passed your exams you can think about things like that,' Maureen murmured, still reading. 'But your dad and I don't know anyone with a yacht, I'm afraid. And I'm sure most yacht owners would want you to have some sort of sailing experience before they'd take you on. Oh, dear, listen to this . . .'

Maureen started to read aloud.

I get the feeling Aunt Grace is pleased to have me around and I think it's a good thing I am.

I was a bit alarmed the other day when she mentioned casually that she'd had a break-in one night just before I arrived.

Apparently when she opened up one morning, she found the till drawer was open and all the money gone. Luckily there wasn't much in there. She refuses to fuss about it and didn't report it to the police. She thinks it was probably just children who came in through the small toilet window at the back, because whoever it was took a lot of fruit and sweeties as well as the money! But as she has no alarm system and no burglar bars, it's a bit of a worry.

Maureen looked worriedly at Jack before continuing.

I also think she's quite lonely in that big house, although she won't admit it, and keeping the shop going takes a lot out of her, even if it isn't busy.

On top of that, she's constantly badgered by a developer who wants to buy the building. He has offered her a lot of money, but she seems to think it's her duty to keep her beloved shop from being demolished and replaced by something modern. She refuses even to talk to the man!

I don't suppose anything I can say would make her consider selling up, although I honestly think she should. Maybe you'd have some influence with her, Mum, and I know she'd love to see you. She talks about you such a lot.

Any chance of a quick visit?

Maureen was overcome by a sudden rush of longing to see Aunt Grace, her old home, the shop, the sea, the sun.

Don't be silly, she told herself. A jaunt to South Africa is the last thing you can afford with the bills piling up and the car making that expensive knocking noise. Instead, she resolved to write a long letter to her aunt that evening, and set out all the advantages of selling up and enjoying her well-earned retirement.

The news of the break-in and the lack of security worried her, even if Aunt Grace took it so casually. Maybe it was a good thing that Patsy was planning to stay longer, after all, and perhaps between the two of them they could persuade Aunt Grace to change her mind.

2

The Writing On The Wall

'Is that coffee you're making, Maureen? Could you make me a cup, too?' It was mid-morning when Archie Wallis strode past Maureen's desk and into his own office, looking tired and harassed.

'Of course, Archie. Coming up.'

Maureen put two chocolate biscuits on a plate and took the steaming cup of coffee through to her boss. He was already on the phone, speaking tersely to someone.

He motioned her to sit opposite him, but kept speaking, so it was impossible for Maureen not to hear what he was saying.

'I know that's what we hoped, but it's not going to happen. I had another call from the bank . . . well, I don't think we have much option here. I'm not a magician and it seems the best thing for everyone in the long run. OK, we'll talk later.' He sighed and replaced the receiver, giving her a wry little smile.

Maureen had an icy feeling that she knew what was coming. She was well aware that things at Wallis Plumbing Supplies were not going well. She'd handled the book-keeping for six years, and for the past twelve months she'd watched Archie Wallis's financial situation gradually become worse and worse.

Three years earlier, a national chain of plumbing wholesalers had opened nearby, and all of their customers had slowly left Wallis's in favour of cheaper prices and special offers that were announced in their flashy half-page advertisements.

At first, Archie had responded by advertising himself, but he couldn't compete with the wholesaler's low prices. Then he'd tried stocking novelty lines, like spa baths and gimmicky taps that played music, but cost-conscious plumbers didn't seem interested in buying them.

Business became a dismal downward spiral with fewer customers, and gradually the stockroom emptied. So much so, that when an order actually came through, the delivery was delayed while new stock was purchased. This chased the customer across town to the enormous wholesaler, where everything was available immediately.

Finally, Wallis's three counter staff had been reduced to just one elderly, retired plumber, and when the junior clerk, Alison, had left to be married, Maureen had shouldered all of the paperwork herself. She had also started taking phone orders, helping out behind the counter and checking deliveries if Archie wasn't in the office. The past three months had been exhausting.

She had wondered how long the company could stagger on in this fashion, but had kept hoping that perhaps someone would buy them out, or that Archie might amalgamate with another business. Anything to keep her job and her regular salary.

'Maureen,' Archie said heavily. 'I expect you know what's been happening. You must have seen the writing on the wall as well as I have.'

Maureen swallowed before replying.

'I have. Things have been very difficult . . . '

'Not difficult. Impossible,' Archie interrupted. 'Our turnover is less than fifteen percent of what we were doing two years ago.'

Maureen nodded.

'I know. But I've been hoping for a miracle, I suppose,' she replied.

'I have, too,' Archie said. 'I've explored every avenue, but it seems I have no alternative but to shut up shop.' He looked out of the window and swallowed. Maureen noticed his lip was trembling. 'After thirty-five years in business I have to give it all up.'

'Oh, Archie, I'm so sorry,' she whispered.

'Helen's not,' he said briefly. 'She's been on at me for years to retire. She wants us to sell the big house and move to the coast to be near her sister. That's what we will probably do once everything is settled.'

'I'm really sorry,' Maureen repeated.

Sorry for the very nice man she worked for, and sorry for herself.

Worried

That evening, when she opened the front door, Maureen had a ridiculous hope that Jack might have started making their tea. She had a pounding headache and would have liked nothing better than to relax in a hot bath, have a light supper of scrambled eggs on toast and an early bed.

But there was no sign of Jack, and no sign that he'd even returned from school. His room was just as he'd left it that morning — the bed unmade and yesterday's clothes all over the floor.

She knew she should teach him a lesson and leave everything as it was, but habit took over and she picked up his dirty things and put them in the laundry bin. Then she swallowed two painkillers and went downstairs to start the tea.

If only Patsy was here, she thought. I'd love to talk to someone about today and discuss what to do for the best. Jack means well, but he's not really mature enough to offer advice.

It was almost eight o'clock when she heard the door open, and she could tell at once that something was amiss. There was no cheerful shout from her son, just a mutter as he headed for the stairs.

'Jack? Where have you been?' She came out of the kitchen, drying her hands on her apron. 'Oh, heavens!'

The right side of Jack's face was badly grazed and his left arm was in a sling. He was white with pain. Maureen rushed up and put her arm around him.

'What happened?' she asked, trying

to stay calm. Had he been in a fight, or been attacked by some thugs? Her heart contracted with anxiety for her son.

'Leave off, Mum. I'm fine,' Jack said through gritted teeth. 'Don't fuss.'

'But what did you do? Did you break your arm? How?'

'It's just a sprain on my wrist,' he replied. 'The nurse at Casualty strapped it up. She said I have nothing to worry about — I was lucky.'

'But what happened?' Maureen demanded.

'I came off Duggie's bike,' he muttered. 'He took a corner a bit fast and skidded. We're fine, but his bike's a write-off.'

Now that she knew he was all right, Maureen's relief turned to fury.

'That wretched boy and his bike are nothing but trouble. How many times have I told you — '

'Leave it, Mum,' Jack interrupted. 'He didn't do it on purpose. I'm fine, so stop fussing about it, OK? I'm going to bed.'

He started limping up the stairs, holding tightly on to the banister.

'Duggie is the wrong sort of friend for you, son,' she called after him helplessly. 'Look what's happened and it's all his fault!'

'Stop nagging, Mum. I'm glad I'm going to Dad's this weekend. At least he doesn't try to run my life!'

His bedroom door slammed shut and left a hollow silence in the hall below.

This has got to be one of the worst days of my life, Maureen thought. If only Patsy would come home.

She walked wearily into the kitchen to make Jack some cocoa.

Single Handed

Next day, Maureen phoned Warren to talk about Jack. 'Warren, are you free on Tuesday evening at seven o'clock? It's Jack's parents' evening and I think that we both should be there. Plus, you and I need to have a talk about Jack, anyway,' she added.

'What's the boy done now?' he asked.

His good-humoured tone made it clear that he would refuse to believe that anything Jack did was more than boyish devilment.

'He had a nasty accident on the back of Duggie's motorbike and ended up in Casualty. He's all right, he went off to school the next day not much the worse for wear,' she told him.

'Boys and bikes, eh?' Warren chuckled. 'Our Jack was born lucky, like me. OK, why don't I pick you up around seven and we can have a talk then? Do you want Rita to come along?'

'Rita? No, I think just the two of us will do.'

Although Rita was the children's stepmother, she was very careful not to interfere. On the weekends that Jack went to stay with Warren, she cooked his favourite food and sometimes slipped him a little extra pocket money, but Jack grumbled that she was a bit strict.

'What do you mean, a bit strict?' Maureen had asked him, slightly amused.

'I have to be home by eleven on Saturday nights! She's pretty old-fashioned, probably because she doesn't have any children of her own.'

Maureen smiled.

'Old-fashioned sounds fine to me,' she said.

She liked what little she knew of Rita.

As she drove to work, she wondered how different things might have been if she'd met Warren as he was now, instead of twenty years before. She'd been so in love with him when they'd first married, and she could see no faults in the handsome, fun-loving Englishman who had swept her off her feet.

The first year of their married life together had been carefree and wonderful, and she and Warren had shared so many dreams of their future together. But she'd soon discovered that he regarded every job as a stepping stone to another opportunity somewhere else. He simply couldn't settle in one place long enough to put down roots. Even after Patsy and Jack were born he moved them from town to town, making it difficult for them to make friends before they moved on again.

At first she had thought of this as ambition, but it was something more. He'd always been a hard worker, but as he climbed the career ladder, he slowly became a workaholic. After a while it was plain to see that his job came first and his family a distant second, but when she complained, he'd insist he was doing it for her and the children.

'You should be grateful I've got some ambition!' he'd say when she begged him to take a week off for a family holiday. 'I can't go swanning off to the seaside — it's our busiest time. You go and have some fun with the kids.'

She and the children saw less and less of him, as he was often working late at night. Finally, when he took a sales job with an international company, which involved travelling to the States for two months out of every three, Maureen realised that she was bringing up Patsy and Jack single-handed. They had drifted apart.

One day, she'd taken a long, hard look at her life and decided that things had to change.

Now that she was no longer dependent on Warren, it was easier to be friends, and things were so much better for everyone. Better for her because she'd landed a good job with Archie Wallis and started to earn a regular income, which meant that she had been able to buy a small house of her own without thinking of packing up and moving ever again. Better for the children because they had a solid, stable home and now saw their father more regularly. And much better for Warren. Within two years of their parting he'd met and married Rita and found an excellent job with a local plastics company that he liked well enough to stay with.

Rita was just what Warren needed a serene, cheerful woman with no children, who appreciated Warren for who he was. He seemed to have lost the intense drive and wanderlust he'd once had, and was content to live with her in his smart house in the best part of town, having Jack and Patsy to stay on alternate weekends.

He spoiled both of his children, she thought as she eased her car into a parking space behind the shop. Perhaps it was his way of making up for not seeing much of them when they were younger. Anyway, there was nothing she could do about that.

She unlocked the shop and started to open up Wallis Plumbing Supplies for the day ahead.

Potential

'Mr and Mrs Henderson? I'm so glad you could come. We really need to discuss Jack's work.'

Miss Lawton looked drawn and tired. Forty students could do that to a person, Maureen thought sympathetically.

'Jack has so much potential, but he's not applying himself at all. Time is getting short, his exams are coming up and he really needs to concentrate on his studies if he's going to pass.'

'I keep telling him,' Maureen murmured. 'I've tried forbidding him to go out in the afternoons, but he's eighteen now and he hardly listens to me.'

'Well, it's quite evident from the work he's handing in that he's putting in the least amount of effort possible. For instance, this science project.'

Miss Lawton pushed a piece of paper across the desk and Maureen recognised Jack's work, with the comment *Careless* written in red ink across the top.

'And history . . . ' Another angry remark in red. Oh, dear.

'So the lad's not academic,' Warren said easily. 'Neither was I.'

Miss Lawton shook her head.

'There's nothing wrong with your

son's brain — he should do better,' she told them. 'It concerns me that he doesn't seem to have any ambition, or much idea about what he wants to do when he leaves school. Have you discussed his future with him?'

'I know he's interested in motors,' Maureen said hesitantly. 'I've always thought he'd enjoy engineering, but he hasn't made up his mind. You know what Jack's like.'

'Yes, I do know what Jack's like,' Miss Lawton replied, without smiling. 'In order to study engineering I'm afraid he'd need at least a C in maths and, so far, he hasn't achieved this. He could, but he hasn't.'

Maureen was shocked. She'd had no idea things were so bad.

'I didn't do well at school, either,' Warren put in. 'I've done all right. It won't be the end of the world if he doesn't pass his exams. I have plenty of contacts in the plastics field, for instance. Jack would make a very good salesman; he's a people person. That's a real gift.'

'Oh, Warren!' Maureen rounded on her ex-husband in annoyance. 'Of course it matters that he passes. If he doesn't his options are so limited and so many doors will be closed to him. And maybe Jack doesn't want to sell plastic bowls for the rest of his life.'

'No need to get upset,' Warren replied comfortably. 'Of course we must encourage him to try his best. We will, Miss Lawton, we will. Jack is spending this next weekend with me and my wife — I'll have a serious talk with him and make him see sense.'

Warren getting serious — I'd like to see that, Maureen thought wryly. As if I haven't had hours of serious talks with Jack already. Let's see how Warren enjoys being the dragon for a change!

Initiative

'Auntie Grace, what on earth is this?' Patsy held up a heavy metal machine with a handle.

'Oh, that's a sausage maker,' her aunt said, looking up from the shelves she was dusting in the shop. 'People around here used to make their own sausages. *Boerewors*. But I haven't had much call for one in a long time.'

Judging by the cobwebs on it, Patsy thought, not for a very long time!

'*Boerewors*?' Patsy queried. 'Is that the sausage we had the other night? It was lovely.'

Aunt Grace nodded.

'Yes, farmer's sausage. They put a lot of spices and herbs in it, so it's much tastier than pork sausage. But all the butchers make it these days, so there's no need for home-made ones.'

'So, can I put this in the bargain bin, then?' Patsy asked hopefully.

'I'm sure you can. Goodness, it's getting quite empty isn't it?'

Patsy smiled in satisfaction. She'd persuaded her aunt to go through her shelves and put aside stock that didn't sell well. Patsy had then put it all into an enormous box in the centre of the floor, so that anyone coming in couldn't avoid seeing her handwritten sign: *50% off! Everything must go!*

The customers loved a bargain, and even people who had only popped in for a packet of cigarettes couldn't resist rummaging through the box.

The sausage machine joined pairs of old-fashioned pointy shoes, drab cardigans, chipped china bowls, plastic boxes without their lids and water-damaged clothes.

The shop was looking considerably emptier, but much tidier.

'Auntie Grace, have you noticed how many women with small children come in here around midday?' Patsy asked.

'There's a little kindergarten just around the corner,' her aunt replied. 'On the way home, the mothers pop in for bread and the kiddies ask for a lolly. That's why I stock those fruit lollies, they're not so expensive.'

Trust Aunt Grace to be thinking of her customers' pockets, Patsy thought.

'Well, I have an idea,' she continued.

'How about stocking more toys and putting them at eye level so the children spot them? You can get those really nice educational toys, and some cheap plastic ones just for fun, and maybe some jigsaw puzzles for rainy days. I bet the mothers would be pleased to be able to buy those here.'

'Do you think they would?'

'I overheard one mother complaining that her son had been invited to a birthday party and that she had to go all the way to Fish Hoek to buy a little birthday present. We could be filling that gap in the market!

'I know just where we could find some, too, Aunt Grace,' Patsy continued. 'There's a toy workshop run by a self-help group up the valley. They're training African women to make the loveliest toys out of wood and they're really cheap. And we'd be helping them if we stocked their stuff. They had dear little rag dolls and cars made out of tin cans . . .'

Grace chuckled.

'How did you hear about that?' she asked. 'You've only been here for a couple of weeks and you already know more places than I do!'

'That's not true!' Patsy laughed. 'I just happened to pass the workshop the other day, and I stopped and went in. Actually, I brought you their price list, just in case.'

'You don't waste any time!' Grace said. 'Let's take a look, then.'

They spent ten happy minutes looking at the bright little pictures and making a list of what to order.

'We'll put the stand right next to the ice-cream freezer,' Patsy said. 'Then they can't miss the toys.'

'Are you sure you've never run a shop before?' her aunt teased. 'You've got all the right ideas.'

Patsy smiled.

'Are you OK by yourself for a few minutes, Aunt Grace?' she asked. 'I want to go upstairs and take a look around.'

'I don't think that there's anything up there,' her aunt said. 'It used to be a storeroom, but I haven't used it for years.'

Patsy had been meaning to see what lay at the top of the narrow staircase for a long time, wondering if the space could be rented out to someone.

When she pushed open the door, she gasped. So much space! Three large rooms covered the whole area of the shop below, one of them opening on to a wide wooden balcony that was edged with a decorative wrought-iron balustrade. The rooms were all empty.

Patsy opened the french doors to the balcony and stood out on it, looking at the view. She could see up and down the main street and over the high wall surrounding the naval dockyard to the boats lying at anchor in the sea. Beyond the big grey-painted navy ships she could see the yacht basin with lines of yachts bobbing gently at their moorings, and the smell of the sea blew towards her in the sunlight.

This is beautiful, she thought. There must be something we can do with this top storey. Some way of making money out of this space and this gorgeous view. But what?

Patsy heard her aunt talking to someone in the shop below, her voice raised in uncharacteristic sharpness. She locked the french doors and quickly ran downstairs, hoping there was no trouble. But the shop was empty except for Grace, breathing heavily, her face flushed.

'That wretched man was here again.' She snorted. 'Richard Hugo, the developer. He won't take no for an answer. Coming in here with a big smile on his face, pretending to be so charming! This building is not for sale and I told him so in no uncertain terms. I don't think he'll be back in a hurry.'

'Good for you, Aunt Grace.'

That's what Grace wanted to hear, but Patsy wasn't certain that she was right to dismiss his offer out of hand. Her aunt couldn't seriously consider running the shop for ever, so maybe she should take the opportunity to sell up and make a big profit while she could.

And I'm not planning on staying for long, Patsy thought, only for another few months or so. When I go back home, how will Aunt Grace manage?

Then she remembered, and looked at her watch.

'Can you lock up on your own, Aunt Grace?' she asked. 'I'm meeting Jeremy down at the docks. He's teaching me to handle a sea kayak.'

Her aunt nodded, smiling.

'Mind yourself on one of those things, now, Patsy. They don't look very stable.'

'Don't worry, I'll wear a life jacket.'

★ ★ ★

That evening, Patsy came back glowing with her achievement.

'It was easy!' she said. 'I loved kayaking. Jeremy says my shoulders might be a bit stiff tomorrow, but I don't mind. If it isn't windy tomorrow we're going to paddle all the way to Fish Hoek and back.'

'That's nice,' her aunt said, distracted.

66

She was reading the paper with her feet up, a glass of sherry on the little table next to her. 'Look at this — it says there was a hold-up last night at the pharmacy on the main road. The robbers got away with a lot of drugs and all of the cameras and sunglasses. Thousands of rand worth. Terrible.'

'Was anyone hurt?' Patsy was shocked.

'No, luckily. But it's almost unheard of here in Simonstown. We've always had a very safe little community here, just the odd handbag stolen from a car or something. Mrs Harrison next door had her washing pinched off the washing line once, but nothing like this.'

'Don't forget that you had a break in, too, Aunt Grace,' Patsy reminded her.

'That doesn't count — they were just naughty children, I'm sure,' Grace replied.

Burgled!

On the way down the hill to the shop the next morning, Grace couldn't help smiling at her great-niece, who was unable to stop bubbling up with ideas for using the top storey.

Before they opened up, Patsy made her aunt stop and look up.

'I can just imagine a coffee shop up there, Aunt Grace,' she said, pointing. 'With little tables and chairs on the balcony and people enjoying the view. It shouldn't be a problem to get someone to run it for us. Or perhaps we could make it into an art gallery. We could invite all the local artists to exhibit their stuff. Then people would have to go through the shop to get upstairs and we'd have all those captive customers!'

Grace shook her head admiringly.

'You're a real bright spark, Patsy,' she said, unlocking the door. 'But setting up a small coffee shop would take a lot of money. And — oh, my heavens! We've been burgled!'

Once again the drawer of the old-fashioned till had been pulled right out and emptied. Empty spaces on the shelves showed that burglars had made off with most of the tinned food, and the clothes rack had been stripped of all the men's jackets and shirts, leaving some dresses and blouses hanging forlornly.

Grace surveyed the damage with a hollow feeling of dismay. Some packets of flour and sugar had been emptied on to the floor, almost in spite, and a bottle of orange juice smashed carelessly on the floor, leaving sticky splinters everywhere.

'Who would do a thing like this?' she murmured, her heart pounding. 'What a mess.'

'They've taken the whole basket of *biltong* and those alarm clocks. We're lucky they left those yacht fittings, they're the most expensive things in the shop,' Patsy continued angrily.

'They probably didn't know what they were, and I expect stainless steel cleats would be difficult to sell. They took all the rope, though.'

Feeling numb, Grace sat down heavily, unable to think. Patsy went through to the back and returned with her face flushed.

'The little toilet window has been smashed open,' she said. 'There are dirty shoe marks all down the wall where they climbed in. Aunt Grace, what's the number of the police station?'

'Oh, my . . . it's written down somewhere . . . ' Grace was too distraught to stand up to find it. 'But they'll take ages to come. It's hardly worth telling them.'

'It's for the insurance,' Patsy said. 'They'll want the police report. Then I'll make you a cup of tea with lots of sugar. They say it's good for shock.'

★   ★   ★

To her surprise, two policemen came around within half an hour of Patsy's call, but as Grace had expected, they didn't hold out much hope of catching the culprits.

'It won't have been the same lot that

held up the chemist,' one of the uniformed men said. 'They were professionals. This could have been teenagers, cheeky little devils. Left you a right mess, didn't they? Can you say exactly what's missing?'

'Not right now,' Grace replied. 'I'll make a list and bring it round to the station later, shall I?'

The other policeman looked at Grace reprovingly.

'I see you haven't any proper form of security. I suggest you put some burglar bars on your lower windows and install a burglar alarm. Do it as soon as possible, because once they know they can get in, they'll be back.' He took out his notebook. 'Let's get the details. I'll give you a case number for your insurance claim.'

'They'll be back?' Patsy said to her aunt once the policemen had gone. 'Aunt Grace, we have to get burglar bars fitted, today if possible.'

'You're right. Oh, dear, where is that phone book now . . . '

'I'll find a local company and call them,' Patsy said. 'You sit down, Aunt Grace, you look done in.'

'Nonsense,' Grace said, getting to her feet with a sigh. 'I'll make a start clearing this broken glass. Where's the broom?'

She moved slowly amongst the devastation, half-heartedly picking up things that could be salvaged or cleaned.

'Perhaps this is a sign,' she said, leaning on her broom. 'Perhaps I should sell up to Richard Hugo. I'm probably being very silly trying to hold on to it.'

News

From: Maureen Henderson
To: PatsyHen@hotmail.com
Sent: April 7
Subject: News
  Hello, Patsy,
  Big changes happening here, for

me, anyway. Remember I told you that Archie's business hadn't been doing very well lately? Well, things came to a head and he has made the decision to sell up and close the business. So that means I am out of a job as of next week!

I'm not that bothered. I know I could find another post fairly easily, but I don't want to make any hasty decisions.

Archie has been very generous and given me what he called 'a little something', and it's enough to tide me over for the next couple of months. Closing up the business has meant a lot more work than usual, and I'm feeling exhausted — I've been getting home after eight o'clock most nights for the last two weeks.

I can't wait too long before I will have to start work again, but I was thinking of maybe going to Greece for a week on one of those package holidays. A bit of sun and relaxation is just what I need right now. Jack *could stay with Dad and Rita for that week, so it shouldn't be a problem.*

Speaking of Jack, he seems to be trying a bit harder at school. I think that accident on Duggie's bike was a bit of a wake-up call and he is spending more time with his books.

It sounds as though you are having a wonderful time, so I'm not going to say how much I miss you. Jack is very envious of your sailing fun. He keeps saying he'll write to you, but he isn't a natural letter writer, I'm afraid!

I had a letter from Aunt Grace this week. She really appreciates having you there to help, sweetheart. I'm trying to persuade her to sell the shop to that man, because it doesn't sound as though she can cope on her own.

Lots of love,
Mum.

Perched on a stool in the internet cafe in Simonstown, Patsy read her mother's e-mail. This is fate taking a hand, she thought. Mum's out of work next week, she has some unexpected money and Aunt Grace needs her.

She started tapping out her reply, hoping her mother would check her e-mails soon and realise the urgency of her request.

From: Patsy Henderson
To: MaureenH@atlantis.co.uk
Sent: April 7
Subject: Bad news from Simonstown

Maureen drew her breath sharply and scrolled down immediately, not printing it out and reading Patsy's letter at leisure, as she usually did.

Hi, Mum.
Don't worry — nothing has hap-pened to Aunt Grace or me, but there was a break-in at the shop a few days ago and the burglars took a lot of stuff. They made an awful mess.
The police were horrified to find that she has no security of any sort, so I spent the entire day trying to

75

arrange for someone to come out and fit burglar bars next week. I have hammered planks over the broken window in the meantime.

I'm really worried about Aunt Grace. I know she is badly shaken up, although she pretends not to be, and since the break-in she hasn't been sleeping and hardly eats a thing. That's so unlike her, as you know. She finally admitted she was feeling ill with all the stress of all the decisions she has had to make.

Poor Aunt Grace, Maureen thought wretchedly. What luck that Patsy was there when it all happened.

Do you remember the developer who wants to buy the building? She is thinking of selling it to him, after all, although I know she'd rather keep the shop going. She says if she sells up she'll be 'giving in' to him.

Personally I think she should sell up, because although I can see big *possibilities for the shop and the upstairs rooms, she's not able to finance any expansion of the shop or start anything new.*

I really wish you could come over here, Mum, even for a week or two, and give her some advice. Aunt Grace needs to discuss this with someone and I'm not the right person.

Just try to stop me, Maureen thought. I wonder if I could get on to the Saturday flight?

Everything seems to fit in so well, what with Archie closing down and you taking a break before starting a new job. I know Aunt Grace would love to see you again.
Lots of love,
Patsy.

Maureen smiled to herself. Of course I'll go over at once, she thought. I'll phone Warren and Rita and ask them if

Jack can stay for a fortnight — that should be long enough to help Aunt Grace sort things out. What luck my passport is up to date after that long weekend to Spain last year.

Her mind leapt ahead to the hundreds of things she would have to arrange, but she couldn't help the overwhelming rush of joy and excitement.

After all these years, she was going home!

3

Going Back

'Now, Jack, you'll do your best to help Rita around the house and not be too much trouble while you're there?'

Jack looked up from packing his duffel bag and grinned easily at his mother.

'Stop fussing, Mum. Rita might be my step-mum, but she and I are old mates,' he said. 'She loves having me to stay. She says I'm a lovely lad and she enjoys cooking for me!'

'Maybe she does,' Maureen said, 'but you've only been there for weekends so far. This is a fortnight. Remember to keep your room tidy and don't forget to put your clothes in the laundry basket every night. Rita's not used to picking up after a great teenage lout like I am.'

'Ah, Mum, admit it, you're going to miss this teenage lout.' Jack hugged her.

'And you're going to miss all this rain and the car not starting properly and the blocked drain . . . aren't you?'

'I might miss my teenage lout, but that's about all,' Maureen said, her voice muffled against his chest. 'I'll just deal with all those other problems when I come back.'

'You're really lucky. Just think of me swotting while you're swimming or sunbathing over there . . . '

'I don't think I'll be doing that at all,' Maureen said. 'From the sounds of it, I'll be helping Auntie Grace pack up her shop and sell it, and I won't have time to do much else. Although it will be lovely going back and seeing everything. All the places I remember.'

'Don't forget that Michael Jackson 'Thriller' poster,' he said. 'I mean, if you were planning on bringing me a souvenir, I'd rather have that than an African mask, any day.'

'Duly noted, love. Come on, is that the lot? Rita's expecting you there by lunchtime.'

She finally bundled him and his gear, including his skateboard and box full of computer games, into the car.

'I don't know why you brought all that stuff,' Maureen said, extremely relieved when the car started on the third try. 'You're there to work. You won't have time for games. Remember, you promised.'

'Sure, Mum. But I might have the odd half-hour off, mightn't I? Dad won't nag me the way you do, but even so, I'll crack open the books every night like a good boy.'

Maureen said nothing, but drove to Warren's big house on the other side of town, praying her car wouldn't cut out at the traffic lights. When she returned, a new starter motor was the first thing she'd attend to.

'This is so good of you, Rita,' Maureen said, while Jack unpacked his clothes in the room upstairs he called his own. 'Now Jack knows he has to study, so I hope he doesn't try to wriggle out of it. His teacher gave him a study programme to follow. Three hours a day, at least.'

'Don't worry about it, Maureen, I'll make sure he sticks to his books.' Rita had a comforting air of calm authority, but Maureen wondered if this would be proof against Jack's beguiling excuses.

'He's a bright lad, he'll pass his exams,' Warren said easily. 'The boy doesn't have to get an A for everything, he just has to get through! Don't stress him about work all the time, Maureen. He'll cope.'

'Nobody's expecting an A from Jack. He has to work hard just to pass, Warren. Please back me up on this one.'

'He will,' Rita said, smiling. 'Warren was just saying last night that he was glad of this chance to be with Jack properly instead of just at the weekend, weren't you, love?'

'Yeah.' Warren looked uncomfortable. 'Look, Maureen, I know I wasn't much good as a father when the kids were younger. And somehow Patsy turned out a little star — with no help from me. All your doing.'

Maureen was surprised at his solemn demeanour.

'But I promise I'll have a good heart-to-heart with the boy and make him see his future's important. I might even persuade him to get an A for something, and surprise us all yet!'

'That would be a nice surprise.' She smiled. 'Let's not hope for the impossible. But it would really help if he knew you won't allow him to fool around any more.'

Off To The Sun

Maureen looked at Warren as she spoke although she was pretty sure it would be Rita who disciplined Jack.

'You just go off and enjoy yourself,' Rita said. 'Have a real break. I envy you, flying away to the sun like that, back to your old home.'

'I'm looking forward to it,' Maureen admitted. 'I expect I'll find a lot of changes, though. I haven't seen my aunt in over twenty years and Patsy says this burglary has aged her quite a lot. And I'll probably be helping to close up her shop, so I'll be pretty busy.'

'Not too busy to send us a postcard, I hope,' Rita said.

'I'll do better than that.' Maureen smiled. 'I'll e-mail Jack . . . can I use your e-mail address, Warren? And I hope he'll write at least one letter to me in the next fortnight!'

'What time's your flight?'

'Eight o'clock tonight,' she said. 'My train to London leaves at two, so I'd better get home and make sure everything's locked up and switched off.'

'It's a pity you're not going for longer,' Warren said. 'You could have rented your house. We have a new salesman down from Scotland starting this week, and he and his family need a place to stay while they look around.'

'I'm sorry I didn't know about that earlier,' Maureen said. 'I could have packed up my things and emptied some cupboards for them. The money would have been useful, but it's all been such a rush.'

* * *

Settled in her seat next to the window in the huge Boeing, Maureen relaxed for the first time that day. There was nothing more she could do about anything and so she sat back and selected a film to watch on the little screen in front of her.

She accepted a drink, kicked off her shoes and tried to concentrate on the romantic comedy she'd chosen, but her mind kept leaping ahead to her arrival in Cape Town.

She knew Patsy would be meeting the plane, and one of her sailing friends called Michael was giving them a lift back to Simonstown.

We arrive at six in the morning so I'll see Table Mountain at dawn, she thought, with a little shiver of anticipation.

I wonder how Auntie Grace is? She's probably still shaken from the burglary and it will be easy to make her see sense and sell the shop. Once I've helped her deal with that developer and made sure she gets a good price, I might be able to persuade her to sell the rambling old house as well, and buy a small unit in a retirement village somewhere. Much safer for her and less to worry about.

And I'll see Patsy soon! Perhaps we'll be able to fly back on the same plane in a fortnight. I wonder if I'll bump into any old school friends? Daniel Clayton . . . Netta Hendricks . . . they've probably all moved away by now. Oh, I hope Jack's going to be all right . . .

The pilot's voice sounded through the cabin.

'Ladies and gentlemen, we are now passing over Nigeria, home to a hundred and thirty million people. If you look down to your left you may be able to distinguish the lights of the capital city, Abuja.'

But Maureen was fast asleep.

Petty Crime

'Now you sit out here and just enjoy the view, Mo, sweetheart.' Aunt Grace commanded. 'I'll pour us each a little glass of wine, shall I? And I'll just check on the lamb curry while I'm at it.'

Mo! No-one had called her that since she'd left all those years ago.

'Thanks, Auntie Grace. Wine sounds lovely.'

She shook her head, smiling. Far from needing her help and support, Auntie Grace was back to her old self. Not only did she intend to restock the shop from the insurance money, but she wanted to do what Patsy had suggested: open a coffee shop in the rooms above. And, whatever happened, she was not going to give Richard Hugo the satisfaction of selling to him.

All this Maureen had learned in the first hour of being back, when she'd unpacked her case and was drinking tea on the verandah.

'So I'm sorry, my darling, but you

didn't need to come back at all,' Aunt Grace had said. 'I don't know what Patsy was thinking of, alarming you like that. Of course, I know she was a bit shaken herself, poor girl, but we're used to this sort of petty crime . . .'

'Petty crime!' Maureen had said indignantly. 'Major burglary, more like. I'm very glad she told me about it. Anyway, I'm delighted you're feeling so positive and I'm just pleased to have had a good excuse to come over. I left it far too long.'

'You did indeed. We have twenty years of catching up to do. I must apologise for not being a very good correspondent, I'm afraid. I find letter-writing really difficult.'

'Me, too. I know I should have written more often . . .'

'An inherited trait, then.' Aunt Grace had smiled. 'But I think we'll do the catching up a bit later. You look ready for a good rest. Twelve hours sitting in a plane must have been very tiring.'

'I managed to sleep a little,' Maureen

had said. 'But they kept coming round and offering food and drinks and the man sitting next to me watched films all night long. I am a bit sleepy, actually. Perhaps I should lie down for half an hour.'

She'd surfaced six hours later, in time for a glass of wine, and feeling wonderfully refreshed.

She leaned back against the rickety cane chair and gazed out across the bay. It was exactly as she remembered it, an enormous sweep of water stretching fifty kilometres across, with a curved blue ridge of mountains in the distance falling down to the sea. The harbour below was filled with grey Naval vessels and next to it, the neat lines of yachts anchored at the marina seemed to have multiplied into an expensive, gleaming armada.

The only change was in the outskirts of the village itself. When she'd left, the old St George's Road had been edged with double-storeyed Victorian buildings and the handsome old hotels, the Lord Nelson and the Britannia, to take care of the thirsts of the Naval men stationed opposite. There were also several other pubs near the Naval base and a scattering of bungalows beyond the shops on the way to Cape Point.

Now, palatial white-painted houses covered the lower slopes of the mountain, some of them built on what looked like impossibly steep, rocky land, and smaller homes spilled along the shore road for several miles towards Cape Point. Pastel coloured town-houses and blocks of flats crept up Red Hill, which she remembered as being completely empty.

'I must go and explore tomorrow, Auntie,' Maureen said, accepting a rich rosé wine in a pretty antique cut glass. 'I can't believe how Simonstown has grown.'

'Yes. Progress.' Aunt Grace sniffed. 'Luckily, they can't touch the old buildings on St George's Street. It's all part of the Historic Mile and we can't even change the colour of our wall paint without permission! But there's nothing to say you can't rip out the insides of the buildings and modernise them in some horrible way.'

'That wretched Hugo fellow should set his sights on somewhere further towards Fish Hoek. All the buildings along the main stretch have historical value, including Whittaker's, of course. But he's not a local man, he doesn't care.'

'Perhaps he just doesn't know, Auntie.' Maureen soothed. 'Not everyone has your sense of the past.'

'Hmph. Maybe I should propose him as a member for our Historical Society! Anyway, Mo, dear, let's celebrate your arrival and all go out for a meal tonight. Patsy's shutting up the shop this afternoon and she should be here any minute. She can suggest a restaurant — I think she's been taken to them all!'

'She seems to have had a wonderful time, socially.' Maureen smiled. 'I can't keep up with the different boys she's mentioned and all the things she's been doing — sailing and climbing and kayaking . . .'

'Ah, she's a great girl,' Grace said. 'I

can't tell you what a help she's been. She's got good ideas and so much energy. She puts in a full day's work behind the counter and then she's off sailing or to a party — or both! There's no stopping her.'

'Here she is now,' Maureen said. 'Hello again, darling!'

'Hi, Mum.' Patsy kissed her. 'You're looking a lot more rested than when you arrived this morning.'

'Wonderful what a little sleep can do. We've decided to celebrate tonight and go out somewhere — you're the expert. Any suggestions?'

'Mmm. Well, do you fancy curry? Steak and chips? There's a fabulous seafood place . . . tell you what, let's walk down to the Main Road and see what we feel like.'

A Second Aunt

'This is lovely, isn't it?' Maureen tucked her arm through her daughter's as they strolled along. 'Smell the sea! I just love being back here. I'd forgotten how pretty everything was with the mountain behind. And so many smart new shops! Even an art gallery. When I lived here, I had to travel all the way to Cape Town to buy a dress!'

'There's a good steakhouse down on the waterfront,' Patsy said. 'How about eating there?'

The night air was cold, and they chose to eat inside rather than on the patio which looked out on to the yachts bobbing about. A big fire glowed in the corner and there was a cheerful buzz of conversation.

'I wish there was a restaurant that served local food,' Patsy said, scanning the menu. 'Aunt Grace, that *boboetie* you made last week was delicious. And there was the fish . . . what was it called?'

'*Snoek!*' Maureen said gleefully. 'Oh, Aunt Grace, do you remember how Rugaya used to make that, with onions and rice and some turmeric? No-one made it as well as she did! I wonder where she is these days?'

Maureen turned to Patsy.

'Rugaya was like a second aunt to me. She was a very traditional Muslim woman and always wore the most beautiful filmy headdresses pinned under her chin. I don't think I ever saw her with her head uncovered. And was she strict! She made me fold my clothes and tidy up my toys, and woe betide me if my manners weren't perfect.'

'Nothing wrong with that,' Aunt Grace said cheerfully. 'See how well you've turned out! Actually, Rugaya pops into the shop every now and then. She's had a very hard time bringing up those two grandchildren of hers, but they're older now. The boy's earning money on a fishing boat and the little girl . . . she must be nearly eighteen by now.'

'I'd love to see her again,' Maureen said. 'And I'd love her to meet Patsy. Right . . . so what are we going to eat?'

* * *

Walking back after their meal, they stopped to look down at the harbour lights.

'Oh — there's Just Nuisance! I'd forgotten they erected a statue of him just before I left for England.'

They crossed the road to Jubilee Square where the bronze statue of the famous Great Dane stood regally looking over their heads, his sailor's cap at his feet.

'A statue to a dog?' Patsy queried. 'I've never seen this before.'

'Able Seaman Just Nuisance! He was the only dog ever enlisted in the Royal Navy,' Maureen said. 'He used to ride on the train with the sailors during the war and they signed him on as an AB so he could have a free rail pass.'

'That's right. I met him during the war when I was a little girl,' Aunt Grace agreed. 'He was the biggest dog I've ever seen, but gentle as a lamb. He loved the men in their Navy bell-bottoms and every time a British boat docked, he'd go on board and make himself at home. He lay across the top of the gangplank so all the sailors had to step over him. That's how he got his name.'

'Why is his head so shiny?' Patsy asked, amused.

'Everyone strokes him for good luck,' Aunt Grace said, absent-mindedly doing the same.

Patsy copied her, with her hand lingering on his head.

'I need some luck,' she said mysteriously.

'Oh? Why's that?'

'It's a secret.' She grinned. 'I'll tell you both soon. If I talk about it, it might never happen.'

★ ★ ★

The next morning, Maureen accompanied her aunt down the hill to open the shop. Just about everyone they met on the way had a word of sympathy or outrage for Grace.

'I heard what happened last week, Miss Whittaker,' one elderly man said. 'Terrible. I'm just glad you weren't in the shop to confront the rascals.'

'Pity I wasn't!' Grace retorted. 'I keep an old cricket bat behind the counter and I would have used it on their heads!'

'You would have, too,' Maureen said. 'But I hate to think what might have happened to you if you had. I'm glad you've got some sort of security now, Auntie.'

Maureen's Memories

As they approached the shop she noticed the new burglar bars and the sign above the door, signalling that the shop was now linked to a security company.

Memories of long afternoons spent in the shop came flooding back and when Aunt Grace opened the door, the half-forgotten smell of the interior made Maureen stop and take a deep, pleasurable breath.

Then an ear-splitting electronic shriek sounded above their heads.

'Oh, drat!' Grace said. 'I forgot to punch the code again. Oh, dear. Now, what was it . . . ?'

She pressed some numbers on the small keypad just inside the door and, mercifully, the shrieking stopped abruptly.

'Wretched thing,' she said briskly. 'Luckily, none of my neighbours takes any notice of that!'

But the security company did. The phone rang immediately and Aunt Grace answered.

'Me again! Sorry, I forgot!' she said cheerfully. It sounded as though she and the security man were already old friends.

Maureen wandered around the room. The shop looked smaller and emptier than she remembered it, although the burglary probably had something to do with the lack of stock. The old wooden counter seemed lower, and she noticed colourful prepacked food had taken the place of the brown paper bags of sugar and flour and tea that she used to enjoy measuring out.

But she could see in an instant that this wasn't a place where people shopped, except if they needed something in a hurry. No-one would want to buy the dreary old sweaters and tracksuits on the racks, and food from the supermarket was far more inviting and probably fresher. And builders surely went to a discount hardware shop to buy a wheelbarrow or thick boots?

The shop, which she'd remembered as being full and busy with customers in and out all the time, seemed stuck in some kind of time warp, and it made her sad to see it. She walked slowly up the stairs and through the empty rooms, her footsteps echoing. Patsy's right, she thought, we could do something with these.

Then she went downstairs and unlocked the wooden stable-door which opened on to a small back courtyard edged with little stone storerooms. The secluded area could have been pretty, but old cartons and empty boxes lay scattered around, the bricks covered in moss and the locks on the storerooms rusted shut.

Maureen remembered playing in the storerooms as a small child, arranging packing cases and cartons and pretending she had a playhouse. This area has such possibilities, she thought, standing in the middle of it and picturing tea tables and pots of geraniums. If we cleaned it up it would be charming.

Time For A Change

Maureen locked the back door again and came back into the shop where Aunt Grace was still on the phone, chatting to the security man.

She looked out on to the street, watching the passers-by. A coach had just disgorged a load of tourists who were wandering along the pavement peering into the shops, and she could hear the sharp twang of American accents.

They made a beeline for a craft market two doors down and some of them went into the new art gallery, but one couple paused at the door of Whittaker's General Dealer and peered into the half-empty shop.

'Oh, sorry, honey, are you closing up?' the woman asked sympathetically. 'Going out of business?'

'Not at all,' Maureen said defensively. 'We've recently had a burglary but we're restocking and staying right here. In fact, if you come back next week, you'll see a lot of wonderful things!'

'That's the spirit,' the husband said. 'This place must be a little gold mine here on the main road. You know what they say about business — it's all position, position, position!'

Maureen smilingly agreed. The situation of the shop was perfect, right in the centre of things. No wonder that

Richard Hugo wanted to get his hands on the building.

'Tell me,' the American continued, 'Is there anywhere nearby we could buy some postcards of this pretty little harbour?'

'We're getting our new stock in tomorrow,' Maureen said quickly, making a mental note to order some as soon as they left. 'But I'm sure they'll have some on the waterfront.'

As they left, she turned to Aunt Grace in excitement.

'Postcards?' her aunt queried. 'They sell them on Jubilee Square, I think. I've never bothered with those.'

'Auntie,' Maureen said, in a rush, 'I know you want to carry on with Whittaker's. I don't blame you, it's practically part of the history of this town! You've been going for so long.'

'Sixty years,' Aunt Grace said. 'My mother opened it in 1946 and just about everyone in Simonstown was a customer.'

'But let's look at who your customers

really are these days. They're tourists ... hundreds of them strolling past every day. And the yachtsmen. Patsy says lots of them come in looking for a snack to take with them while sailing, or odd bits of equipment. Let's change things. Get rid of things that don't sell, like ordinary groceries and clothes, and stock up with what people want.'

Aunt Grace was silent.

'But we've always been a general store,' she said stubbornly. 'Only last week a man came in here and bought a pair of overalls for his gardener.'

'Yes, but how long had you had those overalls on the shelf?' Maureen asked. 'Months, probably. Don't you see, Auntie, we could make this shop buzz again! Get the customers in. We just have to stock the right stuff. Speciality things.'

Maureen could picture the changes she'd make.

'We could paint the place out, put in new fittings, a shiny new counter and resurface the floor, make it cheerful and inviting. Maybe we could turn that old courtyard into a tea garden or something. And upstairs . . . '

Her aunt sighed, looking suddenly older. 'I know you're right, sweetheart. If I were twenty years younger I'd likely jump at it. But I don't think I have the energy to make all the changes you're thinking of. Don't forget, you'll be away back to England in a couple of weeks, and Patsy, too, one of these days. I couldn't handle all that on my own. And another small point is money. I'm getting a nice cheque from the insurance but that won't do more than replace what was stolen.'

Maureen bit her lip. Aunt Grace was probably right. She couldn't handle a sea-change at this stage, not on her own. And even though Patsy planned to stay on, she probably wouldn't want to carry on working in the shop. She'd be looking for more interesting work with better pay.

But still, the possibilities of the shop excited her . . .

She decided to say nothing at present, but while she was standing behind the counter, selling the odd packet of cigarettes and sweets, she did some serious calculations.

★ ★ ★

That evening, Maureen buttonholed Patsy, who was doing the washing-up in the kitchen.

'I'll put the dishes away,' she said, taking a tea towel. 'Patsy, I've been thinking. About Aunt Grace, and the shop, and you. I know you want to stay on longer. Have you considered what sort of job you'd look for?'

'Well, yes.' Patsy's voice was guarded. 'Why do you ask, Mum?'

'I just hate to let that shop go to waste! There's just so much we could do with it. There was an American fellow in the shop today and he commented on what a little gold mine it must be. He wasn't to know that for the past couple of years Aunt Grace has hardly been breaking even! But we could make it a great little business, if we became a speciality shop and restocked with things tourists want to buy.'

Diplomatic

Maureen had so many plans buzzing around in her head that she couldn't wait to share them with her daughter.

'We?' Patsy said. 'Mum, I can't spend the next six months selling souvenirs behind the counter with Aunt Grace! And, actually, I've been meaning to tell you but I just had confirmation today. I have a job. A fabulous job!'

'You have? Where? In Simonstown?'

'Sort of. It's on a yacht, Mum.' Her words tumbled out in an excited rush. 'I've got a post as housekeeper on board the *Sea Freedom*. It's the biggest yacht in the whole club. Sixty feet! I've got to keep it ready to sail at a day's notice, clean up after every trip, and be on board to cook all the meals while the owner's sailing. I get to sail and I'm paid for it! Isn't that the most perfect job?'

Patsy's face was glowing with success but Maureen's heart sank.

'Won't that be dangerous?' she asked hesitantly. 'I mean, that's a huge boat. The skipper — captain, whatever — probably takes it miles out into the ocean!'

'Of course he does,' Patsy said happily. 'It's big enough to cruise across to America if he wants to. The agent mentioned trips up the coast to Durban and a series of races up to a place called Mossel Bay and back again. I think I got the job because I told him I'd been sailing around here on smaller yachts and never got seasick. Apparently the previous housekeeper couldn't cook a thing because she had to lie down whenever they hit bad weather!'

'Well, I just hope the fellow is a good sailor,' Maureen said. 'Is he a local man?'

'Nope, he's from Johannesburg, but he flies down at least once a month to sail. And Mum, another good thing is, I get paid a monthly salary but if he's not sailing, I'm free to do other things. So I guess I could help out at the shop, if Aunt Grace needs me.'

Maureen decided not to discuss her big idea with Patsy or Aunt Grace for the time being. It needed a lot more thought and she'd have to be very diplomatic about it. It would keep.

★ ★ ★

'Patsy Henderson? The new house-keeper for *Sea Freedom*? This is Renata Howell of Metropolitan Properties calling from Johannesburg.'

'Yes?' Patsy said, puzzled.

'I'm Rick's personal assistant. He's asked me to tell you that he and two guests will be flying down and will be ready to sail first thing on Saturday morning. Rick would like you to provision the boat and have it ready for two full days on the water over the week-end.'

'Oh . . . right.' Patsy guessed that Rick must be the owner.

'One of the guests is a vegetarian so will you be sure to have suitable food prepared for him?' The voice was crisp and business-like. 'I'd like your e-mail address, please, so I can send you a list of things that you're expected to do each time Rick or his guests come to sail. Air the bed-linen, check the gas supply for the cooker and so on.'

'Certainly,' Patsy said, trying to sound equally efficient.

'I've already transferred money to your account to purchase whatever you need. You should keep all the slips and mail them to me at the end of every month.'

The PA was frighteningly brisk, and Patsy rang off promising to check her e-mail immediately.

'I won't be coming to the shop this morning, Aunt Grace,' she said. 'I've got to provision *Sea Freedom* for two days' sailing.'

'What fun!' her great-aunt said.

'What are you planning to cook for them?'

'It will have to be something easy to cook while we're tossing around at sea.'

'Why not cook ahead and freeze it?' Aunt Grace suggested.

'Good idea. I bet most sailors are grateful if they get a cup of packet soup,' her mother said. 'You can't go wrong with that delicious butternut and orange soup of yours.'

'And the Thai Vegetarian stir-fry you made us last week was very good,' Aunt Grace put in. 'That man Rick will be thankful he hired a good little cook like you, mark my words!'

'Brilliant!' Patsy exclaimed. 'That could work. We'll only be out at sea for two days.'

She wanted the food to be stylish but simple, and it took her half an hour to work out a shopping list for menus that would suit everyone, including the vegetarian.

If nothing else, she was determined to impress her new employer with her prowess in the kitchen! No, the galley! I must remember to call it a galley, she thought.

Then she went down to the internet café, picked up her e-mailed instructions and caught the train to Fish Hoek where there was a supermarket.

Renata's instructions hadn't mentioned anything specific, she'd simply written *Stock up with enough food and drink*.

'Jam, marmalade, honey, biscuits, crisps, tea, coffee, sugar, dried milk . . . ' Her shopping list seemed endless. 'Bread, butter, salads, eggs, bacon, muesli . . . ' What if they wanted cornflakes for breakfast? Or porridge? She decided against buying any convenience foods like packet soups or instant mashed potato. Everything she served the captain and crew would be fresh and wholesome.

Besides the ingredients for the two main meals, Patsy spent far more money than she'd expected on just the basic necessities. At the last minute she bought two dozen beers and some good red wine, in case the party from Johannesburg wanted to drink something else besides water.

Patsy spent most of Thursday cooking two meals for four people, and freezing them in plastic containers.

Then, on Friday, carrying a big box of dry provisions, she went aboard *Sea Freedom* and unlocked the teak hatch which led below into the main cabin.

* * *

Patsy stood at the bottom of the wooden steps and gazed around in awe. The yacht was luxuriously fitted and very different from the small boats her friends sailed.

The cabin was panelled in gleaming dark wood, with wide, comfortable benches on either side of a long, polished table in the middle. A built-in cupboard in one corner housed a selection of paperbacks, board games and playing cards as well as DVDs.

So there had to be a television! There

was, concealed behind a matching cupboard door, along with a sound system.

Talk about cruising in style! I wonder if this Rick ever pops over to the West Indies or somewhere? Patsy hugged herself with glee at the possibility of a trip like this.

Doors led off to three cabins, each one as big as a small bedroom, fitted with a double bed, bedside lights and thick carpeting.

There was one small cabin aft, with a narrow bunk and a tiny cupboard, which she assumed was for her own use, and two shower rooms and toilets.

When she was appointed, the agent had shown her around briefly, but this time she examined everything carefully, especially in the galley, acquainting herself with the layout and checking the equipment she'd soon be using.

She was delighted with the way everything fitted so neatly, the gas cooker swinging on gimbals so it always stayed level no matter how bad the swell at sea. Six matching plates and mugs were securely stored on a ridged shelf so they couldn't slide off in heavy weather.

Matching cutlery nestled in drawers, with several sharp knives, a tin opener, bottle opener, garlic press . . . everything she could think of needing to prepare food. But in the little herb cupboard she found only salt and pepper. Clearly the previous housekeeper hadn't been a very adventurous cook!

The whole interior of the boat was cleverly planned so that not an inch of space went to waste and there were storage boxes in the most unexpected places. She made up the beds neatly, put out fresh towels and soap in the shower rooms, then turned to unpacking the supplies she'd bought.

First she threw out some mouldy bread and a bottle of congealed tomato sauce, then she wiped the shelves and transferred the packets of coffee, tea and sugar into the special containers marked for them. Everything went behind narrow strips of wood to keep them upright. She was careful to pack the biscuits and everything else into plastic airtight containers so the sea air wouldn't soften them as soon as they were opened. She found herself humming as she worked. It was almost as good as having her own little kitchen!

Finally, after one last look around, Patsy was satisfied she'd made everything as ready as it could be, and she locked the hatchway to the cabin and went home.

A Bad Beginning

'Mum, what do you think 'First thing on Saturday' means? Six o'clock? Seven? I'm terrified of being late. Maybe I should sleep on board?'

'I should think if you're there by six in the morning, you'd be all right. The sun's up by then and I've seen yachts leaving the harbour at first light.'

Maureen was almost as nervous as her daughter.

'Have you packed a waterproof jacket, sweetheart? And a warm sweater? And a complete change of clothes in case you get soaked . . . ?'

'Mum, I'm not part of the crew! Anyway, I don't suppose I'll see much of the sailing, I'll probably have to sit below in the cabin making cups of coffee and sandwiches for everyone. Don't worry, I'll be fine.'

After packing a small bag with her clothes for the weekend, Patsy went to bed early on Friday night and set her alarm for five o'clock the following morning. But visions of burning the meals or forgetting something important kept her tossing and turning until well after midnight, when she finally fell into a restless sleep.

'Patsy! It's nearly eight o'clock!'

Her mother's voice cut sharply into her dreams.

'What happened to your alarm?'

'Oh, no!' Patsy shot out of bed,

dressed hurriedly and ran a comb through her hair in a panic. She scooped up her bag of clothes and the plastic boxes of frozen meals on her way out of the house and ran all the way down the hill to the yacht basin.

She rounded the corner, gasping, to see three people standing on the quay-side next to *Sea Freedom*, surrounded by canvas hold-alls.

That's odd, Patsy thought. I wonder why they haven't gone on board. Surely they could have made themselves a cup of coffee while they waited?

Then she remembered. She had the key to the hatchway.

Two of the men looked at her with amusement as she panted up to them, but the third man, taller than the rest, looked extremely annoyed.

He glanced at his watch.

'You're Patsy Henderson, I presume?'

Her heart sank. She couldn't have imagined a worse start to her new job.

4

First Impressions

Patsy swallowed hard, speechless in the face of the man's obvious annoyance. This wasn't the way she had hoped to meet her new employer.

She'd pictured herself being ready to serve freshly brewed coffee as he came down the quay with his friends and impressing him with her efficiency.

Instead, he was glaring at her, while she stood scarlet-faced and panting from her long run down from Aunt Grace's house on the hill.

'I'm so sorry,' she croaked. 'My alarm didn't go off. I meant to be on board at six o'clock!'

'Six might have been a bit early, but seven would have been good. We've been waiting here for half an hour,' he snapped.

'I'm sorry,' she repeated miserably. But she couldn't help adding, 'I didn't realise I had the only key to the hatchway. I thought you'd be able to open up and make coffee if I was a little late.'

'Yes, well . . . actually I usually do that, but I left my key back in Johannesburg.' His voice softened. 'So I guess I'm partly to blame . . . I'm Rick,' he added unnecessarily, stretching out his hand.

Was that a twinkle starting in his dark brown eyes? Patsy couldn't be sure, but as she stretched out her hand to shake his, the plastic box of frozen soup slipped from her grasp and fell with a clatter on to the quayside.

Rick bent down to pick it up.

'*Butternut and orange soup*,' he read. 'Looks as though you're going to feed us pretty well, Miss Henderson.'

'Please, call me Patsy,' she told him, smiling.

'Are you sure you're used to sailing?' he asked abruptly. 'My previous housekeeper didn't last too long. Cooking in a kitchen is one thing, but preparing a meal at sea is quite another.'

'Don't worry, I can cook anywhere,' Patsy said confidently, wondering if she should tell him that the closest she had ever got to cooking at sea was to open a Thermos of tea on a dinghy.

'Good. Well, just stay out of the way down below when the seas get rough, will you? We've got enough to think about without having a man overboard.'

'Right.' She paused. 'I'm sure that you're all dying for a cup of coffee by now, are you?'

Rick smiled and nodded. He gestured towards his guests.

'I'd better introduce my crew, Martin and Greg. They'll be doing the hard work this weekend, while I give them orders.'

'Dream on, Rick.' The man called Martin smiled and biffed Rick lightly on the shoulder. 'Delighted to meet you, Patsy. I like the sound of that soup. The last time we sailed with this fellow he fed us bread and potato crisps!'

'With tomato ketchup,' Greg added. 'Don't forget Rick's secret passion — tomato ketchup with everything.'

Oh, no, Patsy thought, I hope he doesn't mean that. I haven't brought any.

'I'm afraid when my last housekeeper left we were all a bit hopeless,' Rick told her. 'Admit it, guys, there was nothing to stop you from taking over on the food front if you could have done any better. I was too busy sailing this thing.'

'Yeah, right!' Martin said. 'Believe me, Patsy, your cooking skills are both needed and wanted around here.'

'It's always nice to feel wanted.' She smiled.

She could tell that they were old friends and the easy banter of the crew made her feel welcome. Martin was short and powerfully built, his dark blue eyes fringed with black lashes, and his muscular frame was deeply tanned. Greg was taller, with gingery curls and freckles splashed across his wide round face, and they both looked as if they would be fun to know.

Patsy sensed that Rick was more aloof — rather business-like and not ready actually to be friends with his employee. Which was a pity, she thought, because he was gorgeous; slightly older than the others and with an air of quiet authority that attracted her.

The men stood aside while she stepped on board *Sea Freedom* and unlocked the hatchway. Then she busied herself in the galley, boiling water for coffee while they sorted out their cabins and packed away their hold-alls.

Soon all three men were working above in the cockpit and, as she brewed the coffee and set out the mugs, she heard the throb of the motor.

She went up the stairs with a tray of steaming coffee and a plate of *beskuits*.

The men were seated in the cockpit, with Rick steering the boat slowly out of the marina towards the open sea. Other sailors getting ready to leave waved and called to them and he shouted friendly replies.

'See you in Gordon's Bay!' he yelled. 'Last man across the line buys the beers.'

'Gordon's Bay?' Patsy queried. 'That's right on the other side of False Bay, isn't it?' She could see the mountains in the far distance, coming down to the sea on the opposite side of the huge bay.

'Yes,' Rick said. 'Today's a club race.'

'It's just a fun competition,' Greg added. 'The gun goes off at midday, then it's once around Seal Island and a straight run across the finish line at Gordon's Bay if the wind holds. Most of the boats will sail back here late this afternoon, but we're planning to anchor the night there. Tomorrow we'll carry on to Rooi Els up the coast before travelling back on Sunday night. Is that all right with you?'

'That sounds great!' Patsy replied, not sure how far Rooi Els was. She would have loved to stay up on deck watching the dark blue sea skim smoothly by, but she knew she was there to work. 'Is everyone ready for breakfast?'

'You bet,' Greg said. 'Would that be cornflakes?'

Patsy shook her head.

'Well, I thought I would make mushroom omelettes, but if you'd rather have — '

'No, mushroom omelettes will be fine,' Rick said.

Patsy went below and assembled the ingredients she'd brought and took a deep breath. Her catering career had begun, and even with a tiny stove and very little work space, she was determined to produce the best breakfast of her life. Somehow, she had to make up for the awful first impression she'd made.

Tasty

As Patsy warmed the croissants in the microwave, she was aware of shouting and noises on deck.

Rick was barking commands.

'Pull that halyard. Put some muscle into it, guys!'

Then footsteps pattered across the deck above the cabin and there were sounds of another sail being released.

'Number two jib!' Rick shouted. 'Hank it quickly, Greg. OK, sheets through the fair lead and winch them, Martin.'

Patsy had no idea what he was saying. Since she'd arrived in Simonstown she'd sailed plenty of dinghies with her friends, but the only orders she had been required to obey were 'Coming about', 'Duck!' and 'Mind the boom!'

She'd learned pretty quickly to bend double to avoid the sail as the skipper shoved the rudder to one side and turned the boat rapidly, then she'd jump quickly to the other side and hang on to one of the stays while the sail filled with wind and they were off across the water again. But everything Rick was shouting could have been in Greek!

Suddenly all was silent except for the swish of the water past their bows. The motor was switched off, the sails were hoisted and they were sailing with the wind.

Patsy couldn't resist climbing the stairs and looking about her. Above her head the enormous foresail billowed tautly in the stiff breeze and ahead of it the triangular foresail was trim, red and green streamers flying in the wind. Simonstown harbour was receding into the distance at a great rate and all around lay the swell of the deep blue sea.

'Good job, guys,' Rick said. 'Ah, Patsy, is breakfast ready?'

'Yes,' she replied, wondering how she was going to carry the plates up the steps. 'I suppose you'll have to eat on your laps up here?'

'Not at all,' Rick said. 'I'll just switch to auto-pilot. We're miles from anything else at the moment.'

Soon all three men were seated around the polished table in the main cabin, making short work of orange juice, mushroom omelettes, warmed croissants and a fresh pot of coffee. It could almost have been a corner of an up-market coffee shop, instead of inside a boat.

Patsy watched them nervously from the galley. Why didn't they say something? Had she put too much salt in the eggs?

'Oops, I forgot the honey.' She took the pot and put it next to the marmalade already on the table. 'Um, is everything all right?'

'Nope,' Greg said. 'There's something missing.'

'What?' Oh, horrors, did Rick really want ketchup?

'You,' he said. 'The cook has to eat with the rest of the crew. It's the rule on board this boat.'

'Oh!' Relief swept over Patsy and she grinned shyly. 'All right. I'll know for next time.' She glanced at Rick but he said nothing.

'Patsy,' Martin said solemnly, 'this is

the tastiest breakfast I've had since I left home. Will you marry me?'

As she broke into giggles, she had a feeling that being the housekeeper on board *Sea Freedom* would turn out to be one of the best jobs she'd ever had, anywhere in the world. If only her employer would be as laid back as his crew, then it would be perfect. His distant manner made her feel like she was there on sufferance.

Security

Grace closed the front door of Whittaker's, being careful to set the security alarm before she did so, and drew the two bolts and snapped the new padlocks on.

She sighed. She hated the new security gadgets she'd been forced to install, but she knew it was essential these days. And she had to admit she felt a lot safer with it, and the burglar bars at the back and the electric fencing across the wall. But it's like being in jail, she thought crossly.

Mo said it was the same in England these days so she shouldn't complain. Things had changed everywhere and she just had to accept it.

Walking along St George's Street to meet her niece, Grace brightened.

The row of handsome old buildings curving down the road gladdened her heart and if she ignored the motor cars parked along the kerb, she could have been strolling along the road a hundred years ago.

She remembered back to the war years when horse-drawn carts were common along this road, and how she and her little brother had saved apples and bread to feed the horses as they delivered firewood and sold vegetables door to door. Their favourites had been the two enormous white Clydesdales that pulled the municipal rubbish cart.

I pity any horse trying to come along this road now, she thought. All these tourist coaches would push them right off.

A voice broke into her reverie.

'Hello, Miss Whittaker. I hear young Mo is back with you for a visit?'

It was Henry Morton, the librarian. People said no-one sneezed in Simonstown without Henry knowing about it. He'd manned the desk in the library for almost as long as Grace had stood behind the counter in Whittaker's and they were old friends.

'And her daughter, Patsy,' Grace said cheerfully. 'Aren't I the lucky one? I'm meeting Mo for a little sherry down on the waterfront. I know she'd love to see you again — would you like to join us?'

'Not this evening, Grace,' Henry said. 'It's the Historical Society's get-together in the museum. Had you forgotten?'

'Oh, my goodness,' Grace said guiltily. 'I had. It went clean out of my mind. Would you give my apologies, Henry, and tell them my time with Mo is precious, but I'll definitely be there next month. And you can tell them all that that developer is still after me to sell, but I'm standing firm!'

'Good for you, Grace,' Henry said. 'I have never thought for a moment that you would give in.'

Getting It Right

Smiling, Grace quickened her pace and arrived at the restaurant on the waterfront just as Maureen was sitting down.

'Two dry sherries, please,' Mo said to the waitress. 'Oh, isn't this perfect? What a view!'

They were seated on the patio overlooking the small jetty where young people were setting out in their sleek yellow sea kayaks. Seagulls swooped and cried and, in the distance, some big yachts were returning to harbour as the sun set and the sea turned to silver.

'It's so wonderful having you home, Mo,' Grace said, patting her hand.

131

'You're full of good ideas. I would never come here and have a drink on my own. Think what I would be missing.'

'I'm glad I'm good for something,' Maureen joked. 'Even if it's leading you astray!'

'I wish that you could stay longer, darling,' Grace said. 'If only you didn't have to rush back to England and look for a new job, or have all that trouble with your car — '

'Actually, Auntie,' Maureen interrupted, 'that's what I wanted to talk to you about. I've been doing a lot of thinking. Maybe I could stay here a little bit longer and help you get the shop right? Jack could stay on with Warren and Rita, and — '

'What do you mean, get it right?' Grace asked suspiciously. 'I know you have all those high-flown ideas to make it into some kind of tourist Mecca, but it would all cost a lot of money. The shop's fine as it is. Nothing fancy, but people know Whittaker's and they know what to expect when they come in.'

'I don't mean anything too wildly different, really,' Maureen soothed. 'Just stock up a few new lines that tourists would like to buy. Stop wasting shelf space on the things that never sell . . . '

'I sold a wheelbarrow today,' Grace said defiantly. 'Not a tourist line at all! We've always been a general dealer, Mo. My mother started it and she kept whatever people needed. I wouldn't want to make big changes. Not at my time of life.'

'That's why I'm suggesting I stay on longer. Maybe for six months or so. We could think of some way to use those rooms above the shop to generate some income. Between us, with Patsy's help, we could really turn the business around.'

'But Patsy has a job,' Grace said stubbornly. 'She's off on that boat these days.'

'Only at the weekends, and not every one at that,' Maureen said patiently. 'I know she'll be willing to help.'

Grace sipped her sherry, deep in

thought. She would love to have Mo stay longer. For ever, preferably, although she knew this was unlikely. On the other hand — could she herself handle a whole new shop once her niece had left? She had no doubt that, if she agreed, Mo would make sweeping changes which, in her heart, Grace knew were needed.

Even while at school, Mo had always been very sure of herself, clear thinking and logical, and always able to win an argument by sheer force of character. Bossy, too. Grace smiled as she remembered. I suppose that's why they elected her head girl, she thought.

'I'll think about it,' she said eventually. 'You know there's nothing that would make me happier than to have you stay on with me. But I'd have to consider the cost. All these ideas of yours would mean spending money I don't have.'

'I could help, Aunt Grace. I'd love to,' Maureen blurted out. 'I've got some extra cash.'

'Oh, yes?'

'When I left Archie Wallis he was very generous. And when I converted my pounds sterling into South African rand, I was amazed! I've never had so much money in the bank.'

'And that's just where it should stay,' Grace said firmly. 'You'll need every penny when you get home. Didn't you say that your car was giving you trouble?'

'Yes, but I've had another idea. If I stayed for six months, I could arrange to rent out my house in Witham. The rent would make a nice little nest egg to come home to, and I would love to use some of my extra money to help make a few changes at Whittaker's.'

Grace approved of her niece's sound financial sense.

And the idea of a new image for the shop began to excite her — if only she could persuade Mo to stay for longer than six months. She didn't have a job waiting for her and she was clearly enjoying being back in Simonstown.

Inspiration

Then Grace had a flash of inspiration that offered the perfect solution. She couldn't bring herself to accept money from Mo, but what if she offered to make her niece a partner in the business? If she accepted, she'd have to stay! And she had no doubt that under Mo's firm guidance, everything they did in Whittaker's would be successful.

But there's no sense in rushing her, she thought cautiously. I'll sleep on it and see how best to approach the idea in the morning.

'Please, Aunt Grace, consider it,' Maureen wheedled. 'After all, you stand in the shop every day as it is. Wouldn't it be better if you were kept busy selling things instead of, well, just standing around?'

'Oh, get on with you!' Grace paused. 'Well, I suppose it does make good sense to use those top two rooms. Patsy thought of an art gallery.'

'Yes!' Maureen agreed at once. 'And

we could serve refreshments up there, and we wouldn't have to do a thing. We could sell home-made cakes that the church guild could make for us, so they'd be benefiting, too. We could hire a young person to serve the coffee and have local artists' paintings hanging on the walls . . . '

'Don't get carried away. I haven't agreed yet!' Grace said. 'We have to consider all the work it would entail. So let's say no more about it for now. Another sherry?'

Maureen shook her head.

'No, thanks, I think we should be getting home,' she said regretfully. 'Patsy will be wondering where we've got to.'

Warm Regards

They walked arm in arm along the darkened high street. All the shops were closed and Jubilee Square was deserted of cars and tourist coaches. A soft breeze played through the trees and, down below, the rows of yachts bobbed gently at their moorings. The statue of Just Nuisance remained silhouetted against the purple night sky, the dog's bronze nose pointing for ever towards the mountain.

The two of them had already sat down to supper when Patsy rushed in, her face flushed.

'Sorry I'm late, Mum. I was down at the yacht club with Steve, telling the gang about my job. They are all jealous of me!' she said, slipping into her chair around the dining-room table. 'Steve says *Sea Freedom* will probably take the Commodore's Cup this year. They were first over the line at Gordon's Bay, which means they've won every race of the season so far.'

'Well, I'm not surprised. It's such a big boat,' Maureen said. She had taken a walk down to the yacht club earlier and had a good look at it.

Patsy giggled.

'Mum, I mean it's won everything in

its class. Rick and the boys don't compete against little dinghies! Anyway, I can't wait until the next race at the end of the month.' She turned her attention to her food. 'Yummy, this smells great. What is it, Auntie Grace?'

'It's called *waterblommetjie bredie*,' Aunt Grace replied. 'It's one of Rugaya's old recipes. It's lamb stew, but these things that look like flowers are — well, they're flowers! Water flowers from some sort of plant that grows in the rivers and dams around here. They give it a nice flavour, I think.'

'Speaking of Rugaya,' Maureen began, 'I met her in the street this afternoon. It was lovely to see her again. She hasn't changed a bit.

'She had her granddaughter, Mellie, with her,' she went on. 'What an attractive girl she is. She told me she plans to go to university, but she has to find a job for a year or two to afford the fees.'

'That's what her brother, Rafe, has been doing,' Grace said. 'He's been

139

crewing on a fishing boat and apparently has enough saved to start his studies next year. Those two are so determined, I really admire them both.'

Maureen ruefully thought of Jack, refusing to take his studies seriously with no thought of his future. She wondered what Rugaya's magic formula was, to produce two such hard-working grandchildren.

Grace cleared her throat.

'Patsy, my dear, your mother and I have been talking about the shop. She's very keen that we should make a few changes there, but this might involve you as well, so we need to discuss it.'

Patsy glanced at her mother who gave her a small, conspirational grin. Maureen had known it was only a matter of time before her aunt came round.

★　★　★

Dear Warren and Rita. I hope all is going well with you both and that Jack is not giving you any problems with regard to his studies. I know how difficult it can be to persuade him to open a book! I had a short e-mail from him saying how much he liked being with you both. He says you make a mean chicken curry, Rita, so that is praise indeed from him!

As you know, I expected to be here for a fortnight to help my aunt sell up and retire, but she is an amazing woman and won't hear of it. The shop itself is in a very good position on the main road, but over the years it has been slowly losing money.

If she made a few changes and catered more for the passing trade of tourists she would do very well: in fact, the old shop could be a little gold mine!

So Patsy and I have decided to brighten up the walls with a lick of paint and help her to expand the business. If it all goes as we hope it will, she'll be able to afford a couple of sales assistants and then she could perhaps only work half days behind the counter. I'm afraid that retirement is not a word in Aunt Grace's dictionary!

So, the reason for this e-mail is to ask you if you would be able to have Jack stay with you for a further six months.

I know his exams start next week, but Rita, you are such a calm person I am sure you would be good at helping him to cope with all the stress.

Warren, I remember you mentioned a young couple in your company who needed somewhere to stay for a few weeks. As I am going to be away for longer than I thought, I wondered if they were still looking for somewhere, and if so, perhaps they could rent my house for a couple of months? I don't like to think of it standing empty, and the rent would be useful when I come back. I'd be very grateful if you could arrange that for me.

Maureen leaned back and read what she'd written. It sounded rather abrupt, but she'd never been much good at letters. She added a bit about exploring her old home town and how much Patsy was enjoying herself before pressing *Send*.

Warren can hardly refuse, she thought. After all, he is Jack's father and he's always resented only seeing him every second weekend. This could be good for both of them.

Then she wrote a second e-mail to Jack, telling him of her plans.

Just do your best and I'm sure you'll do well, sweetheart. Remember, don't try to stay up all night to cram at the last minute. Getting a good night's sleep before the exam is so important. When I get home we can discuss what you want to do next year. Of course this will depend a lot on your results. Perhaps you should take a gap year and work at some sort of job until you are sure of what you would like to do?

She pictured Jack pulling a face as he read this. She knew he secretly hoped that his father would pay for him to travel, as he had done for Patsy. But Warren had made it clear that this was a reward for their daughter doing so well in her studies.

Jack was completely unlike Patsy, who had been a mature, sensible teenager who took easily to responsibility.

I wonder if he'll be upset that I won't be there for him while he's studying, Maureen mused. Probably not. Rita will most likely spoil him and humour him far better than I would. I'd probably end up nagging him as usual and we'd have those awful scenes again.

Yet she couldn't help feeling guilty, as if she was somehow ducking her responsibilities to her son.

Doubt

'Don't be daft, Mo,' Aunt Grace told her when she voiced her anxieties. 'Your Jack's a big boy. Warren and Rita will make sure he gets enough sleep and

144

doesn't skip meals. His schoolwork is all up to him, really, isn't it?'

But Maureen couldn't prevent a hollow feeling of doubt that Jack wasn't going to do well enough in his exams. And then what would he do with himself? Be a plastics salesman like Warren? Not if she could help it. She was determined that Jack would study further and get proper training in something he enjoyed doing. But what that would be she had no idea. And neither, she knew, did Jack.

The two e-mailed replies she received the next day made her even more uneasy.

The first was from Rita.

Jack is welcome to stay on longer with us, of course, but I feel I should tell you that he has been neglecting his studies, despite my best efforts to encourage him. He started off with good intentions but he seems to have so many distractions — mainly two friends who persist in coming round and persuading him to go off with them. I'd like to forbid him, but I can't really as it's not my place. I'm only his stepmother, as he has reminded me more than once.

Oh, Jack, Maureen grieved, imagining the scenes. How could he be so rude to Rita, who only has his best interests at heart?

Warren has spoken to him about coming home at a reasonable hour, but nothing seems to get through to this lad. You seem worried about the stress the exams will cause him, but I have to say that I don't think that he is under any stress at all. He is totally ignoring the fact that he sits maths next week!

Furious

Her ex-husband's note was even more terse.

Rita and I have done our best, but Jack seems determined to fool around. He is upsetting Rita with his bad attitude and another six months of this behaviour is asking a lot of us, although, of course, we will let him stay here until you come home. You obviously have been too easy-going with him over the years and as a result he has no discipline or work ethic in his life.

This from Warren? Who never stopped telling her she was too harsh on the boy and he'd come right without her nagging him? Maureen was furious at his remarks and immediately decided that it was a good thing that Warren saw for himself just how very annoying their teenage son could be.

Re' your house. Andy Roberts, the new salesman I mentioned, is very keen to rent it, as it's practically next door to their daughter's new school. I will arrange to see him tonight, show him around and give him the keys. He and his wife are a very nice young couple and I think they will make excellent tenants. Please let me know as soon as you can what rent you would want for it.

Well, that was one good thing, at least.

Jack hadn't replied to her e-mail and she'd spent the whole day fretting. It didn't sound as though he was making any sort of effort to co-operate as he'd said he would. She felt a sudden longing to speak to her son and to try to sort things out, so that evening she took a deep breath and dialled Warren's number. To her surprise, Jack answered.

'Hey, Duggie. How's it going, man?'

'It's not Duggie. It's Mum,' she said, hoping that she didn't sound immediately annoyed.

'Oh, sorry, Mum. I was expecting a call.

'So you're staying over there a bit longer? That's cool.'

'I'm just staying for six months, to help out and fix the shop. But, Jack, I'm worried about you. Dad says you're not working as hard as you should, and — '

'Don't worry, Mum. Y'know, Dad's taking this whole exam thing too seriously, and Rita's being a real pain, going on about little things like me not making my bed.'

Maureen sighed.

'She just wants you to behave in a responsible way and to be polite,' she said. 'She's doing us both a favour, Jack, looking after you while I'm away.'

'Mum, I don't need looking after!'

The conversation wasn't going as Maureen had hoped, and an overseas call was too expensive to waste on arguments.

'Jack,' she said patiently, 'just help Rita out with the washing up and things like that, and do some schoolwork.'

Perhaps I've made the wrong decision staying on, she thought later. What if he fails all of his exams just because he's unhappy?

Warren doesn't sound sympathetic and Rita's obviously getting a bit fed up with him. Are they giving him the support he needs, she wondered.

No, it was Jack's fault! After all, Rita could hardly lock him in his room to study. At his age, it had to be his own decision.

Maureen's mind went round and round in unhappy circles until she fell into a fitful doze.

In the morning she looked out of her window at the white clouds scudding across the bay beyond the gum tree. She knew she'd made the right choice.

Going home to Jack wouldn't change his attitude to his schoolwork, and Aunt Grace needed her.

Getting Started

Maureen could tell that her aunt still had a few lingering doubts about modernising Whittaker's and she was careful to discuss every little change so that Grace wouldn't feel that they were moving too fast.

The first thing, she decided, should be to have a proper round-table discussion about what they wanted to do.

Both her children had always laughed at her habit of making lists for everything, but she felt that reinventing Whittaker's warranted buying an extra-thick new notebook for all their ideas.

One night after supper, she turned with pleasure to the first clean page and on the top wrote *To do*.

'Right. What's the first thing we should tackle?'

'I think that we should paint the shop inside a really bright white. And we should sand down all that old brown wood that makes the place look so gloomy. It'll look wonderful.'

Aunt Grace nodded.

'I agree. More light and space . . . '

'Now, what sort of new lines should we carry?' Maureen continued. 'What do tourists want the most?'

'Handicrafts,' Patsy said at once. 'But

ours should be different — unusual, even. There's that toy workshop up the valley. I told you about those African women, didn't I, Mum? Everything we've bought from them has sold almost the same day.'

Maureen made a note in her book.

'I saw some beautiful bead-covered bowls being sold on the pavement in Fish Hoek, and I think that they would do well, too. And if we could find a good potter willing to let us keep their work on a sale or return basis, then that's even better,' Maureen added.

'What's that?' Patsy asked.

'We put their pottery on our shelves and if we sell them they get their money, less our commission,' Aunt Grace said. 'And if they haven't sold after a month or two, we give them back.'

Maureen had some ideas for the local painters, too, but she didn't want to throw too many suggestions into the ring just yet, so she said nothing.

Patsy looked thoughtful.

'We could carry some sort of Just

Nuisance souvenir!' she said. 'Every tourist loves the story of that dog and I noticed most other shops have them.'

'Ours should be different, then,' Maureen put in. 'I really want everything we sell to be unique.'

Every idea sparked off another and Maureen's list grew longer and longer.

New carrier bags with shop name in bold lettering.

Find cheapest source of good quality souvenir cloths and tea-towels.

Ask about potters who could supply their products.

'What about antiques?' Aunt Grace asked tentatively. 'I do love old things.'

Maureen nodded excitedly, glad that Aunt Grace was getting involved.

'Oh, yes, that's a good idea. We could have a special antique collectibles corner and you can have all the fun of checking the car boot sales to see what bargains you can find!' she said. She just knew that it was going to be a success.

'Tomorrow we'll go and see anyone who produces handcrafts,' she continued, taking the empty plates from the table.

'If I didn't know better I'd say you've been running your own business all your life,' Grace said affectionately. 'It must be in your blood. Do you know, you're the third generation of Whittaker women to stand behind that counter?'

'And so I'm the fourth!' Patsy said. 'Even if I'm technically a Henderson. Isn't that great? It's Dynasty stuff!'

This seemed to be the perfect moment to broach the subject that was uppermost in Grace's mind. She took a deep breath.

'Mo, my dear,' she began. 'How would you feel about becoming a partner in Whittaker's? That way, you wouldn't be lending me the money, or giving it. You'd be investing your money in your own business.'

'Oh, Mum, that's a great idea!' Patsy cried, delighted. 'It would be a real family business, then! You could just stay on here for ever and take over when Aunt Grace wants to retire.'

'A partner in Whittaker's?' Maureen murmured, her mind racing ahead.

The idea was instantly appealing. She was loving the challenge of making changes and she was enjoying being back in South Africa. No job she could find in England would give her the satisfaction she was getting from the shop.

But stay here for longer? Years? What about Jack? She couldn't expect Warren and Rita to have him stay with them indefinitely, not after their e-mails. Perhaps once the exams were over Jack could study something at a college that had student housing.

Aunt Grace was looking at her with a hopeful little smile. Maureen made her decision. She gave a huge smile and hugged her aunt fiercely.

'Thank you, Aunt Grace. I'd be honoured to be your partner,' she said. 'I can't think of anything I'd like better!'

Catching Up

Maureen crossed the road and walked briskly past Jubilee Square. It was a week since she'd signed the papers which made her a full partner in the shop, and she still hadn't plucked up the courage to mention it to Jack. Not while he's in the thick of his exams, she told herself. There'll be plenty of time when they are over.

She passed a group of Japanese tourists who were photographing each other standing next to the statue of Just Nuisance, when she heard someone calling her name.

'Mo Whittaker?'

She swung around to face a tall, tanned man with a look of delighted disbelief on his face.

'Daniel Clayton?'

It was odd how, after twenty years, she could immediately recognise the boy who had been sports captain three years above her in school. Even more remarkable was the fact that he remembered her, a lowly junior, when he'd been captain of the rugby team and athlete of the year.

She'd worshipped him from afar, of course, along with the rest of the girls in her class, and she remembered how thrilled she'd been when he'd asked her to have a soda with him one afternoon. She'd been standing behind the counter in the shop and he'd come in and bought one, still in his school uniform.

As an afterthought he'd bought her one, too, and stood chatting casually about rugby while he gulped down his drink.

She smiled to herself, remembering how she'd boasted to her friends that he'd bought her a drink, making it sound like some sort of date. She'd kept the empty can for a long time as a souvenir of being chatted up by someone so awe inspiring.

'I thought you'd moved away ages ago,' he said. 'I don't think I've seen you for . . . '

'Twenty years!' she finished. 'I went overseas on a backpacking holiday and settled there. But I'm home now, helping my aunt in the shop.'

It was funny how easy it was to call it home, she reflected. Witham seemed very far away.

'Miss Whittaker, isn't she? Whittaker's General Dealers? That place has been going ever since I can remember.'

Maureen nodded.

'I've joined her as a partner and we're making a few changes,' she told him. 'My daughter's here, too, until she goes back to the UK to study.'

'Let's have a coffee and catch up,' he suggested, much to Maureen's delight.

They seated themselves outside the small tearoom on the Square and smiled at each other.

Daniel's face was tanned and weather-beaten and his thick thatch of hair was flecked with grey, but he was still as good looking as she remembered, his narrow face lit by his twinkling brown eyes.

'So, tell me what you're doing these days,' she said.

'I've done a bit of everything, but

now I run a tuna boat from Kalk Bay,' he said. 'In good weather I take tourists out beyond Cape Point for game fishing. Marlin, bonita, tuna, that sort of thing.' That accounted for his tan. 'American clients, mostly. I'm kept pretty busy. What about you?'

'Nothing as interesting, I'm afraid,' she said. 'I was a book-keeper in a plumber's wholesaler for five years. When that job came to an end last month, I decided to come out and visit Aunt Grace. And here I am!'

'OK, that takes care of the now. Fill me in on the past twenty years.'

Maureen smiled. For the next ten minutes she told him about her life in the UK, glossing over the years before her divorce and describing the pleasures of living in a small English town. Something about the interested, sympathetic way he listened encouraged her to open up more than she intended and she found herself sharing her pride in Patsy, as well as her anxieties about Jack.

'If he doesn't pass his exams I don't know what he'll do,' she ended. 'I want him to have a good training for a decent career. Oh, dear, I don't know why I'm telling you all of my worries. Typical mother. I'm sorry!'

'Don't be. Jack sounds as though he has some growing up to do, that's all. Lots of boys don't decide what to do with their lives until they're well into their twenties. I was exactly the same.'

'But you've ended up all right. I mean, you're happy with what you're doing now?' Maureen was curious.

'I love it, but it took me a long time to find what I wanted to do. Along the way I made a few bad mistakes. One of those was my marriage.' He looked away, grimacing ruefully.

'You're married?' Of course he would be.

'I was. We married too young and too hastily and repented at leisure, as they say. It was a mutual decision to call it a day seven years later.'

'I'm sorry,' she murmured.

He was silent.

Daniel paid the bill and they left the tearoom.

'Well, I really must be off,' Maureen said. 'I'm on my way to meet a potter who lives down the road. Priscilla Harman. I've heard her work is good and I want to persuade her to let us sell her things in our shop.'

'Priscilla? Her stuff is excellent,' he replied. 'She's a local character. She's quite famous and sells a lot of her work to the art galleries in Cape Town. In fact, she prefers to be called a ceramic artist, not a potter.'

'Well, maybe she'd like to display some ceramic art in a local shop for a change,' Maureen said. 'Goodbye, Dan, it was lovely to meet you again.'

She turned to go but Daniel caught her hand.

'Hang on, Mo! You can't just walk away and vanish from my life. Maybe you'd like to come out for dinner with me one evening this week?'

'I'd love to,' she replied.

'Good.' His grip was warm and reassuring. 'I'll phone you at your aunt's.'

As Maureen walked away she couldn't help grinning. A date with Daniel Clayton at last! Twenty years too late and with a very different Daniel, but still, it was a date! This would be the first time she'd agreed to go out with a man since her divorce. She hoped Patsy would approve.

Grounded

Priscilla Harman lived in a small cottage overlooking the sea on the edge of town. A sign on the gate said *Studio at the back*.

Maureen followed the brick path around the house to where a large white-washed building stood amidst the overgrown garden, the big wooden doors ajar.

From inside came the sound of opera music, with someone singing along in a husky voice, rather off-key.

'Hello?' Maureen knocked tentatively. 'Priscilla Harman?'

A small, fierce woman was hunched over a potter's wheel, her thick grey hair in a long plait behind her back. She was concentrating on a tall clay cylinder taking shape under her hands and she didn't look up.

'Who wants me?' she barked. 'I'm working. I'm not buying Christmas cards and I'm not interested in doing any market surveys, either.'

'I'm not selling. I'm hoping to buy. Well, not exactly buy . . .'

Priscilla looked up.

'You're from England? I thought you were one of those pests who come round from door to door. When people know you work from home they never leave you alone.'

She allowed the wheel to slow down gradually and stop spinning. She wiped her hands roughly on a cloth.

'Do I really sound so English?' Maureen asked in surprise. 'I was born here in Simonstown, but I've been living overseas for ages. I'm Maureen Henderson, Grace Whittaker's niece.'

'Ah, Whittaker's — I love that old shop, it's part of this town's history.'

'Yes, I know, but we want to modernise it a bit inside.' Maureen explained her mission.

'So we're hoping that you would let us display a few of your pieces on a sale or return basis,' she said. 'Your pottery is really beautiful. There's something different about it.'

Spectacular

The pots and bowls standing around were glazed in deep, rich reds and vibrant oranges with flashes of brilliant yellows.

'But I'm not interested in doing sale or return. I can sell just about everything I make to the galleries in Cape Town. Interior designers like my larger pieces,' Priscilla said.

'I can see why. But you could sell

your work in our shop for the same price as the big galleries and we would only take fifteen per cent commission.'

'Really? It might be worth thinking about, I suppose.'

Maureen stroked the shining surface of an enormous scarlet and purple platter, imagining lemons and oranges piled high on it. No wonder interior designers bought Priscilla's pieces — they were spectacular. Her mind leaped ahead, already inviting selected customers to buy direct from the shop instead of the galleries.

'And we're very well positioned for the tourists,' Maureen persuaded. 'We have a lot of passing trade.'

It was surprising that just brightening up the interior with a coat of white paint meant that far more people were popping in to see what was on offer.

'And most of them don't have time to go into galleries in Cape Town, but if they saw your stuff they wouldn't be able to resist it,' she wheedled.

'Let's have a cup of tea and talk

about it,' Priscilla said.

Maureen sat on an old rattan chair draped with an Indian throw and looked around. The shelves were lined with unglazed bowls and platters, as well as some finished ware. Buckets of mixed glazes and bags of powder stood on the floor and an enormous kiln took up one whole wall at the far end of the room.

The opera music had given way to some folk singing and Priscilla hummed along while she brewed the tea. She served home-made ginger snaps with the tea in her own pottery mugs and they were delicious.

By the time the cups were cold, both women were getting on well and Priscilla had agreed to deliver ten small pots, bowls and jugs to Whittaker's.

'We'll see how it goes,' she said. 'I'll price the things slightly below what they go for in Cape Town. And any breakages are to your account.'

'Of course,' Maureen agreed. 'You won't be sorry. I promise!'

Miserable

She couldn't wait to get back to tell Patsy and Aunt Grace about her success. If people knew Priscilla Harman was displaying her work in the shop, other crafters would follow suit, she was sure.

But Patsy was waiting on the verandah for her when she returned. She waved to her mother and ran down to meet her at the gate, looking anxious and upset.

'Jack's on the phone, Mum. He sounds awfully miserable.'

Maureen ran up the steps and into the hall, her heart pounding.

'Jack, what's wrong?'

'Everything,' Jack said sulkily, his voice as clear as if he was phoning from round the corner. 'Dad says I'm grounded. He won't let me leave the house except to sit the exams. He's treating me like a child, and Rita keeps fussing over me. I can't stand living here any more, Mum. I wish I was at home with you. Can you tell Aunt Grace that you've changed your mind and you're coming back?'

He sounded like a little boy again and Maureen felt torn apart. Her son was admitting that he needed her and was begging her to come home. How could she refuse him?

But how could she agree? Patsy stood watching her, an odd look in her eye. And, behind her, Aunt Grace was expressionless.

'Jack . . . ' Maureen croaked. 'I — I'll phone you in ten minutes.'

She put down the receiver and burst into tears.

5

Wake-up Call

Maureen sat down heavily, tears streaming down her face. 'Jack needs me at home!'

Patsy snorted.

'Mum, that's absolute nonsense,' she said angrily. 'He's not getting his own way with Dad and Rita and he thinks that you'll come running back to hold his hand the minute he asks you to. He's eighteen years old, not eight!'

'I know. But these exams are so important and he sounded so miserable. He can't be expected to work if he's unhappy,' Maureen replied.

Patsy reached out and held her mother's hand.

'Mum, listen to me. Jack will do anything to get out of doing a bit of work, you know that. He's looking for excuses. He probably hasn't done nearly enough studying and now he thinks if he doesn't do well he'll be able to blame the fact he was unhappy. He'll make you feel guilty because you weren't there. Can't you see he's got you around his little finger?'

'Oh. Patsy.' Maureen murmured. 'It was different for you. You found school so easy. Jack needs a lot of encouragement and — '

'I'm sorry, but all Jack needs is a good wake-up call!' Patsy snapped. 'Nothing you can do at this stage will make the slightest bit of difference to his results. You can't go flying back to him now — you have an obligation to Auntie Grace. The shop, remember? Partners?'

Maureen was silent, her thoughts in turmoil.

'Mum! How can you even consider going home?'

Maureen had never seen Patsy like this, her face flushed with anger. It struck her suddenly that Patsy might have been jealous of the way her younger brother had taken up more of her mother's time while they were growing up. Jack had always needed extra attention for his problems, while Patsy had been independent from an early age and had bubbled through life causing her almost no worries.

And Maureen knew her daughter was blessed with clear vision and was probably spot on in her opinion.

'You're right, Patsy,' she said abruptly. 'I can't consider leaving now. Jack is being thoroughly unreasonable to expect it. I'll phone him and tell him so. He must sort things out with his dad and Rita.'

Aunt Grace smiled and patted her shoulder.

'You know, he sounded quite distraught, but I think when he phoned he'd just had a big argument with Warren. He'll probably get over it tomorrow. You give him a call, and Patsy and I will do something about supper.'

She led the way to the kitchen and left Maureen alone.

She steeled herself for a scene and dialled Warren's number, expecting Jack to pick up immediately. To her surprise, Rita answered after several rings.

'Oh, hello, Maureen, how nice to hear from you. Everything going well?'

'Yes, fine, thanks. I wanted to speak to Jack,' she said, puzzled. 'He phoned a few minutes ago and he sounded upset. Something about a fight with his dad.'

Rita laughed.

'Oh, that daft Jack! He and Warren had a big barney at tea, but now they're friends again, of course. It's been a bit of a rollercoaster in this house, as we told you, but things are going a lot better.'

Her son hadn't sounded as though he agreed with this, Maureen thought.

'Jack's very edgy with exams, of course, and his nerves get the better of him sometimes, but we quite understand,' Rita continued. 'Right now they are both in the study. Warren's showing

Jack something on the computer. I'll call him.'

There was silence on the line before Jack answered cheerfully.

'Hi, Mum! Dad's just found this wicked site with questions and answers from old history exams. I'm printing it out and I'll try to memorise them. Dad reckons I'm sure to get some of them in the paper next week.'

Maureen was nonplussed.

'So you're OK to stay on there, after all? You don't need me to come home?' she asked.

'No, I'm fine. Don't worry, Mum. I suppose I must have sounded a bit fed up, but you know how Dad gets up my nose sometimes. But we're cool now.'

'That's good,' she said crossly, 'because I wasn't going to come over, anyway. And it wasn't fair of you to ask me, Jack. Patsy and I were both very upset by your call, and now it seems it was all for nothing!'

'I'm sorry, Mum,' he said humbly. 'I don't really expect you to drop everything and come back. I'm fine with you staying another six months.'

'I'm glad to hear that,' she said with a sigh. 'I'm staying on quite a bit longer. Aunt Grace and I have become partners in the business, but I'll write and tell you all the details. You just concentrate on passing those exams, and no more fights with your dad, all right?'

'That's cool, Mum. You stay as long as you like — I've got plans for after the exams, too. Bye!'

'Well, really,' Maureen muttered, hugely relieved, but still annoyed with herself for becoming so upset. 'That boy!'

A Date

After the supper things were cleared away, Grace took out a red leather album with black paper, the pictures separated by yellowed tissue paper.

'Tomorrow's the monthly meeting of the Historical Society,' she said. 'They're having a lecture on the old Naval burial ground at Seaforth, and I suddenly remembered an old photo I have of your grandfather, Mo, in his uniform just before he embarked. You know there's a plaque there in memory of his boat that went down with all hands, off Jutland? I thought they might like to see this.'

Maureen looked at the old brown photograph, with the inscription in white ink below: *Able Seaman Bertie Whittaker, 1940*. It showed a young man in dark bell-bottoms, smiling confidently into the camera.

'He was a good-looking man, wasn't he?' Maureen said. 'I think I see a bit of Jack in him.'

'It's sad, I can hardly remember him,' Grace said. 'I was only four when he left and he never came back.'

'Let's have a look at your other photos, Auntie Grace.' Patsy flicked through the pictures, smiling at the old fashions. 'You were such a pretty little girl, Auntie. I love this hat!'

'That picture was taken in 1947 and

I was all dressed up to meet the King and Queen,' Grace told her.

Patsy was amazed.

'You met the royal family?' she asked excitedly.

'No, but I was quite sure I was going to!' Grace chuckled. 'They came to South Africa with the two princesses and visited the Naval dockyards here and everyone went to watch. Of course, I just caught a glimpse of them as they drove past. All the children were given little Union Jack flags to wave. I've still got mine, somewhere.'

'What's this?' Patsy pointed to a picture of a small girl with her arm around an enormous Great Dane.

Aunt Grace smiled.

'Oh, that's me with Just Nuisance. The only dog ever to be officially enlisted in the Navy! During the war he used to wander around Simonstown quite freely and I always saved a fish paste sandwich for him. He didn't usually let children get very close, but for some reason he let me stroke him.'

Patsy looked thoughtful.

'You know, we could use this photograph in the shop window,' she mused. 'He was such a famous dog, but there aren't many pictures of him around. I bet this is unique.'

Maureen was aware that she herself was always thinking about the shop and the changes that they would make, but she hadn't thought her daughter was too concerned.

Patsy was full of surprises and she was looking forward to the two of them working together. What was it that Patsy had said? The family shop was dynasty stuff!

* * *

'So, do I get to meet this fabulous man of yours this evening?' Patsy asked impishly. 'Or are you going to keep him a secret for ever?'

'Oh, Patsy, don't be silly! Of course Dan's not a secret. And he's not fabulous. He's just a nice man that I knew a hundred years ago, and we're going out for a meal.'

'Come on, Mum, he's a date!' Patsy said. 'This is the third time you've been out with him, and he must be fabulous or you wouldn't have bought a new dress. Which looks great, by the way. It really suits you.'

'Thanks,' Maureen murmured. Far from being disapproving, Patsy had been thrilled when she had mentioned meeting Daniel Clayton again, but up till now she'd always been out whenever Dan called. 'What do you think? Hair up, or down?'

'Up,' Patsy replied. 'Let me do it, Mum. You always leave bits hanging loose.'

Maureen looked at her reflection, soothed by Patsy's firm brush strokes. I do look good, she thought happily. I've lost some weight and blue is just my colour. I've picked up a tan, too, even though I'm more in the shop than out of it these days.

'Now, just relax and enjoy yourself tonight, Mum,' Patsy said reprovingly.

'Sometimes I worry about you. I mean, it's been six years since you and Dad parted, and he's found Rita and now he's very happy. But you don't let anyone get near to you. No man, anyway.'

A lecture like this from Patsy!

'I haven't met anyone I liked well enough to want to get close to them,' Maureen answered truthfully. 'I hardly met anyone behind that computer in the back office with Archie.'

'What about Mr Forbes, Jack's history teacher? I could see he fancied you,' Patsy said. 'And that insurance man who kept coming round last year, Richard or Robert . . . he was nice and I could see he liked you.'

Maureen nodded thoughtfully.

'But there was no . . . Oh, I don't know. I shouldn't expect bells and fireworks at my time of life, I suppose. But there has to be more than just liking someone, don't you think?' she said eventually.

'Of course, you're right.' Patsy grinned mischievously. 'Liking's a good start, though.

Fireworks sound even better. So maybe Dan's the man?'

'Dan's just a friend.'

But was there the beginning of something more than friendship? Maureen thought she could feel something deeper between them. Not that she had any intention of admitting this to Patsy just yet.

'Oh, there's his knock. You go and let him in, love. I'll be along in a minute once I've put on some lipstick. You can give him the once-over and tell me later if he wins the Patsy Henderson stamp of approval!'

But Maureen couldn't suppress a little frisson of excitement as she took a last look in the mirror. There might not be fireworks with Dan, but she had to admit to a little sparkler inside!

At Ease

'That's quite a girl you've got there,' Dan said, sitting opposite Maureen in the dimly lit restaurant. 'No wonder you're proud of her.'

'I hope she didn't give you the third degree?' she asked.

Dan smiled.

'Not at all. We had a good chat. She tells me she has a part-time job on a boat.'

'Yes, on *Sea Freedom*. Don't you belong to the yacht club?' Maureen asked. 'I thought everyone did around here.'

'Not me. I keep my boat at Kalk Bay, in the fishing harbour there. I'm a working man, Mo, not one of your weekend sailors! When I've finished the day my hands are full of engine oil and I smell of fish. I wouldn't last two minutes in that club!' He laughed.

'You clean up pretty well, though,' she teased.

'Thank you, ma'am. You're not looking too bad yourself!'

Maureen smiled. She felt so at ease with him, almost as though she'd known him all her life, yet she was only getting to know him now. They'd been out for coffee several times, and he'd taken her to lunch at a seafood restaurant on the beach where they'd eaten crab and watched a group of whales blowing and diving fifty yards from their table.

Tonight they were dining elegantly in what once had been an eighteenth century farmhouse and was now a trendy restaurant. It was lit by hundreds of candles around the walls and on the table, with the soft light flickering off the antiques and classical music playing softly in the background.

It had been years since Maureen had been so pampered and she couldn't help feeling a little guilty. She knew Dan wasn't a rich man.

'This is such a lovely place,' she observed. 'You're spoiling me!'

'I want to,' he said, leaning over and pressing her hand. There was no mistaking the feeling behind his words and the warmth of his grasp. She met his eyes and smiled, confused.

'I can't think of anyone I'd rather spoil,' he said softly. 'You've become very dear to me, Maureen.'

She let her hand stay where it was, secure under his own. She felt the rough calluses on his palm and instinctively caressed them with her thumb, not knowing how to reply.

'Working man's hands,' he said. 'Does it bother you that I'm not one of your office types?'

'Of course not! Besides, I couldn't imagine you sitting behind a desk — it wouldn't suit you at all,' she reassured him.

'You're right. I'd really like you to come out on my boat one day, with the fishermen. See what I do.'

Maureen giggled.

'Oh, yes, so I could bait the hooks for them with rotten fish heads?' she teased.

'No, I've got young Rafe for those sorts of jobs. You could just sit back and admire the view.'

'Rafe?' she queried. 'That wouldn't

be Rafe Daniels, would it?'

'It would. He's been with me for two years, but he's off to university and it's going to be difficult to replace him. Why, do you know the lad?'

Maureen shook her head.

'No, but I know his granny, Rugaya Daniels. And I've met his sister, Mellie. She's a sweet girl. I believe she's also planning to study.'

Dan took a deep breath, still holding her hand.

'Mo, look, I'm not very good with words, but I just wanted you to know that since we've met up again, I — I know that you're the only woman I want to be with.'

'Oh.' Maureen was at a loss for words. 'Dan, I — '

'Shush. Don't say anything.' He pressed his finger to her lips with a lop-sided grin. 'I thought I should tell you, so you know where we stand. And when you decide how you feel, you can tell me, OK?'

A Goodnight Kiss

Dan was a practical man and not given to flowery speeches, but Maureen was deeply touched. She was used to Warren, with his glib tongue and salesman's patter to cover every situation, but Dan's few words rang with sincerity.

She was spared any further conversation by the waiter who came to take their order. Dan visibly relaxed and picked up the menu.

'So, what do you fancy? Fillet of ostrich? Crayfish? I see they have venison tonight, how about that?' he asked.

For the rest of the evening they discussed neutral subjects; the progress in the shop, his experiences with some German tourists who'd chartered his boat, and the fact that Jack's exams were over at last. But there was an indefinable tension that hadn't been there before.

When he took her home, the house

was in darkness, apart from a light that Aunt Grace had left on in the hall.

'It's way past my bedtime,' Maureen said lightly. 'Thank you, Ian. This was a lovely evening.'

She leaned up to kiss him gently on the cheek, but he took her firmly in his arms and kissed her properly. She felt herself responding, leaning into his tall, muscular frame and enjoying the strength of his arms around her. It felt so right and their kiss went on and on for what seemed like minutes.

When they broke apart, Maureen stared at him, breathless.

'Hey, Dan,' she croaked.

'Hey, Mo.' He took her chin gently in his hand. 'Is that your answer then? To how you feel about me?'

'Maybe,' she said, smiling. 'But goodnight for now.'

She went inside and shut the door, her heart pounding and a huge smile on her face.

So maybe there were fireworks, after all!

Perfect

The carpenter Dan had found for them was busy hammering up shelves, so Maureen and Grace took a break from the noise in the shop by going outside to the back courtyard. Three small storerooms, filled with years of old stored junk, had been cleared out and painted and were ready for use. But for what?

'Storage space so close to the main road would be very useful for the right person,' Maureen said. 'We'll put up a sign advertising the space to let and I'm sure someone would be interested. And this courtyard's paved so prettily with old bricks. They took trouble with the details in the old days, didn't they?'

She looked around.

'You know, I've been thinking that this would make a perfect little tea garden. If we whitewashed the walls, we could easily fit four tables in here, with umbrellas. We could buy those little wrought-iron chairs, put pots of geraniums against the wall — it would be perfect!'

'A tea garden means a lot of extra work,' Grace protested, but Maureen stopped her.

'Not if we start small. We could hire a young girl to make the drinks and serve the customers, and with only four tables, there would probably never be more than eight or ten people at one time. We wouldn't need to offer a huge variety. Just coffee and tea, and if we found someone to supply us with fresh muffins every morning, the word would soon get around.'

Grace smiled at her niece's enthusiasm.

'You make it sound so easy! Well, why don't you work out how much it will cost and we'll discuss it.'

Maureen made a note to do her sums that evening.

Inside the shop, controlled chaos reigned, but only until the new shelves were installed and painted. Then they would become the area she already thought of as their gift section. A new consignment of brightly painted wooden toys was waiting to be unpacked along with some uneven hand-blown glass bowls and carved wooden platters, hand-made jewellery and delicate pictures made from dried seaweed.

Grace had suggested a special area for tourists, so a big display of postcards already made a colourful corner. The shop was taking shape very nicely and when Priscilla's pottery came, which was due to arrive the next day, she had a wide shelf ready for her pieces.

'I'm just off to the library, Aunt Grace,' Maureen said. 'I thought I could put a little note on the community board about our back rooms while I'm there. Will you be all right on your own for a while?'

'Mo, sweetheart, I've been on my own in this shop for years and years. Why wouldn't I be all right? Off you go.'

Maureen detected a note of impatience in her aunt's voice and smiled.

'Of course you'll be fine. I just meant that if a coach load of tourists arrives all at once you might not be able to handle the rush. I won't be long.'

I hope I'm not being too bossy, she thought, walking towards the town centre, but she can't blame me for being a bit anxious with all the changes we've made. It's amazing the way she's learned to operate the new electronic till so quickly. And getting to know all the new stock and remembering where it is on the shelves. On the other hand, why am I so surprised? Aunt Grace was always as sharp as a needle.

'Morning, Maureen!'

Rugaya waved at her and crossed the street, her long gown billowing in the wind, her granddaughter alongside. Mellie looked every inch the modern miss, Maureen noted. She was wearing jeans and a sparkly sweater with stripy neon socks and trainers.

'Hi, Rugaya. Hi, Mellie. How's the job-hunting going?'

She remembered the girl was hoping

to find regular work so she could save towards her university fees.

'Nothing yet.' Mellie pulled a face. 'I've applied for loads of jobs, but everyone wants experience and I don't have any. All I've ever done is help Gran with cooking.'

'But she got an A for five of her subjects last term,' Rugaya said proudly. 'I keep telling her she'll find something soon!'

Maureen had a sudden thought. Mellie would be perfect!

'Can you make tea and coffee?' she asked.

'Of course,' Mellie said, puzzled.

'Then how would you like to be in charge of our new tea garden? I'm hoping to have it up and running by next week.'

An Offering

She watched Mellie's face light up as she clutched Rugaya's arm in delight.

Sums or not, the tea garden would have to open now!

'Why don't you both come round to the shop tomorrow and we can talk about it?'

'A tea garden?' Rugaya queried. 'You mean that little space outside at the back of the shop?'

Maureen nodded.

'It would just be a small one to start with, and only in the summer. We'll only serve muffins or something simple. If it's a success, we could expand it upstairs in winter and get some more tables, but we'll have to see.'

'Muffins?' Rugaya pretended to look insulted. 'And what is wrong with my *melkert*? And my *koeksusters*? And my cinnamon spice biscuits?'

'Oh, Rugaya! Absolutely nothing! Why didn't I think of it? You're the best baker I know. You could supply the goodies. Would you, really?'

'No problem, Maureen. Cooking is how I earn my living! I've been catering for dinner parties for a long time, making curry and that sort of thing. But I'd appreciate this chance to do something more regular.'

'When Gran and I come over tomorrow, we'll bring a price list with us,' Mellie said firmly.

'That's an excellent idea,' Maureen said. 'A price list will save time. I'll see you both tomorrow!'

She walked on to the library, humming to herself. All their ideas for the shop seemed to be falling into place. Now all she needed was good news about Jack's exam results.

A Great Start

Patsy was busy packing the small refrigerator on board *Sea Freedom* with the essentials for a weekend up the coast. Beer, white wine and Greg's favourite tipple, a cream and honey liqueur, which he sipped late at night under the stars.

She brought a big box of supplies on board. For the evening meal she planned to do chicken, using one of Rugaya's delicious, delicately flavoured Malay curry recipes. For Greg, who didn't eat meat, she'd use the same recipe with an assortment of vegetables. For dessert she'd already made an apple tart in Grace's kitchen, lightly sprinkled with sugar and cinnamon.

Looking around her little domain below deck, she was well pleased. Over the past weekends she'd arranged everything just as she liked it, buying a lot of spices and condiments that she needed. At the end of every sailing trip she received fulsome compliments from the crew and knew she'd made a success of being the cook.

She still wished Rick wouldn't be so stiff, though. While she already thought of the other two crew members as friends, Rick, although always pleasant, seemed determined to keep their relationship on a business footing.

She heard the men's voices on deck and straightened up, closing the fridge door.

'Hi, Martin. Hi, Greg,' she called. 'The beer's all packed away and ready when you are.'

'Got your priorities right, I see.' Greg grinned, taking the stairs down into the cabin two at a time. He was followed by a small, dark-haired girl.

'Patsy, meet Linda Howard. Linda, this is Patsy — be nice to this girl if you want breakfast!'

'Hi.' Linda grinned at her. 'I'm not sure if I should even think about food. I'm terrified of getting seasick.'

'Is this your first time sailing?' Patsy was sympathetic. 'Maybe you'd better stick to dry toast and see how you feel.'

'Never mind the toast, I could use one of those cold beers right now,' Greg said.

'Listen, mate, first we leave the harbour, then we have breakfast, then we crack open the beers!' Martin retorted, tossing his bag in his cabin.

The girls exchanged amused glances.

'Can I help you?' Linda asked. 'I'd rather be useful down here than fall overboard on my first trip!'

'Thanks,' Patsy said, glad to have feminine company for a change. 'You could beat the eggs, if you like. Are we racing today, do you know?'

'Nope,' Rick said, clattering down the stairs. 'There isn't a race scheduled. I thought we'd cruise up the west coast and overnight at Langebaan in the lagoon there. Maybe catch a couple of crayfish at Dassen Island and have them for supper.'

'Catch them?' Greg scoffed. 'Your way of catching crayfish is with a couple of bottles of wine!'

'Old sailing secret,' Rick said to Patsy. 'You'll see.'

It was perfect sailing weather, with a light breeze lifting the mainsail, and they were underway in minutes. By now Patsy was accustomed to the routine of hoisting the sails and leaving the harbour, and by the time the three men were done with their tasks, the girls were ready with the breakfast of muesli, scrambled eggs with fried tomatoes, and toast and honey.

'Another great start to the day,' Martin said, surveying the table and pouring himself some orange juice. 'Patsy, remember that my offer of marriage still holds.'

'You only love me for my cooking,' she teased. 'I don't intend to marry someone who'd keep me barefoot and in the kitchen!'

'You tell him,' Greg said. 'So what do you do, Patsy, when you're not keeping us fed and watered?'

'I help my mum and my great-aunt in their shop in Simonstown. It's been in the family for ages and when my mum came over she decided to stay on a while and make a lot of changes. So they need me right now, but in a year or so I'd like to do a course in catering, and run my own business one day.'

'Would you go back to England to study?'

'I'm not sure.' When Patsy thought about going home, she couldn't imagine fitting back into her old life. 'I suppose I could do the course at college here just as easily.'

I hope Mum decides to stay for a long time, she thought, then I won't have to make any decisions soon.

Linda, who had been toying with a piece of dry toast and saying nothing, suddenly started to look very pale.

'Why don't you go up on deck and get some fresh air?' Patsy suggested, recognising the signs. 'Take big, deep breaths and don't look at the horizon.'

Honestly, Greg could have introduced her to sailing a bit more gently, she thought crossly. It's always choppy around Cape Point, and we're away for two whole days. What if she's seasick the whole time?

The others went above deck while Patsy washed the breakfast things and packed everything neatly away. By the time she was finished, they were around Cape Point and sailing downwind in a stiff south-easter. To Patsy's relief, Linda looked a great deal more cheerful.

'At this rate we'll reach Dassen Island

well before lunch,' Martin said, peering at the instruments. 'Eight knots, pretty good.'

Rick was standing at the wheel, scanning the horizon as *Sea Freedom* scythed through the swell and the land shrank away to a thin blue line.

'OK, boys, up spinnaker!' Rick barked, and Greg and Martin leaped to their feet, scrambling to the front as quickly as they could, their canvas shoes clinging to the sharp angle of the deck, and yanked the rope that released the spinnaker from its bag.

The huge red and blue triangle billowed out and immediately their speed increased dramatically.

'Like it?' Rick was grinning at her.

'Oh, yes!' She'd never felt anything like this. Even in the races they hadn't gone this fast. She felt a surge of exhilaration.

'Come and sit here.' Rick indicated the bench next to him. 'I'll switch to autopilot for a while. It's all straight ahead for a bit.'

The five of them sat together in the cockpit, enjoying the sun on their faces and chatting comfortably. Linda was clearly nervous being at sea and Greg kept up a continuing flow of teasing and banter to put her at ease.

'This is the life,' Rick said, his eyes half closed.

He looks so much younger when he's relaxed like this, Patsy thought. All the tight lines have gone from around his mouth.

'I'd like to keep right on sailing up the coast to the Med and never come back. Cruise around the islands off Croatia. How does that sound?'

'Ha! I reckon you'd be back in a week, suffering withdrawal symptoms,' Greg said laconically, his arm around Linda. 'Patsy, you're looking at a driven man. He's such a workaholic that if we didn't drag him kicking and screaming down to Cape Town for a bit of sailing every now and again, he'd probably sleep in his office.'

'Not true.' Rick opened his eyes and

smiled at her. 'Actually, I'd love to live here and sail every weekend.'

'It's all the wine,' Greg said. 'If I lived here I'd visit a different wine estate every chance I got and start my own wine cellar.'

'No, it's all the sun and sea,' Martin argued. 'Whatever beach you go to, there are people swimming any time of the day, although I'm sure they're meant to be at work like the rest of us!'

'They're probably tourists,' Patsy said. 'Our shop gets a lot of visitors coming in and buying souvenirs and postcards. The poor things spend the day in an air-conditioned coach going around the Peninsula, so if they have a day off from touring I bet they head straight to the beach. I know I would.' She hesitated. 'So what sort of work do you do, Martin?'

'I'm a financial adviser in a trust company. And Greg here earns his pennies as a supermarket manager.'

'And Rick?'

'I do a bit of — hey! Watch out!'

Amazing

Right next to them a whale surfaced with a snort, its great grey back glistening above a ring of foam frothing around it as it shot to the top of the water. Linda gave a shriek of fear.

'It's going to blow!'

Unable to dodge, they stood help-lessly as the whale spouted a fountain of water from its blow hole, drenching them in an instant. Then it seemed to wallow in the water next to them and Patsy could see its little eye focusing on them almost humorously, before it slid beneath the surface again.

'That was amazing. I never dreamed I'd get that up close and personal with a whale,' she gasped.

'We were pretty lucky,' Rick said, watching it dive, leaving a ripple of bubbles in its wake. 'If it had come up underneath us we would have been in real trouble. I've seen what happens to yachts that run into a whale.'

For the rest of the way up to Dassen

Island, he switched off autopilot and kept a good look out.

Patsy went below to make coffee and warm the muffins for elevenses. Linda followed her down to change her wet clothes.

'That was quite enough excitement for me,' she said nervously. 'I was terrified. But you seemed to enjoy it.'

'I did. It was amazing!' Patsy replied.

'You really like sailing then? Greg told me you kayak, as well? Have you always been such an outdoors person?'

Patsy shook her head.

'Not really. But I love it. You know, you gave me an idea earlier. I could study here instead of going back home.'

'Wouldn't you get homesick? I could never live in another country. I'd miss my friends and family too much.'

Patsy considered. From this distance, Witham seemed too tame, and almost too orderly.

'I expect my mother will go back in a couple of years, so I might, too,' she said slowly. 'But living here is great. I'd

203

miss this weekend job and I'd miss being able to surf, and climb, and I've made so many friends . . . '

'And Rick's one of them? I've noticed!'

'Oh, no!' Patsy said hurriedly. 'Not really. He's my boss. As far as he's concerned I just work for him.'

'I'm not so sure,' Linda said shrewdly. 'I saw the way he looked at you. And I've known Rick for ages. He's a very private person and never shows his feelings, and ever since Evelyn he's been very wary of girls in any shape or form.'

'Evelyn?' Patsy queried.

'She was his fiancée. They broke up a couple of years ago. She was totally wrong for him, of course, all his friends could see that. But not Rick. She dumped him for a mega-rich Saudi investor.'

'Poor Rick.'

So perhaps she'd mistaken a defensive shell for coldness. Patsy felt oddly comforted by this thought.

When they reached the sheltered water off Dassen Island, Rick anchored in the little bay and whistled loudly. From a small building close to the rocky shore an old man appeared, waved enthusiastically and pushed a rowing boat out towards them.

These waters were dark with floating kelp, a thick seaweed that made rowing difficult, and to Patsy's surprise the old man suddenly stopped rowing and jumped overboard into the middle of it.

'What is he doing? This water's freezing!' Patsy exclaimed.

'Oh, he knows we'll give him something to keep him warm,' Martin joked, and from a bag he then produced two bottles of sweet red sherry and held them aloft.

'One bottle, three crayfish,' he explained briefly. 'The crayfish live under that kelp and he just has to pull them out. There are hundreds down there.'

Within minutes the man was back in his boat, soaking wet but grinning broadly, and heading towards *Sea Freedom*. He reached up and handed

Rick a bag which moved jerkily and Rick leaned down and gave him the sherry.

'Thanks, Petrus,' Rick said. 'These look good. Enjoy yourself tonight, OK?'

Petrus's wide, gap-toothed grin told them he probably wasn't going to wait until evening to warm himself.

Patsy peered into the sack. Six huge red crayfish snapped their tails at her and waved their feelers threateningly and she closed it quickly. How on earth would she be expected to prepare these?

'Don't worry,' Rick said, looking at her expression in amusement. 'Crayfish are our department. We'll keep these babies until we get to Langebaan and *braai* them on coals on the beach there. Tonight, the cook's job is to collect the firewood.'

'Oh, good.'

I can do firewood, Patsy thought, but not those terrifying things!

Evening was falling as they rounded a rocky headland and entered the calmer waters of the lagoon. The wind had dropped and they motored along quietly, keeping to the deep channel in the middle. Patsy saw a sprawl of houses on the shore, but they continued onwards past the village, until a cliff loomed up in front of them above a small strip of sandy beach. There was no sign of life except for the seagulls swooping and shrieking across the face of the rocks above.

Rick cut the motor and Greg lowered the anchor with a splash.

'Right,' Rick said. 'Let's show our cook how to *braai* a crayfish, guys. I hope you brought your bathers, girls, because we're swimming across to that beach.'

'As long as someone else carries those crayfish.' Patsy grinned. She slipped down to her tiny cabin and changed quickly, then collected a few things from the galley to add to the meal.

'I can't swim very well,' Linda said nervously, changing into the briefest bikini Patsy had ever seen. 'I hope Greg will give me a piggy-back.'

'I'm sure he'd love to,' she replied. 'Have you and Greg been going out for a while?'

'Yes, but I've a feeling that bringing me down to sail with him was some sort of test. If it was, I've failed miserably! Seasick for the first hour and then scared of that whale . . . and I'm not sure about eating on the beach. What about all those insects? And don't crabs walk around at night?'

'Well, I can see the way Greg looks at you, too. I'm sure you've passed every test in his book! Never mind the insects — think of supper over a fire on the beach under the stars. Can't get more romantic than that,' Patsy said, laughing.

This job just got better and better. How could she ever think of going back to Witham?

Charming

'Can I help, or would you just like to browse for a bit?'

While she'd been serving two German tourists who were buying carved wooden zebras, Maureen had noticed the tall, good-looking man studying Priscilla Harman's ceramics. The brilliant, deep colours glowed invitingly against the wall and everyone who came in was drawn to them. Although they were expensive, the big platters and enormous fruit bowls were some of their best sellers, and Priscilla had already had to restock the shelves twice.

'These are beautiful,' the man murmured. He held up a deep crimson bowl splashed with shades of brighter scarlet. 'I can just imagine lemons in this. Or oranges.'

'They'd look perfect,' Maureen agreed. 'Are you an interior designer? We have a lot of them coming in here for Priscilla's pieces.'

The man shook his head, returning the bowl to the shelf.

'Not at all. But I've been in here before and not seen anything like this.

Miss Whittaker has made some changes, I see.'

'Yes, quite a lot,' Maureen replied, smiling. 'Are you local, then? I haven't seen you around.'

'No, I'm from Johannesburg,' he said. 'Let me introduce myself. Richard Hugo.'

He leaned across the counter and shook Maureen's hand firmly.

Richard Hugo! She looked into his twinkling brown eyes and wondered how this charming, good-looking man could be the ogre that Aunt Grace had described.

'Maureen Henderson. I'm Grace Whittaker's niece and her new partner in the business.'

His eyes widened briefly. Was it her imagination or did Richard Hugo look disconcerted? As well he might, she thought; he can obviously see straight away that he can't bully me!

Mr Hugo continued.

'So your aunt has probably told you of my interest in buying this building,' he said pleasantly. 'What do you think of the idea?'

'As I know my aunt has told you many times, Mr Hugo, it's not for sale. Especially not now that I am involved. We've got a lot of plans for expansion and absolutely no intention of selling. Ever. Now, are you interested in purchasing that bowl?'

That's the best way to deal with him, she thought. Short and sharp.

But he didn't seem put off at all.

'Ever is a long time,' he said laconically. 'I'm sure we could come to some sort of arrangement that would suit us both. I've offered your aunt a lot of money for this place which, as I'm sure you're aware, is in dire need of major repairs.

'With that money you could set up somewhere else along this road and still have capital in the bank. You could rent premises more suited to displaying your things, now that you've changed the image of the shop. And done a very good job of it, too,' he added. 'I must compliment you on the new look.'

'Don't try your soft soap with me,' Maureen said angrily. 'We'll get round to the repairs as and when we're able to. In the meantime we're very happy right here.'

'You look like a sensible woman,' he said. 'Think about the financial aspect of it. Your aunt isn't a young woman any longer and financial security would mean a lot to her. You're going to return to the UK in a year or two — '

'What makes you think I'd do that?' Maureen was indignant. How dare this young man tell her what her plans were, when she didn't know them herself?

'I was born in this country and I might very well decide to stay permanently.' As she said it out loud, Maureen realised it was true. She couldn't imagine herself returning to England. 'Anyway, I don't know why you're so keen to buy this building. It's a beautiful example of Victorian architecture and it's protected by the Historical Society, so you wouldn't be able to tear it down and build something horrible and new.'

'Why does everyone in Cape Town seem to think that 'new' means 'horrible'?' He looked impatient. 'I'm quite sure there are ways of changing the mind of the Historical Society and then you'd see how I could turn 'new' into beautiful.'

'The people of the Historical Society aren't open to bribery, which is probably what you have in mind!' she snapped.

He shook his head, amused.

'I don't do bribery, I'm afraid. But there are plenty of ways of persuading people. However, please consider what I've said, and here's my card if you should wish to contact me.'

Tender

He shook her hand warmly, as though they'd already come to a friendly agreement, and turned to go.

At the door he paused.

'You know, you're not maximising your assets. Why don't you do something with the upstairs rooms?'

'We intend to,' Maureen snarled. 'And we don't need you to tell us. Good day!'

She was still fuming two minutes later when Patsy burst through the door, looking guilty.

'Mum! I'm sorry, I overslept! Why didn't you wake me?'

'You looked so peaceful, love. And you came back so late from your sailing that I thought you could do with a nice lie-in. Besides, Mondays are never very busy.'

'Thanks,' Patsy replied. 'Yesterday was a long day. We had to beat against the wind all the way back from Langebaan, and that made us quite slow.'

'You're starting to sound like a proper sailor,' her mother said. 'I thought you spent all your time below deck making food for the crew!'

'No, I just pop down ten minutes

before every meal. Miss Efficiency, that's me! The rest of the time I'm up on deck, working on my tan. Although every now and then I'm allowed to help loop up a rope or something. Oops, I mean, sheet.'

Maureen looked baffled but Patsy rattled on enthusiastically.

'And on Saturday night I didn't even have to cook. We had a *braai* on the beach. It was fabulous, Mum. It was one of those warm nights and Rick and the boys made a huge fire, and while we sat around waiting for it to die down to coals we had a sing-song. Rick's got a lovely singing voice.'

'Sounds as if he's not such a monster after all,' Maureen teased.

Patsy flushed.

'I never said he was. Just kind of cool and distant. But I think I got to know him better this weekend. When he's relaxed he's actually very nice.'

She wasn't going to tell her mother that they'd ended the evening by falling asleep around the fire, and somehow her head had fallen comfortably on to Rick's shoulder. She'd jerked awake to find him looking at her with a strangely tender expression, but he'd immediately straightened up.

'It's too cold for you girls to get wet and swim back now,' he'd said briskly. 'I'll fetch the tender.'

Charming

Without waiting, he'd waded back into the water and untied the small aluminium cockleshell from the front of the deck and rowed back to the beach. They'd covered the dead coals with sand, packed up their rubbish and returned to *Sea Freedom* to sleep until well after sun-up.

But although he'd hardly spoken to her on the trip back to Simonstown, Patsy had a feeling that things had subtly changed between them.

'What's this?' Patsy read the business card on the shop counter. '*Richard*

Hugo, Property Developer? Was that man here again, Mum?'

'Yes, he's just left,' Maureen said. 'Pity you missed him.'

'Auntie Grace can't stand him,' Patsy replied. 'He sounds awful.'

'I wouldn't say awful,' Maureen admitted slowly. 'He actually seemed very nice. Charming, even. One of those men who is used to getting exactly what he wants in life. But he's going to be sadly disappointed because he's not getting Whittaker's!'

Patsy was about to toss the card into the bin when she noticed the e-mail address written in the corner.

richardh.metroproperty@telkomza. com.

She went cold all over. Richard Hugo's e-mail address was the same as Rick's.

6

Furious

Richard Hugo, property developer, and Rick, owner of *Sea Freedom* were the same man! Patsy's hand shook and she dropped the business card on to the counter, her mouth dry.

How could I have been so stupid, she thought. I've worked for Rick for months and never asked his surname. I've started to like him more and more — and now it turns out he's that horrible man who's been trying to twist Aunt Grace's arm! He must've been laughing at me all this time. She was suddenly furious.

'Mum, when did he leave? This Richard Hugo?'

'Just before you came in. As I said, you missed him by a whisker.'

'Right. I'll be back soon. I'm going to go for a walk.'

Without stopping to explain, Patsy hurried out of the shop and looked down the street towards the centre of town. In the distance she could just make out Rick's lanky frame striding along the pavement towards the little green sports car parked under a palm tree. His Cape Town wheels, he called them. Patsy broke into a run and caught up with him as he was opening the door.

'Hey, Rick. Wait for me!' she called, panting.

'Patsy? Good morning!' He looked at her quizzically and then grimaced slightly. 'OK, I know what you're going to say. I've just met your mother, haven't I?'

'You have. But I'll say it anyway. You've been making my great-aunt's life a misery by badgering her to sell the shop. Now you're starting on my mum! Why can't you realise that money can't buy everything, you — you property developer!'

Rick checked his watch.

'Oh, dear. The worst insult, obviously. Look, let's have a cup of coffee and I'll explain.'

But Patsy wasn't finished.

'Explain what? That you've been pretending to be someone else and the whole time you're the man who wants to tear down our building and put up some horrible modern rubbish? And take away our family business? Can't you appreciate the charm of these old buildings?' The words poured out, unstoppable. 'No, you're probably too busy thinking about the money you'd make if you could just push this deal through! Well, it's not going to happen.' She took a deep breath, feeling treacherous tears of anger close to the surface. 'And I was beginning to think that you were so nice.'

'Well, that's one good thing,' he said softly. 'Because I've liked you from the first day we met.'

'You have?' To her annoyance, she felt herself blushing.

'Come on, Patsy. Please, let's sit

down like sensible people and discuss this. There's a coffee shop right across the road. Hear me out.'

Patsy hesitated before nodding, and allowed Rick to lead the way across the road.

She sat stony-faced as the waitress took their order.

'A pot of coffee, please,' he said. 'And croissants for two, don't you think, Patsy? I don't know about you, but I missed breakfast and I'm starving.'

How can he sound so cool and unruffled, she seethed, refusing to smile at him.

'Right,' he said evenly, leaning back with his arms folded. 'For starters, I have never pretended to be anyone else but who I am. This weekend you asked me what I did and I was about to tell you when we ran into that whale, remember? Secondly, I had absolutely no idea you were related to Miss Whittaker. Only when I spoke to your mother about ten minutes ago did I realise the family connection.'

Patsy was silent, furiously thinking back.

Rick was right, of course. He'd never deliberately hidden anything about himself, he'd simply never discussed his work in Johannesburg. And she'd never known his surname because she'd always called him Rick and hadn't taken the trouble to ask!

'Well, even so — how can you harass my great-aunt like that? You're supposed to be a respectable businessman!'

Rick looked thunderous, but was prevented from responding by the waitress arriving with their order.

She smiled at Patsy, placing the coffee pot next to her.

Rick continued seriously.

'Now, don't be daft, Patsy. Of course I'm a businessman. Quite a successful one as it happens. But don't ever accuse me of harassing people. I simply want to buy the building she happens to own. I'd be doing her a favour, taking it off her hands. As I've just told your mother, if Miss Whittaker sold to me, she'd have a very nice sum to invest. And she could rent premises somewhere else in the street without any worries about maintenance.'

Patsy made a face.

'That's how you see it,' she said angrily. 'People here have a sense of history and they don't want it destroyed. Aunt Grace is proud to own that building — her mother bought it just after the war. Before that, it belonged to a ships' chandler and she's got the title deeds that go right back to 1850. Can't you see it's a piece of history?'

'I can see it's a piece of history with bad cracks and a leaking tin roof,' he retorted. 'I didn't think you were so concerned with old things, Patsy.'

'I didn't know I was, until I met Aunt Grace,' she allowed. 'She's taught me to see the beauty in old things. Anyway, didn't you know it's a listed building? You have to get permission to do anything. They'd never allow you to knock it down.'

He shook his head and looked at her

almost pityingly.

'Patsy, I hate to say this but you're being rather naïve. There isn't much you can't get done in this world if you know the right people. Besides, councillors love progress! They love to see things being developed because it increases the value of the properties as well as the look of the place. I intend to turn it into an exclusive little hotel, which would be a huge improvement.'

Patsy frowned.

'A hotel? But that building's not big enough for a hotel, surely?'

'Not on its own, no. But — ' Rick seemed to think better of it. He held up his hand with a sudden, disarming grin. 'Look, we're never going to see eye to eye on this. Just accept the fact that I don't give up easily when I want something. Now, forget all about it and let's enjoy our breakfast.'

She stared at him mutinously, but it was hard to resist that grin and the coffee smelled wonderful.

'OK, no more about it for now,' Patsy

agreed. 'But no matter what you offer, Aunt Grace won't sell and you'll have to eat your words in the end.'

'You're as stubborn as your aunt!' He laughed. 'And, Patsy, there's nothing personal in this. In my book, business and pleasure are strictly separate. Are we all right?'

Patsy stared, baffled.

'All right?' she asked.

'I mean, is everything OK between you and me? You won't suddenly decide that you don't want to work on *Sea Freedom* any more, will you? I don't want you harbouring all sorts of hard feelings about this monster you're working for.'

Patsy giggled.

'Yes, everything's fine between you and me.'

His eyes held hers and she felt a little tremor of excitement as she tried to read his expression.

'Good. Patsy, are you busy for the rest of the morning?'

'Well, I should be getting back to the

shop to give Mum a hand,' she began, but Rick looked boyishly hopeful, so she added, 'I'm sure she could do without me for an hour or two. What did you have in mind?'

'How about a guided tour of Simonstown? I've not really seen much of the place beyond the yacht club.'

Patsy grinned in delight. Suddenly, a whole morning in Rick's company seemed very attractive.

'One cook's tour coming up! Your itinerary includes a swim with the penguins and a drive around the mountains to have lunch at Cape Point. Just make sure you avoid the baboons!'

'Sounds good to me.' Rick smiled. 'And maybe dinner tonight? I'm booked on the midnight flight back to Johannesburg.'

Patsy knew that she would love to have dinner with him, but what if he got bored with her company before then? What if she ran out of things to say?

But looking at Rick's smile she couldn't think of any reason why a dinner date with him wouldn't be the perfect ending to the day.

Although what her mother and her aunt would say when they found out she'd been working for the enemy all this time, and had chosen to spend the day in his company, she didn't like to think.

Appalling

'Hey, man. How's it going?' Jack asked. 'Seen Duggie this morning?'

His friend Andy shook his head.

'Nope, he's off collecting stock for his stall. I never thought I'd see old Duggie working so hard. He reckons he's making a fortune on the market selling those car parts.'

'Is he? I wonder if he needs a bit of help?'

'Maybe,' Andy replied. 'You should ask him.'

Selling second-hand car parts didn't hold much appeal, but since receiving his exam results, the usually cheerful Jack had been as close to being depressed as he'd ever been.

To no-one's surprise but his own, he'd discovered he didn't qualify for entry to any college that he would have preferred. For some months he'd been secretly planning to study design engineering — something he'd heard about at a careers evening at school — but he realised too late that he'd need at least a B for mathematics to get on to the course. Maths had never been his strong point. In fact, he had to admit that, scholastically, he hadn't had any strong points, but it hadn't seemed to matter. Until now.

'You could have done a lot better than this,' his father had said. He had been remarkably unsympathetic when he'd learned of his son's results. 'These marks are appalling.'

'Maybe I can sit some of the subjects over again,' Jack had mumbled.

'I doubt they'll allow you to, with these results,' came his father's reply.

'We can ask, I suppose. Or maybe we could look at some sort of apprenticeship.'

'Apprenticeship? I don't want to learn a trade!' Jack had said sulkily. 'That would mean years of earning peanuts.' He had a vision of himself in oily blue overalls with dirty fingernails, and wondered what the girls at school would do if they saw him. Laugh, probably, or ignore him.

His father continued.

'And the trouble is, of course, you'd have to work hard to get somewhere. It probably wouldn't suit you.'

Jack squirmed at the sarcastic tone in his father's voice.

'In the meantime, see if you can find some sort of work until we decide what you're going to do with yourself. Your mother's going to be furious.'

Jack didn't even want to think about the e-mail he'd received from his mother.

Her disappointment made him feel so ashamed he'd deleted it without printing it out. Even now his face flushed when her words came back to him:

We both know that if you had done as you promised and applied yourself, you could have passed everything. I've always had such faith in you, Jack, and I really expected more from you, my boy. You have not only let me down, but worse still, you've let yourself down.

Jack thrust his hands into his pockets and walked on gloomily. Rita had sent him to town to buy sausages for supper, but mainly, Jack suspected, to get him out from under her feet. Hanging around the house these days with Rita expecting him to help with the housework was no fun.

Busy

When he'd been to the butcher, he turned and sauntered off towards the market. All his mates seemed to be busy with their lives and there was no-one to phone to suggest a game of pool.

May as well see what old Duggie's up to, he thought.

To his amazement, Duggie had a busy stall, piled high with a haphazard collection of metal bits and pieces and he was surrounded by customers. Jack recognised several gear boxes and carburettors, water pumps and starter motors, as well as a neat pile of car radios. His interest quickened.

'Hey, Jack, haven't seen you around!' Duggie gave Jack a high five then turned his attention to a customer. 'That's only ten pounds. It's German made, sir, a bargain at the price. It would cost you at least fifty new. Thank you.' He smoothly slipped the note into a cash box and turned back to Jack. 'Fancy helping me out a bit here, mate? I could use another pair of hands this morning.'

'Sure.' Jack put the sausages under the trestle and surveyed the table. 'Hey, that's an old Jag steering wheel, isn't it? Cool! Where'd you get all this stuff?'

'Here and there. Breakers' yards,

mostly.' Duggie's mobile shrilled and he turned away.

A man grabbed Jack's attention.

'Son, how much for this water pump?' he asked. 'And would it fit a Peugeot?'

'Yes,' Jack replied. 'But remember to fit a new sealing ring when you install it, and check your fan blades. If they are out of balance they can damage the pump in a couple of weeks.'

'Right,' the man said gratefully.

'That'll be ten pounds, please,' Jack said, consulting Duggie's scrawled price list.

'Ta.' The customer grinned and paid up.

'Hey, man, you've got the touch!' Duggie beamed at him. 'Nice work. Was that a line you were spinning that fellow about the fan blades?'

'No,' Jack said in surprise. 'My dad's taught me quite a lot about motors. He changes the oil and does most of his own servicing.'

'Listen, man, you're waiting to go to college or something, aren't you? If you have some free time, would you like to work here for a bit?'

'Sure!' Jack replied eagerly. 'You mean, every day?'

Duggie nodded.

'I could do with the help and you seem to know what you're talking about. I often get calls about good stuff that's available and up to now I've had to pack up the stall and collect it straight away. If you were here to watch the stall, I'd have no problem. My sales would probably double.'

'Would you pay me?' Jack asked cagily.

'Of course!'

When Duggie told him how much he would be paid, it was all he could do not to whoop with amazement.

'That sounds OK,' he said, trying to sound casual. 'See you tomorrow.'

Not Quite Right

That evening, his father and Rita were suitably impressed, enough to forgive him for forgetting to bring the sausages home from the market.

'I'll be managing the stall,' he told them. 'I'll have a free hand to price things and I'll be advising customers about the right parts and so on. Money for jam, eh, Dad?'

'It sounds good,' Warren said. 'I didn't know your friend Duggie was in business.'

'Oh, Duggie's got lots of irons in the fire,' Jack said airily, although he wasn't too sure what those irons were. Duggie had always made a habit of disappearing at odd times, but he usually had plenty of money to flash around so whatever he was up to, it was profitable.

'I'm so glad you've found something, love.' Rita beamed. 'It'll keep you busy while you decide what you're going to do later on. And you'll earn some pocket money, too.'

Jack enjoyed manning the stall. Every morning he helped to unpack the boxes of parts and set them out, wiping off the worst of the greasy dirt. More often than not Duggie would go off and leave him in charge, coming back later in the morning with an assortment of new things to sell. One time, he triumphantly brought five car radios.

'Top of the line stuff, this is,' he said. 'Cost a fortune if you had to buy them new. These'll be gone by the end of the day, you'll see.'

There were several regular visitors to the stall who came every couple of days to inspect the stock, and soon Jack got to recognise them. One in particular, a thin man with a moustache who wore a bright red beanie, was a good customer and never haggled about the prices.

'Where's Duggie?' he asked one morning. 'I need a tail-light for a 2005 model Beamer, 330 series. In a hurry.'

'Um — he's coming back at about twelve, I think,' Jack said. 'I'll tell him then.'

'Not good enough, mate. Phone him and ask him to get it for me this morning. Tell him Charlie wants it.'

Jack did as he was told, but he wondered how Duggie could be expected to find something at such short notice. Of course, the breaker's yard might have just what Charlie wanted, but it would be a long shot.

'Series 330 tail-light? No problem,' Duggie said when Jack told him. 'Tell Charlie he can collect it by midday.'

Jack turned back to face Charlie.

'You're in luck,' he said. 'He can get it.'

'Luck? Is that what he's calling it these days?' The man laughed shortly.

Jack couldn't think what Charlie meant and resolved to ask Duggie more about the supply side of the stall when he had the chance.

'Aren't you Warren Henderson's boy?' A burly man in a grey topcoat put down the car radio he'd been examining and shook his hand. 'Jimmy Rogers. I know your dad from the Rotary Club. So, you're involved with Duggie Scott, eh?'

'I'm the stall mana — well, I'm helping him,' Jack said. 'Are you interested in that radio? I can let you have it for a good price.'

'Just browsing.' The man picked up several car parts and put them down again. Jack noticed he seemed to be writing something.

Then he tipped his hat to Jack and was about to leave the stall when he came back over to Jack and spoke in his ear.

'I wouldn't stay involved with Duggie Scott for too long, my lad.'

Then he turned on his heel and left the market.

That's odd, Jack thought. Maybe he's a rival parts dealer, trying to make trouble for Duggie. But for the rest of the day he had an uneasy feeling that something wasn't quite right.

Special Delivery

As Patsy had expected, when Aunt Grace discovered that Richard Hugo and Patsy's boss were one and the same, her reaction was explosive.

'How can you even think of carrying on working for that dreadful man? I don't see how you can set foot on his wretched boat again!'

'Aunt Grace, he's not what you imagine,' Patsy said patiently. 'He's really very nice. He had no idea that I was connected to the shop and as far as he's concerned, making you an offer to buy it is just business.'

'Ha! That snake in the grass is probably going to try to use you to persuade me to sell to him.'

'He wouldn't do that. Anyway, I told him you'd never budge and he's wasting his time,' Patsy placated.

'And wanting to put up a hotel! Is the man mad?'

Grace was still snorting with anger when a uniformed man walked into the shop carrying an enormous bunch of roses.

'Miss Whittaker? A delivery for you.'

'Me? Who on earth could they be from?' Grace wondered. 'Patsy, you read the note. I haven't got my glasses.'

Grace buried her nose in the blooms and inhaled deeply.

'These are the real thing,' she said, pleased. 'Lovely old-fashioned perfume. So, who sent them, Patsy?'

Patsy smiled as she read the card.

'They're from Rick, Auntie.'

Miss Whittaker,

Please accept these with my deepest apologies for any anxiety my proposition has unwittingly caused you. However, I still hope to persuade you that we can do business. I'm afraid you will find the Hugo family motto is Nous ne cédons jamais! *Regards,*

Richard Hugo.

'Family motto, indeed.' Aunt Grace sniffed. 'What does that fancy phrase mean?'

'We never give up, I think,' Patsy said. 'His family was French, originally. They came out four hundred years ago with the Huguenots. His brother still runs the vineyard out in the country that's been in the family ever since they arrived. It's called Mont Liberté. Hugo is an old French name.'

'Seems he told you a lot about himself. But if his family's lived here so long, why has he no sense of history, I wonder? Still, he does make a handsome apology!' Grace admitted.

Patsy could see her aunt was secretly pleased with the bouquet and when they were shutting up for the day, Aunt Grace said casually, 'No sense in leaving these here in the shop. I may as well take them home.'

Arrested

Now the roses were arranged in a wide silver bowl on the sideboard, scenting the warm night air that drifted in through the open french doors. Maureen, Patsy and Grace were sitting at the dining-room table playing Scrabble. Grace, as usual, was winning.

Maureen was a hundred points behind and her mind wasn't on the game. She waited for Aunt Grace to think of a word and sighed inwardly as her thoughts drifted back to Jack and how badly he'd failed his exams.

Although his recent e-mails were full of bravado, she was sure he must be feeling depressed. He'd mentioned helping that awful Duggie on the market and seemed to think she'd be pleased that he was working. But the sooner he finished with Duggie the better. And no matter how often she asked him if he had any firm ideas of what he wanted to do, he'd answer with short and cheerful e-mails and completely ignore her questions. Maddening!

'Handsome,' Grace said triumphantly. 'On a double word score and I used all seven letters, so that's an extra fifty for me! Come on, Mo, you're not concentrating.'

'Sorry,' Maureen said, pulling herself back into the room.

'And Patsy?' Aunt Grace's eyes

twinkled at her over her glasses. 'You're miles away, too. That little smile on your face — if I didn't know better, I'd say you were thinking of some young man!'

'Not at all, Aunt Grace,' Patsy said, promptly using her X to make *EXACTLY* on a triple score. 'I'm just happy that you gave me that E and let me beat you!'

But Maureen and Patsy exchanged understanding smiles.

It was true that since spending the day with Rick, Patsy had felt bubbly inside every time she re-lived their trip around the Peninsula, and caught herself humming and smiling for no reason.

He'd been surprisingly relaxed, warm and open, and had wanted to know all about her home in England and her travels since leaving. In turn he'd described his own carefree, almost idyllic childhood amongst the Hugo family's vineyards, riding bareback with his brother over the mountains and swimming in the river that crossed their farm. But when she asked how he could bear to leave the farm for life in the big city, his face had tightened and she'd glimpsed the old, controlled Rick she'd first met.

'I'm the younger son,' was all he would say. 'And in all fairy tales, younger sons have to make their own way in the world.'

Patsy had the definite impression that further discussion on this subject was closed. But she knew their relationship had subtly shifted gear and they'd become a lot closer that day.

She'd been expecting a kiss when he said goodbye to her before he left to catch his plane, but he'd only taken her hand and said, 'Thank you for a wonderful time, Patsy. I've enjoyed every minute of my cook's tour. I hope you haven't caught the sun too much.' He put his finger on her nose teasingly. 'But it suits you.'

'I look like Rudolph the red-nosed reindeer, I suppose,' she mumbled. 'Good-night, Rick. See you when we sail again.'

Not exactly a scintillating answer, but the best she'd been able to come up with at short notice!

But she hugged herself gleefully whenever she thought of seeing him again and checked her e-mails impatiently to see when he'd be coming back to Simonstown.

And she hadn't been able to hide her mood from her mother, who knew her very well. The day afterwards, Maureen had walked down to the shop with her.

'So, are you and Rick getting to know each other better?' she asked casually.

'Oh, very subtle, Mum! What you're actually wanting to know is . . . '

'Are you falling for this man, sweetheart?'

Patsy smiled at her mother's direct question.

'I haven't fallen for him. I don't know what gave you that idea,' she replied. 'It's just that I've got to know him better and he's not too bad.'

'Patsy!' Maureen exclaimed. 'This is me, your mum!'

'Oh . . . ' Patsy hesitated. 'Well, maybe a little bit. But I know I'm being silly to even think that anything can come of it. He's older than me and he's rich and successful and he has a whole other life up in Johannesburg. Why should he even look at me?'

'I can think of lots of reasons,' Maureen said warmly. 'And I can certainly see why you're smitten. I liked him very much, until I found out who he was! But you're right, he moves in different circles and he's a sophisticated man. You're still young and I don't want you to get hurt, my love.'

'Don't worry, Mum. I've no intention of getting serious.'

But now, as Maureen looked at her daughter triumphantly placing her tiles on to the board, she could tell that Patsy was glowing with the kind of happiness that comes from being in love. Even if she didn't know it.

'How about the winner making us a cup of tea?' she asked. 'You're both too good for me tonight.'

'Good idea,' Patsy said, standing up. 'Anyone for a chocolate biscuit as well?'

Just then the phone rang in the hall.

'Who can be phoning at this hour? I'll get it,' Patsy called. 'Hello? Oh, Dad? How are you? Yes, she's here. I'll call her.'

She came back into the dining-room frowning, but Maureen was already hurrying through.

'It's Dad. He sounds a bit odd.'

Maureen picked up the phone.

'Warren? Is there anything wrong? Is it Jack? Is he all right?'

Visions of him lying in hospital after a motorbike accident shot through her head. She couldn't bear it, she'd have to go back . . .

'Yes, it's Jack.' Warren's voice was cold and abrupt. 'He was brought back home this evening by my old friend Jimmy Rogers of the CID, just one small step away from being arrested and thrown in jail.'

'Arrested?' Maureen's knees went weak and she sat down heavily. 'For what?'

'Handling stolen goods. It appears that the police have had their eye on his friend Duggie for months. He's been using that market stall of his to off-load motor parts from stolen cars.'

Patsy came quietly into the hall.

'What's wrong?' she mouthed, her eyes like saucers.

Narrow Escape

Maureen shushed her with her hand, but Patsy put her arm around her mother and held her ear close to the phone, trying to listen to Warren.

'But surely Jack didn't know they were stolen? He would never — '

'You can't say what that boy would do!' Warren interrupted. 'He's been hanging around the wrong sort of crowd for too long, Maureen. You should have put a stop to it. Forbidden him to see them.'

'Oh, Warren, don't be unfair! I tried so often to warn him off Duggie, but he wouldn't listen. You know how stubborn he can be.'

'Well, Duggie and another friend of his are under lock and key tonight, and the only reason Jack was released with a caution is because Jimmy and I know each other from way back. He's left it up to me to handle things this time, so let me tell you, he's a very lucky boy.'

Maureen cleared her throat.

'What are you going to do?' Her voice shook.

'Do? What can I do?' Warren sighed. 'He's in his room now, sulking,' he continued. 'He doesn't realise what a narrow escape he's had, thanks to my contacts.'

'Warren, let me speak to him, please.'

She heard Warren shouting for Jack and turned to Patsy, her eyes filling with tears.

'It's awful,' she whispered. 'Jack was selling stolen car parts for Duggie and he nearly got arrested. Dad's furious, of course.'

Patsy was sympathetic.

'Poor old Jack. He's so trusting. You never liked Duggie, did you?' Patsy was silent. 'You were right about him.'

'What good did my disapproval do?' Maureen sighed. 'Jack just didn't listen.'

Patsy had a sudden thought.

'Mum,' she said. 'Why doesn't he come out here? Then he could get away from all that crowd. He's been dying to come over and I'm sure he could get a job here as a waiter or something.'

Maureen's face lit up.

'Patsy, you're a genius! Of course that's the answer . . . I'll have to speak to Aunt Grace, but I'm sure she wouldn't mind.'

Maureen waited impatiently for Jack to come on the line. When he did, his voice was hesitant.

'Hi, Mum,' he said quietly. 'I suppose Dad's told you?'

'Yes, of course he did.'

'I didn't know the stuff was nicked. Honest. Duggie offered me work and I thought it would be a good way to earn some money, you know?' Jack sounded miserable.

Maureen sighed and had a feeling that it would be a long story.

'Listen, Jack, it sounds as though you went into something without thinking. But I haven't got time to discuss everything over the phone. How would you feel about coming out to Cape Town?'

Jack was silent.

'What? Now?' he said eventually.

'Just as soon as you can get your passport organised.'

'Fantastic! I'd love to do that!' He cheered up immediately. 'All those beaches, and maybe I'd get to sail on Patsy's yacht . . .'

'It's not going to be a holiday for you, my boy. We'll find you a proper job here and you can pay me back for the air fare out of your earnings,' Maureen told him.

'Right, yes, of course. That'll be great, Mum. Thanks a million!'

Smiling at his enthusiasm, Maureen

relaxed a little. She was sure this was the right thing to do and she was certain that Warren would agree. If nothing else, he'd probably be glad to get his troublesome son out of the house so easily.

'Ask your dad to talk to me again, please,' she said. 'We need to make the arrangements.'

Good Influence

Sometimes, even with the three of them in the shop, it was hard to cope with the rush of customers. That Friday afternoon was one of them. Tourists seemed to find their way in droves, and when twenty or more of them were milling around inside as they were just now, Maureen had to take a deep breath to stop feeling panicky.

But somehow they were all being sorted out, with money paid, purchases wrapped and then shepherded back to their bus by their tour guide. Only then could Maureen, Patsy and Aunt Grace relax.

'I'm not complaining, but I wish they'd come in twos and threes, not such a crowd! I think we all need a cup of coffee to recover,' Maureen said.

'Three cups coming up!' Mellie said, catching the tail end of the conversation.

Mellie was busier with every passing day. Exactly as they'd hoped, customers who popped in to the shop to browse stopped for coffee. She served them with charm and efficiency and handled the money easily.

'When's your brother arriving, Patsy?' Mellie asked. 'Will he be working in the shop, too?'

'Who, Jack?' Patsy laughed. 'I can't see my little brother being much help. He'd eat all the *melktert* and give the wrong change. He's coming next week but he'll have to find a job somewhere else!'

'Oh, I don't know,' Maureen argued. 'Jack could learn to be very helpful behind the counter. He's got a way with people and he's got experience selling things these past few weeks . . . '

Her voice trailed off, remembering just what Jack had been doing. Selling stolen goods to motor mechanics on a market stall was hardly the same as dealing with tourists!

'No, well, perhaps not. But he'll find something in Simonstown, I'm sure.'

'I'm looking forward to meeting him,' Mellie said. 'And I must introduce him to Rafe. I'm sure they'll get on well.'

Her brother had been into the shop to see his sister the week before, and Maureen had been impressed by the quietly spoken, pleasant young man who was getting ready to study law. If Jack was to become friends with Rafe, she was sure the older boy would be a good influence on her son. He was taller than Mellie and didn't have her outgoing, friendly ways, but Dan had never stopped singing his praises.

'He's the best crew I've ever had,' he'd said. 'Rafe's got brains as well as brawn and I have never found that combination before. I don't know how I'm going to replace him. But, of course, I'm pleased for him that he's going to study. I know he'll do well.'

Maureen enjoyed a warm glow just thinking about Dan. Since their dinner together they'd been out several times and she'd come to depend on him as the man she'd spend her evenings with. Films, the theatre, dinners out, either by themselves or with his friends — Maureen hadn't had such a full social life since before she was married!

'The shelves look as though a swarm of locusts have come through here,' Aunt Grace said briskly. 'I'll fetch more stuff from the stockroom.'

Short Notice

Just then, as if summoned by her thoughts, Dan walked through the door. He was still in his sea boots and working clothes, but Maureen thought

254

again how attractive his tanned, narrow face was under his slightly raffish denim cap.

'Afternoon, ladies.' His smile included them all. 'Is the tea garden still open? Any chance of a cuppa, Mellie?'

'Of course, Mr Clayton.' Mellie had a soft spot for Dan. 'And a piece of *melktert*?'

'If your gran made it, certainly! By the way, I like your new window display. Very eye-catching.'

Patsy had taken the old sepia coloured photo of Aunt Grace aged six, with her arm around the enormous dog and had had it enlarged to a metre high. It had pride of place in the windows, forming the backdrop to an ever-changing display of colourful goods.

'I love watching their faces when they discover that I'm the sweet little girl,' Aunt Grace said wickedly. 'The looks of disbelief!'

Patsy started to collect her things.

'Do you mind if I go off early? I got an e-mail to say we're racing again this weekend and I have to provision the boat.'

'Off you go.' Her aunt smiled. 'I'm sure we can manage without you for the rest of the afternoon.'

Patsy gave her mother a conspiratorial grin. She made no secret of the fact that she approved of Dan and hoped something more serious would develop between them.

As Patsy left, Dan took the tray from Mellie and followed Maureen through to the little area at the back.

Once she and Mellie had cleaned it up, the high, moss-speckled stone walls and the pots of geraniums made a charming, intimate space with only four small tables for customers.

'Hard day?' he asked Maureen, taking her hand in his.

'Very. Five bus loads of tourists, one after the other. But we're handling it, and business is really taking off.'

Dan squeezed her hand.

'Are you too tired to come out with me tonight?'

'Never too tired to go out with you.'
She grinned. 'What did you have in
mind?'

Dan returned her smile.

'I know it's short notice, but the
widow of a friend of mine is in town
just for one evening and she's invited us
to dinner at the Mount Nelson. That
very posh old hotel in Cape Town.'

'Us?' Maureen was confused.

'Well, when she invited me I told her
I'd bring my partner. And that's you.'
He looked at her steadily. 'Isn't it?'

Merry Widow

Maureen never knew what to say when
Dan got serious. She was too busy
fighting the fluttering butterflies in her
tummy, not ready to take the next step
that Dan so obviously wanted. She told
herself there was all the time in the
world and it was far better to take
things slowly.

'Anyway,' he continued briskly, 'Ella

257

was married to an old mate of mine who died in a motor accident about five years ago. Tragic. They were a great couple and sadly they had no kids, so now she's all alone. At the time I helped her out a bit with his estate, selling his car and that sort of thing. Then she moved off to Durban and I lost touch. Seems she's thinking of moving back to the Cape.'

Maureen frowned.

'Are you sure you don't want to have dinner with her on your own? You'll have lots to talk about and she probably isn't interested in having me around,' she said.

'Nonsense. I wouldn't enjoy it without you. Besides, she said she'd book a table for four so it sounds as though she has a man with her. Actually, I can't imagine Ella alone for long. She's a real live-wire, full of fun. She used to be on the stage, a professional dancer. Did a bit of modelling, too, I think, before she was married.'

'Oh, my,' Maureen said mischievously. 'In that case I'd better put on full war paint and wear my best party dress!'

Dan smiled.

'No need for that,' he said. 'You always look good to me.'

But the thought of a merry widow coming back into Dan's life made her feel a little uneasy. She looked into his smiling eyes and was hit by a wave of jealousy.

A live-wire, full-of-fun dancer who used to be a model?

Full war paint, definitely!

7

Inadequate

Looking around the elegant restaurant bathed in candlelight, Maureen was glad she'd pulled out all the stops for this evening. She'd chosen her prettiest dark-blue silk dress and washed her hair before Dan picked her up for the drive through to Cape Town for dinner. She'd borrowed Aunt Grace's diamond stud earrings and Patsy had insisted on doing her make-up, so she felt that she was looking her best to meet Dan's live-wire lady friend.

The stately old Mount Nelson Hotel, set in a landscaped garden at the foot of Table Mountain, was almost intimidating with its towering, white-pillared entrance and sweeping driveway up to the carved front doors.

With a solemn salute, the uniformed

doorman had ushered Maureen and Dan into the foyer, which was gleaming with antique furniture and ablaze with bowls of pink and scarlet protea flowers. There was an air of quiet, subdued luxury.

Dan was looking around uncertainly.

'Ella said to meet her in the bar,' he muttered, just as a woman in a shimmering red cocktail dress rushed up and threw her arms around him.

'Danny! How wonderful to see you again! Looking so handsome, just as I remembered! And this must be Maureen!' Ella spoke in husky, breathless exclamations, her red-nailed hand clutching Dan's arm as she smiled at Maureen. 'Lovely to meet you! Come and say hello to Alfred.'

She led them into the bar where a rather portly man in a three-piece suit was perched uncomfortably on a bar stool.

'Alfred, meet Dan Clayton, my very oldest and dearest friend and confidant. Dan, meet Alfred le Roux, my very clever financial adviser. He's making me rich, isn't that nice? Oh, and this is Maureen . . . um . . . '

'Henderson,' Maureen finished crisply. Ella had certainly made it sound as if Dan was a lot more important to her than he'd said.

'Right, will we have some champagne to celebrate? Alfred, catch the barman's eye. Tell him we want a bottle of his best champagne!'

Maureen felt exhausted just listening to her rattling on, as Aunt Grace would have called it.

But Dan seemed totally charmed and Alfred acted as though her every wish was his command. Maureen listened silently while the two of them chatted about old times. She caught Alfred's eye and they smiled sympathetically at each other, two people on the edge of a charmed circle for two.

Ella was an extremely beautiful woman, with her dark auburn hair swept up into a chignon. She had a slim, toned body with a suntan that could only have come from hours on the beach or expensive treatments in a beauty salon.

Maureen consoled herself by thinking that Ella would probably make any woman feel inadequate by comparison, let alone one who was tired after a busy day behind a counter and was still battling to lose some extra weight from around her hips!

Once in the dining-room, Ella insisted that Maureen sit next to Alfred.

'Dan tells me you've got a little shop,' she said. 'So you and Alfred can talk to each other about business! He's marvellous at business, aren't you, Alfie?'

Dan winked at Maureen.

'Don't let her get under your skin. I'd forgotten what a bossy-boots she can be sometimes,' he whispered, squeezing her hand as they sat down opposite each other.

Maureen hadn't meant to look as upset as she felt and she smiled back.

'Not to worry. I'm going to enjoy a

fantastic meal and let the two of you get on with nostalgia night,' she said, slipping into the chair held out for her by the waiter. 'And who knows, maybe Alfred can give me some business tips?'

'Doubt that, I'm a financial consultant — I don't know a thing about business!' Alfred wheezed as he laughed at his own joke. 'I can tell you're from England, aren't you? How do you like it over here?'

'I'm loving it,' Maureen replied. 'But I'm not exactly a visitor.'

She went on to tell him about herself and Aunt Grace and the shop. He seemed interested, and was an easy person to talk to, but Maureen couldn't help listening with half an ear to the conversation between Dan and Ella across the candelit table.

It sounded very much to her as though Ella was hoping to involve Dan in her plans to settle back in the Cape.

'I was thinking of somewhere along the coast,' she said.

'Up against the mountain at Kalk Bay or Fish Hoek. Or even Simonstown, although that's a bit far from the city if I want to go to the theatre. But I must have a view of the sea! That's essential, don't you agree, Maureen?'

With a brilliant smile she suddenly included Maureen in the conversation.

'Oh, yes. Definitely. A view of the sea is lovely,' she said hastily. 'Have you thought of looking for a place on the other side of the mountains — Sea Point or Camps Bay?'

As far away from Dan as possible!

'No, too far away from all my friends,' Ella said firmly, as though reading her mind. 'Friends are so important. Especially now that I live alone. Neville and I had so many friends when we lived here, but I wonder how many of them will be interested in just little me, all on my own?'

'Why shouldn't they be?' Maureen asked. Whatever else she thought of Ella, she was certainly good at conversation and she had no doubt her glamorous good looks would make her a popular dinner guest.

'Oh, you'd be surprised. Widows have a hard time of it, you know. Nobody wants a spare woman at their dinner party!'

'Nonsense, Ella,' Dan said firmly. 'Everyone will be very happy you've come back. I am, for one.'

'Ah, you're a sweet man, Dan! I know I can always count on you . . . aren't I lucky!'

She put her hand on Dan's arm and squeezed gently, smiling up at him.

Leave him alone, Maureen snarled silently. He's mine!

But looking at Dan's bemused expression, she wondered if he still was. Things didn't improve when they finished their excellent meal and moved to the Palm Room for coffee.

A trio of musicians played classical

music quietly in a corner and they chose a table nearby.

'Ah, Debussy,' Ella said dreamily, sinking back into a comfortable arm-chair and gazing up at the ceiling, a position that showed off her delicate jaw line and slender throat. 'I love that arrangement. Dan, have you been to any concerts recently?'

Dan shook his head.

'Not had the time,' he said. 'We mostly go to see films if we get a chance, don't we, Maureen?'

'Films? Oh, but surely you miss going to the concerts in the City Hall? We always used to go, you and me and Neville, don't you remember?' Ella persisted.

'Yes.' Dan nodded. 'But I've got out of the habit, somehow.'

Ella turned to Maureen.

'Regular as clockwork, every Wednes-day evening,' she said. 'The City Orchestra plays beautiful music. You should make him go, Maureen. He loves classical music, don't you, Dan?'

'Does he?' Maureen was surprised. Dan kept CDs of the Beatles and Bob Dylan in his car and usually played those while they travelled anywhere.

'Well, some of it.' Dan smiled. 'Mozart, Beethoven, Vivaldi. I've never learned to like opera, though. Perhaps we should go together next week, Mo, and see if we enjoy it?'

'If I can,' she said abruptly. 'I might have to go over the books with Aunt Grace.'

Concert Date

For some reason she felt hurt, discovering that Dan had never shared his love of classical music with her.

'Wednesday,' Ella said. 'I'll get us tickets, shall I, Dan? And if Maureen finds that she can come, I'll buy an extra one. They're doing an evening of Schubert, I believe.'

'Give me a good film any day,' Alfred said comfortably. 'Any music without a good strong beat just sends me to sleep!'

'Me, too,' Maureen said defiantly. 'I'd take a good rock concert over a few violins scraping away, myself.'

Now why did I say that, she thought miserably. Dan looked at her in astonishment.

'Didn't know you felt like that, Mo,' he said slowly. 'Well, we must see if there's a concert on soon for you!'

Maureen could think of nothing worse than sitting through the racket of a rock concert with a bunch of screaming adolescents! She wished the evening would end and they could just go home. She could talk to Dan and tell him it was all a joke, that she was perfectly willing to give classical music concerts a try.

But Ella insisted on a liqueur with their coffee, and it was long past midnight before they left the hotel.

Maureen was too tired to correct Dan's impression and on the long drive back to Simonstown she listened with dismay as he told her what a brave woman Ella was and how well she coped with being on her own.

Oh, really, she thought crossly. You've never told me how well *I* cope and I've got a lot more on my plate than Ella!

Then she realised that she was being stupidly jealous and said nothing. She was fast asleep when they arrived at Aunt Grace's house and Dan woke her by turning up the volume of 'Blue Suede Shoes' on his CD player.

'Wake up, sleepyhead.' He grinned. 'I'll call you later in the week.'

I expect he would have played a Mozart concerto if I had been Ella, she thought resentfully as he escorted her slowly up the stairs to the front door. She felt cross all over again.

★ ★ ★

'Great breakfast, Auntie Grace!' Jack beamed at his great-aunt who ruffled his hair affectionately as she collected his plate.

'Glad you enjoyed it, my boy. You could do with some meat on those bones!'

'Ah, it was all the hard work I've been doing back home.' Jack grinned. 'If you keep feeding me like this I'll soon fatten up.'

'She's not going to,' Patsy said pertly. 'Next week it's your turn to cook, Jack. We all take turns — this is a working household, remember?'

'Don't tease the lad,' Grace said comfortably. 'I'm quite happy to make breakfast for my one and only great-nephew! What are your plans for today, Jack?'

All three women looked at him expectantly. Maureen with her heart full of love and relief that Jack was with her again, Aunt Grace in undisguised admiration for her handsome great-nephew, and Patsy with the usual mixture of affection and annoyance that she reserved for her brother.

'I thought I'd just take a wander around the town and then walk to the beach. Patsy told me how she swam in amongst the penguins — that sounded pretty cool.'

'Remember the sun cream, Jack,' Maureen warned. 'You've only been here a week and you're not used to the sun.'

Jack turned to Patsy.

'Do you want to come with me, sis? It'll be no fun on my own.'

Patsy shook her head.

'I can't today, Jack. I'm working at the shop, remember? Speaking of which, aren't you supposed to be looking for a job?'

'Mum said to take a couple of weeks off and then look,' he replied easily.

'Actually, I said one week,' Maureen said. 'That's long enough for you to get your bearings around here. You need to start looking for work soon.'

'I will.' Jack sighed. 'But I want to take the train into Cape Town and explore. Take the cable car up Table Mountain.'

'That isn't cheap,' Patsy told him. 'I

planned to do that, too, when I first arrived, but in the end I climbed it with some guys from the yacht club. It only took us three hours. The view at the summit is fantastic. You can see for miles!'

'Three hours?' Jack exclaimed. 'I'd rather go by cable car. Have you been up there, Mum? Maybe you and I could go together?'

'Sounds good,' Maureen replied. 'But I haven't time to chat. I need to open the shop. Jack, when you've finished your coffee, would you be a dear and wash up? And don't forget to make your bed.'

'I'll come with you,' Grace said. 'I'll just get my bag . . .'

Bossy

Alone in the big dining-room, Jack grimaced at Patsy.

'Nothing changes,' he said disconsolately. 'She still treats me like a kid.'

'Well,' Patsy said, 'considering you didn't make your bed yesterday or the day before, I guess she thinks you need reminding. Come on, I'll give you a hand with the washing up before I go.'

Patsy was delighted that Jack had come out to join them, although he still irritated her. But Patsy had been away from home for a year and now it felt good to have all her family around her.

But I suppose I'll never feel that our family is whole, she thought, with Dad married to Rita.

'How was it at Dad's, Jack?' she queried. 'How did you get on with Rita?'

'OK, I suppose. Actually, she was pretty nice to me, especially after that business with Duggie. It was Dad who got so upset. She's a bit of a cleanliness freak, but once I got past that . . . '

'Oh, you mean like expecting you to clean your room and pick up your clothes?' Patsy laughed. 'We do the same thing here, so you'd better get used to it. Aunt Grace is too nice to say anything, but Mum feels that as we're living in her house we shouldn't be a burden.'

Jack frowned.

'I thought Aunt Grace would have a maid,' he said. 'Doesn't everyone around here?'

'Nope,' Patsy replied. 'While Mum was growing up Aunt Grace had a housekeeper called Rugaya, but now Rugaya bakes for the shop and her granddaughter, Mellie, helps Mum and Aunt Grace in the tea garden.'

Jack's eyes lit up.

'Granddaughter? How old is she?' he asked.

'About eighteen. But she's not your type at all, Jack!' His sister grinned. 'She's clever and hard-working and she's aiming to go to university next year. She hasn't got time for a layabout like you!'

Jack was obviously insulted.

'I might not be cut out for the academic stuff, but I'm going to run my own business one day. It's the only way to make big bucks.'

'Oh, yeah. Right.' Patsy shook her head in exasperation. 'But until that happy day comes around you'd better find some sort of work as soon as you can.'

'I'll look properly tomorrow, I promise,' Jack said. 'Well, I'm off to check out those penguins.'

'Don't forget to make your bed before you leave,' Patsy called after him.

'Why are all the women in my family so bossy?' he grumbled. Then he saw her expression. 'I'm going to! I'm going to!'

That evening, as they set out the Scrabble board, Maureen noticed Jack wincing in pain.

'What's the matter, son?'

'Sunburn,' he said ruefully. 'I fell asleep on the sand and when I woke up I was a piece of toast.'

His back was flaming red and hot to touch.

'That needs bicarb,' Aunt Grace said. 'Mix up a thick paste of the stuff, Mo, it will take all the sting out of the pain. And don't be without your shirt for a couple of days, Jack, or you'll blister and then you'll be really sore.'

Maureen gently patted the soothing mixture on to his back while Jack flinched and squirmed. He's filled out since I last saw him, she thought. My little lad is really growing up.

'I'm being as gentle as I can,' she told him. 'You'd better stay indoors and out of the sun tomorrow.'

'Maybe you could come down to the shop and unpack those wire toys that arrived today?' Patsy said. 'And the top floor needs sweeping. That'll keep you from getting bored!'

'I won't be bored,' Jack protested. 'I will come, though, I'd like to help out. Maybe I should get a job at your shop, Mum?'

'I don't think so,' Maureen said firmly. 'But you'll be very welcome. We could use the extra pair of hands.'

'Oh, perhaps we *could* find a permanent post for Jack?' Aunt Grace beamed at him. 'A big strong lad like you would be very useful. I'm sure you'd be good with the customers, once you got to know the stock.'

'Aunt Grace, Jack needs to get out into the world and find a job that can lead somewhere,' Maureen interrupted.

'I don't want him to stay behind the counter with us. Besides, if we pay him his wages, that's not exactly bringing money into the family, is it?'

Aunt Grace winked at Jack and patted his head.

'I'm sure we can find you something, lad,' she whispered. 'Don't you worry.'

Patsy grinned to herself. Aunt Grace was totally smitten with Jack!

★ ★ ★

Maureen always enjoyed the early morning walk down to open up the shop. Before the sun rose, the sea across the huge bay was still perfectly calm, with a pearly-grey sheen, and in the harbour the orderly rows of yachts rode quietly on the water. As she walked past the sleeping houses she breathed in the fragrant, earthy smell of the mountain above her and thought how happy she was to be living here again. And now Jack was with them, she was sure everything would work out.

He just needs to find the right job, she thought. It's too late to register at a technical college, but we can do that next year, when he's decided what he wants to do.

Maybe he should speak to Dan about his future.

Accident

She hadn't seen Dan for more than a week, not since the dinner with Ella. This wasn't unusual — Dan often took fishing parties out for three or four days at a time, but she'd expected him to phone her before now.

Then she remembered it was Wednesday and he was going to the concert with Ella. He hadn't called to ask if she could make it.

He must have forgotten about me now Ella's back in town, she thought with a pang. Or maybe she told him she didn't really want me along. She was a little rude, telling him she would buy just two tickets! Well, I didn't want to go, anyway.

Yes, I did. Dan just didn't want me to go with them, obviously.

She was aware that she was being childish but she couldn't help it, and by the time she'd unlocked the shop door, her happy mood had evaporated.

Mellie was the next to arrive, neat and attractive in her jeans and bright sparkly T-shirt and carrying a pile of boxes. She hung up her sweater and put on a cute frilly apron.

'That's new,' Maureen observed. 'Whose idea was that?'

'Granny's. She thinks I should wear some sort of uniform if I'm a waitress.'

Maureen smiled.

'Well, as far as I'm concerned you're

manager of our tea garden and managers don't have to wear aprons! Unless you want to protect your clothes, of course,' she told her.

'Oh, good.' Mellie whipped off the apron and stuffed it into her bag with a grin. 'Manager, right? That sounds pretty cool.

'Granny made extra *koeksusters* today, because I told her they were all gone by lunchtime yesterday. And I've brought seven *melkterts* and two ginger loaves as well as the fruit pies.'

'We're really increasing our sales,' Maureen said thoughtfully. 'Two months ago you only sold one *melktert*.'

'I know. These days people even want to buy an extra one to take home,' Mellie said. 'But there's never enough. Anyway, here's today's bill.'

She stuck it on to the spike next to the coffee machine and went through to the little garden at the back to set the tables.

Ever the business lady, Maureen thought. She knew Mellie kept a book where she always entered everything her grandmother baked for the shop, how much the ingredients had cost, when she was paid and how much profit this represented.

By eleven o'clock the shop was buzzing with customers.

A coach-load of Japanese tourists were queueing politely at the till to pay Maureen for their armfuls of souvenirs, with Patsy and Aunt Grace wrapping and packaging their purchases in the new green paper bags with the Whittaker's name in white.

★ ★ ★

Maureen didn't see Jack's arrival. She heard it.

One of Priscilla's magnificent ceramic platters hit the floor with a crash and smashed into a thousand brilliant-coloured pieces. There was instant silence in the shop, with all heads turned towards Jack, who stood scarlet with embarrassment.

'Sorry, Mum. I dropped it,' he mumbled.

'I can see that,' Maureen said levelly,

trying to keep her voice quiet. All the irritation she'd felt for Jack while he was at school came flooding back. 'But why did you pick it up in the first place? Didn't you see the sign *Please Do Not Touch*? Did you think that didn't apply to you?'

'Oh, Mo, don't fuss, it was an accident,' Aunt Grace whispered hurriedly, although she looked as dismayed as Maureen felt. 'Patsy, there's a broom in the storeroom. Be a sweetheart and fetch it.'

'Jack, you heard Aunt Grace. There's a broom in the storeroom,' Patsy said coldly. She had no intention of sweeping up Jack's very expensive disaster. Priscilla's things were so pricey that Maureen never let a customer pick them up. She always insisted on carefully lifting the plates and bowls down herself.

'That way, if there's ever an accident, I'll know who to blame,' she'd said.

This had been the first time anything had been broken and, of course, it had to be the most expensive item on the shelf.

Jack bent down to sweep up the pieces into the dustpan.

As he carried the third pan of shattered fragments to the back, Maureen followed him. She searched amongst the pieces and found what she was looking for. The price sticker.

'Read that,' she said, tight lipped.

'*Three thousand rand*?' Jack whispered. 'For a *plate*?'

'Not just a plate, Jack, it's a Priscilla Harman platter, hand-painted with her new gold lustre. It's a work of art and costs as much as your plane ticket from England!'

Jack swallowed.

'I'll pay you back, Mum. I will, just as soon as I get a job.'

'Indeed you will. You can add it to the price of your air fare, which you're also going to repay. I think you'd better find work as soon as you can. No more lying around the beach for you from now on.'

She was determined not to make it too easy for him by telling him it was insured. Jack needed to learn a lesson and the sooner he did, the better. But looking at his stricken expression, Maureen couldn't help relenting and gave her chastened son a swift hug.

'Never mind now, what's done is done and it was an accident. Did you come down to give us a hand?' she asked.

'Yes. Maybe I'd better go upstairs and sweep the floor. I can't do much damage in an empty room.'

Jack recovered his spirits and was whistling as he pushed the broom briskly across the big empty space upstairs, when a very pretty girl put her head around the door.

'Hi,' she said, coming in with a tray. 'I'm Mellie. You must be Jack.'

She handed him a steaming cup of coffee and a thick plaited confection that spurted ginger-flavoured syrup when he bit into the crisp outer crust.

'Wow,' he said. 'Did you make this?'

'No, my granny did. She's a caterer. I'm the manager of the tea garden down below.'

'Oh, right.'

Jack couldn't stop looking at Mellie with her long, shiny black hair and her dark eyes fringed with long, thick lashes. She was quite simply the most beautiful girl he'd ever set eyes upon. He *had* to keep her up here, talk to her and get to know her!

She seemed in no hurry to go downstairs, either. She opened the french doors on to the wrought iron verandah and sat on the railing, looking down over the street. He strolled over and joined her, leaning on the railing and studying her profile.

'You make a great cup of coffee, Mellie. What do you do when you're not working here? In the evenings, I mean.'

'I help my gran with her baking. I do the books for her catering business and I help her with the housework,' she replied.

'No, I mean for fun. Do you like the movies?'

'Not really. They're very expensive. We have a video at home and sometimes we hire films. But Rafe and I — he's my brother — we prefer to read in the evenings.'

Jack had never met a girl who preferred to spend her evenings reading.

'I love reading, too,' he said immediately.

'You do? That's great! Who's your favourite author?'

Jack was put on the spot.

'Oh, well, I can't choose one in particular . . . '

Jack had never been a great reader.

'I've been reading the Russian authors recently,' Mellie continued. 'We did a play by Chekhov at school and I liked it so much I've been reading Tolstoy.'

'Oh.' How was he ever going to find something to talk about with Mellie? Jack was desperate.

'So, what do you want to study next

year?' he asked eventually. 'My sister says you're going to university.'

'Yes, I hope to. Business Science, if I can get enough money together. Then I'd like to get a job with one of the big corporations, to see how they run things. Then I want to start my own business. What do you plan to do?'

Phew, this girl had it all worked out, her whole life! She was so confident and knew exactly what she wanted. Jack didn't know what to answer and felt like an idiot.

'I don't know.'

Mellie was incredulous, her dark eyes laughing.

'Come on, Jack! Don't you have ambitions in life? You must have some dream, something you really want to do?'

Ambition

The only thing Jack wanted to do at this moment was to get to know Mellie better. And to have her think well of him. Suddenly, Mellie's good opinion became the most important thing in the world to Jack.

He racked his brains, trying to think of some ambition he could claim to have that would impress her.

'Of course I've got ambitions,' he said grandly. 'I want to own a yacht.'

Mellie burst out laughing.

'That's just something you want to *buy*! I mean, what do you want to *do* with your life?'

'I haven't decided.'

If she wasn't so cute, this would sound like a conversation with his mother.

'If you haven't decided, that's fine. It's better not to rush in and study something you're not interested in. Why not do what my brother Rafe did? When he left school he couldn't decide if he wanted to be a doctor or a lawyer, so he took a job that earned him some money and after three years he's now decided to do law. Plus, he's earned most of his university fees.'

'You're absolutely right,' Jack said. 'That's exactly what I'll do.'

When Mellie suggested it, it made such good sense.

'I'd better get downstairs and see if anyone wants some tea. But I've got yesterday's paper, so let's look and see if there's a job that might suit you.'

When Maureen went outside later, she found the two of them poring over the classifieds.

'I'm helping Jack find a job,' Mellie said, a red pen in her hand. 'He wants to start work as soon as he can.'

Maureen could have hugged her!

Rough Day

Patsy hurriedly wiped the small work-top of her little galley and put away the last of the washed coffee cups. She could already see the masts of the other yachts in the harbour as they slowly motored past to their own mooring, the sails of *Sea Freedom* stowed neatly in the forward hold.

They'd had a rough day on the bay, with the wind gusting at gale force and causing the boat to heel over at a frightening angle. In weather like that Patsy preferred to be up on deck, clutching a sheet and jammed between Martin and Greg on the side of the boat, her legs hanging over the side and getting drenched. Staying down below on her own was no fun and she revelled in the exhilaration of the wild wind and huge waves that splashed them all, including Rick grasping the wheel. But it was a relief to be back in calm waters.

She finished locking up the galley and came up on deck in time to say goodbye to Martin and Greg, who were heading back to the airport to catch their plane to Johannesburg.

'Greg, say hi to Linda for me,' she said. 'When are you bringing her down again?'

'Probably next week. I think the sailing bug has bitten her.' He laughed. 'She went out and bought loads of cute sailing gear and she's looking for a chance to wear it!'

'I'll look forward to seeing her again.' Patsy smiled.

She was about to leave the boat, too, when Rick cleared his throat.

'Do you feel like a trip into the country?' he asked her. 'I've got some family business to attend to on the farm before I fly back tomorrow. I thought you might enjoy the drive.'

'I'd love that. Your farm's out at Fransch Hoek, isn't it? Over the mountains? I've never been that far.'

'Not *my* farm. It's my brother's farm now,' he said abruptly. 'But it's very beautiful. Vineyards and oak trees. I'm sure you'll like it,' he added.

★ ★ ★

The little green sports car made short work of the drive through to Cape Town, with Rick skilfully weaving between the slower moving traffic.

Once clear of the city and heading

north on to the four-lane freeway towards the line of blue mountains in the distance, he put his foot down and roared ahead.

Patsy loved speed and with Rick at the wheel she relaxed and enjoyed the wind in her hair, completely confident in his driving ability. She was almost disappointed when they left the freeway and he slowed down to climb the mountain pass.

Towering rocky mountains rose steeply on either side of the narrow winding road, with farmhouses perched on the lower slopes, surrounded by regimented green vineyards. Beautiful old oak trees stretched their branches across and formed a dark green tunnel, and as they headed down into the Fransch Hoek valley, everything spread out below was green and lush. The farmhouses, gleaming white in the glare of the afternoon sun, were surrounded by smaller, white-washed labourers' cottages.

'Most of the farmhouses here were built in the 1600s,' Rick said. 'The

Catholic French government at the time was persecuting the Protestants. Many of them emigrated to this valley and were given free land to start wine farms. Therefore a lot of people here have French surnames.'

'Like Hugo,' Patsy said. 'It must be lovely to have a family going way, way back, all living in the same place for generations. You must have a wonderful sense of — I don't know — roots?'

'If you like that sort of thing,' he said briefly. 'Here we are.'

Tranquillity

He swung the car smoothly past some handsome white gateposts and up a long paved driveway, motoring slowly to the front of a gracious, old gabled farmhouse, and parked in the deep shade of several old oaks.

Patsy drew a deep breath and looked around her.

The enormous house was thickly

thatched, with four-inch deep sash windows on either side of the massive front door, which opened on to a wide verandah. Comfortable old sofas and armchairs were grouped invitingly around a low table where someone had left a pile of books.

The shade from the majestic oaks dappled the white-washed walls and Patsy felt as if she'd stepped back in time. The feeling of peace and tranquillity was almost overwhelming. The only sound was the gentle, insistent cooing of the doves on the roof above.

She shaded her eyes and looked up at the gable, decorated with bunches of plaster grapes surrounding the date *1699*.

'Is that when the house was built?' she asked. 'That's over three hundred years old! It's so beautiful.'

'Yes, it is,' Rick said quietly.

'How could you ever bear to leave?' she asked impetuously. 'If I lived here I'd stay for ever. Didn't you want to be a wine farmer?'

Rick grimaced slightly.

'Patsy, what I wanted and what the Hugo tradition is are two very different things. In this family — oh, there's my brother, Andre.'

A tall, thin man appeared at the open front door in khaki shorts and an open-necked T-shirt. He looked like an older, skinnier version of Rick with the same slightly reserved manner, but without his brother's confident mien.

'It's My Farm, Richard'

'Hello, Richard.' He clapped him on the shoulder with a slight smile before turning to Patsy, his hand outstretched.

'Andre Hugo. Good afternoon.'

'Patsy Henderson,' she said, smiling. 'What a beautiful home you have.'

'Thank you. It suits me fine.'

Me? Surely he had a family to enjoy all of this?

'It's been a while, Richard. Well, come and sit down. Tea?'

'Is Maria still making her famous

lemonade? I think we'd prefer that in this heat,' Rick replied.

'I'll organise it.'

Andre disappeared into the cool gloom of the house, leaving Patsy and Rick together on the sofa.

'Maria's been working for our family since I was a baby,' he said. 'Both of her sons grew up here and now they work on the farm.'

Just then a small dark woman hurried out of the house and stopped in front of him, her arms open wide with her smile nearly splitting her face.

'Mister Richard! I am so happy to see you!'

She flung her arms around Rick, who uncoiled himself from the depths of the sofa and gave her an enormous hug in return.

'Great to see you, too, Maria,' he said affectionately.

'Too long you stay away from us!' she exclaimed. She looked down at Patsy, a twinkle in her eye. 'And now you bring your girlfriend, too? Very nice!'

'Oh, no, I'm not — I mean, I'm just a friend,' Patsy said hurriedly.

Rick smiled.

'She's a very hot and thirsty friend, Maria. Do you have any of your lemonade in the fridge?'

'Of course, Mr Richard. And some ginger cake I made this morning. It's good that you come to eat it. Mr Andre, he doesn't like to eat my food these days.'

She gave her employer a reproachful look.

'Nonsense, Maria. If I ate everything you cooked I'd be the size of a house,' Andre said.

Rick looked at his brother.

'You've lost a bit of weight, Andre,' he said. 'Everything OK?'

'Of course. I've been busy with the spraying. This heat takes it out of me.'

'How's the crop looking this year?' Rick asked.

'Pretty good. Those Chardonnay I planted three years ago are starting to bear.'

Patsy looked mystified.

'Chardonnay is a type of grape,' Rick explained. 'It makes an excellent wine once it's been aged in oak for a year or two.'

'Oh, lovely. Do you make your own wine here on the farm, Andre?'

'No, I send the whole crop to the co-op.' Andre glanced at Rick almost as though he expected his next comment.

'Who buy it for peanuts! If you'd only rebuild the winery like Dad intended and produce our own Mont Liberte label. Like every other wine estate does around here. When are you going to get your nose out of a book and get your act together?'

'It's my decision, Richard.' Andre turned to Patsy. 'Selling direct to the co-op is a lot easier and more convenient. They collect grapes from lots of the vineyards and make wine by blending them together. A winery on the estate would be a lot of extra work.'

Rick interrupted.

'But for three centuries the Hugos

have bottled and sold their own wine from this estate,' he said. 'Until the fire destroyed the old winery just before Dad passed away.' He glared at his brother in undisguised disgust. 'You know it was Dad's dying wish that you rebuild it and start bottling Mont Liberte wines again. Dad won awards for our wine. So did Grandad.'

'It's my farm, Richard. I can run it the way I want to,' Andre repeated levelly.

The tension between the brothers made Patsy distinctly uncomfortable, and she wished she could leave them and explore her surroundings.

As if reading her thoughts, Rick said easily, 'Why don't you go for a walk, Patsy, and have a look at the vineyards? There's a river beyond that barn. I've got some papers to sign so give me half an hour.'

She escaped thankfully and headed for the cool of the river. As she passed a big kitchen garden, Maria straightened up and waved to her.

'I pick tomatoes for Mr Richard and you to take when you go,' she said, a big basket on her arm. 'Mr Richard likes tomatoes from the farm.'

'They look lovely,' Patsy said. 'Home-grown tomatoes taste much better than shop-bought, don't they?'

Maria nodded in agreement.

'Are you staying in Johannesburg like Mr Richard?' Maria was clearly interested in finding out more about the girlfriend!

'No, Cape Town. I work for Mr — er, Rick, on his boat. I'm his cook.'

'Like me! I cook for the old Mrs Hugo and all the family. Now I cook just for Mr Andre. Forty years I'm cooking here,' she told Patsy.

'I expect you're a far better cook than I am.' Patsy smiled. 'So, Mr Andre isn't married?'

'No, he never marry. Now he not so young any more, I don't think he ever find a woman. We need children here again.' She grinned broadly. 'Maybe you and Mr Richard . . . ?'

'I'm just a friend, Maria,' Patsy insisted, embarrassed. 'This must have been a wonderful place to grow up. Rick said he used to ride a lot.'

'Yes, him and Mr Andre. Long ago, those boys used to have big parties. Everyone in the valley come.' Maria was silent, remembering. 'Now Mr Andre, he doesn't ride, he doesn't have parties, he doesn't do anything. He just read his books and he stand on his head.'

'Stand on his head? Whatever for?' Patsy was confused.

'He do that thing — yoga. He say it makes him strong.' Maria clearly thought this a waste of time. Then she burst out, 'Mr Andre, he never go out to look at the vines properly. And he doesn't eat any more. Like a little bird, he pecks at my food. I think perhaps Mr Andre is sick.'

Sick? Andre had certainly sounded dispirited when he spoke and he didn't seem to have the energy that Rick exuded, but sick?

'He says it's the heat, Maria. Maybe he just finds it too hot to eat?'

'No, you must tell Mr Richard.' Maria clutched her arm. 'I think there is something wrong with his brother.'

A Job For Jack

'So, Jack, any luck with finding something in the paper?' Maureen asked the following evening. She was in the big kitchen, busy preparing a supper of chicken stir fry, with Jack hulling strawberries into a bowl. 'Hang on there, leave some for the rest of us!'

Jack sighed heavily and dropped the strawberry he was holding.

'No, nothing. Everyone wants experience or some sort of qualifications. But Mellie reckons there's a small local paper that comes out once a week and it's full of positions vacant around this area. So I'll wait and see.'

Maureen always enjoyed the evening meal around Aunt Grace's big shiny table. Grace still used the same cruet set Maureen remembered as a child. The linen napkins and old bone-handled cutlery were probably the same ones her grandmother had used when Aunt Grace was a child. Maureen loved the feeling of continuity and roots, something she'd never felt in England.

She wished now that she'd managed to have a formal meal with her own children more often, with real conversation. But life in Witham had been so hectic, there never seemed time. Usually supper had been a hurried affair, often in front of the TV. I enjoy being without a TV, she thought, there's more time to do things.

Dan's Proposal

They were just clearing away the plates when there was a knock on the door.

'I'll get it,' Patsy said. She came back, smiling, with Dan in tow.

'I told him he was just in time for the strawberries!' she said.

'Take a seat, Dan.' Maureen's heart flipped but she only kissed him briefly. She hadn't seen him since the evening at the hotel and wondered how things stood between them now that Ella was around. Should she ask him about the concert?

'Thanks. Evening, all.'

He hadn't mentioned that he would drop by, but he drew up a chair and started talking to Jack. He'd met Jack the day after he arrived and Maureen was pleased to see they'd immediately got on well.

'So, how's the job-hunting going, lad?' he asked. 'Find anything suitable?'

'Not yet,' Jack replied. 'I'm waiting for the local paper — '

'You'll only find jobs for waiters and bicycle couriers in that rag,' Dan said. 'You want a proper job, don't you?'

'Well, yes, but I wouldn't mind being a waiter! They get good tips,' Jack replied. 'And it would be evening work

305

so I could do my own thing during the day.'

'Yeah, like sleep late!' Patsy had no illusions about her little brother.

'OK. Fair enough.' Dan grimaced, but caught Maureen's eye and changed the subject. 'Lovely strawberries, Mo.'

After the meal, Patsy hurried off to meet some of her sailing club friends down at the clubhouse.

Grace looked at Maureen.

'Jack and I will do the dishes. Why don't you and Dan go and sit outside on the *stoep* and we'll bring the coffee later?'

Maureen settled on the old cane sofa, and Dan joined her, his arm around her shoulder. She snuggled comfortably against him, gazing down at the twinkling lights of the harbour below.

'How was the concert?' she asked hesitantly.

'Oh, I really enjoyed it. I wish you could have come, Mo.'

'I would have liked to go, but Ella didn't exactly make me feel welcome!'

'But she told me — oh, never mind. I'll look out for the next good programme and we can go together.'

'Has Ella found somewhere to live yet?' Maureen asked.

Dan nodded.

'Actually, she wants me to go and look at a place in Kalk Bay. I think she's quite keen to make an offer on it but wants my opinion first. She says it has a great view of the fishing boats.'

So she'll be able to watch your boat coming home every day, Maureen thought.

'That sounds nice,' she replied, determined to find something nice to say about his friend. 'Um . . . she's very beautiful, isn't she? And she seems so full of enthusiasm for everything!'

'She is. She's quite exhausting,' Dan agreed.

Maureen was delighted to hear this.

'Oh, I don't know,' she demurred. 'She's interested in so many things.'

Dan took her hand in his.

'Enough about Ella,' he said. 'There's

something I want to ask you.'

His voice was suddenly serious and the word 'proposal' flashed through Maureen's mind. This time, she had no doubt at all what her answer would be, and she turned to him with a smile, her heart racing.

'I thought I'd run my idea past you first, before I speak to him. What would you think of Jack becoming my crew and learning the business of big game fishing from the bottom up? It would be very hard work. Do you think he's up to it?'

8

One of The Crew

Maureen swallowed, overcome by a huge feeling of anticlimax. How could I have been so daft as to think he'd propose now that Ella's around, she thought bleakly.

But a job for Jack — a real one — that would be a wonderful solution to the problem of finding employment for him.

'I think he'd jump at the chance to crew for you, Dan,' she said slowly, straightening up and slipping out from under the embrace of his arm. 'He'd be silly not to. It's very kind of you to think of him.'

'Not at all. I need someone quite urgently and Jack's a big strapping boy,' he said briskly. 'But I heard him saying how he liked to sleep late and so on, and there'd be none of that if he signed on with me.'

'No, of course not. He's still on holiday, that's why he sleeps in a bit. I'd make sure he was down at the harbour on time every day — I'll buy him an alarm clock if need be!' she promised.

Maureen could picture Jack on board the boat, revelling in a proper job, no matter how hard the work. And being in the fresh air out at sea all day would be a bonus.

'It's no nine-to-five work, either,' Dan went on. 'On days when I've got a party of game fishermen on board, he'd have to be down at Kalk Bay by six o'clock, and he won't get back home until maybe ten at night, after he's cleaned the boat and checked the engines. Some clients like to take a run up the coast, so we could be away for three or four days at a time. It's tough work, Mo. He'll get wet and cold and he'll use muscles he never knew he had.'

Maureen nodded.

'I think it would be good for Jack, I really do,' she replied.

'Well, as long as he's not afraid of hard work, he could earn good money with me. The fishing parties usually give the crew big tips, too, if they're happy with their catch.'

This sounds perfect, Maureen thought, smiling brightly.

'I'll speak to him about it as soon as I can, then,' Dan said. 'I didn't want to suggest anything until I knew you approved. It can be dangerous work out there, Mo, in the high seas around Cape Point.'

She looked up, startled. She hadn't imagined anything else but motoring out across the rolling swells of the bay.

'Dangerous?'

'I don't go out looking for trouble, of course,' Dan explained. 'I always check the weather forecasts. But we sometimes go up to fifty kilometres off the Point and a storm can blow up out of nowhere. They don't call this the Cape of Storms for nothing.'

'Patsy seems to love sailing in bad weather,' Maureen said. 'But it's up to Jack. If he thinks he can handle it, he will. I'll make sure he gives it his best shot.'

Dan smiled appreciatively and he replaced his arm around her shoulders and took her hand in his.

'But whatever happens with Jack, if it doesn't work out for any reason, you and I will still be OK, won't we?' Dan looked worried.

'Of course. I'm very grateful you're prepared to give Jack a chance.'

'A chance at what?' Jack said, coming out on to the verandah with the coffee, followed by Grace with a plate of cinnamon biscuits.

Dan grinned.

'How would you like a job crewing on my boat?' he asked.

'Really? That would be wicked!' Jack said, putting down the tray with a thump and nearly spilling the coffee.

'Right. Be at Kalk Bay harbour at six tomorrow morning and we'll discuss the details. Did you make these biscuits, Miss Whittaker? They are delicious.'

'No, these are one of Rugaya's specialties.' Grace smiled. 'Did I hear you offer Jack a job, Dan?'

Dan obviously hadn't intended talking about the job in front of Grace, but he couldn't avoid answering.

'That's right, Miss Whittaker. Crewing for me. I was telling Mo it would be hard work and we'll see how it goes.'

'I'm not afraid of work, Dan, honestly,' Jack put in. 'I'm good with engines, too. You'll see.'

Jack couldn't keep the grin from his face. He caught his mother's eye and gave her a thumbs up sign. She winked back. Everything was going to be fine for Jack now, she was sure.

Refusal

'I'm just popping out for a minute, Mo,' Grace called. Maureen noticed that Grace had dressed in her good blue suit and was wearing her special pearl earrings, a sure sign that she wasn't just going to the library, but she didn't ask.

She would have been surprised to know that her aunt was walking next door to Messrs Ebrahim and Patel, Gentlemen's Outfitters and Tailors of Naval Uniforms to His Majesty's Armed Forces.

The chipped gilt sign above the shop was very old, and dated from before the war. His Majesty's Armed Forces no longer required Naval uniforms from Messrs Ebrahim and Patel, but no-one had got around to changing the sign, and Mr Ebrahim had been buried in the Muslim cemetery thirty years earlier.

Raj Patel, the son of the original owner, now ran the shop, selling off-the-peg men's clothes. His father had trained him as a tailor, but for a long time there had been almost no call for suits and he and his wife, Suraya, stocked a lot of beachwear and casual shoes.

Grace stopped and looked at the window display, which consisted of a mannequin wearing a pair of floral shorts and a vivid yellow and green Hawaiian shirt, all covered in a thin film of dust. The Patels could do with a bit of help from Mo, too, she thought.

She pushed open the door which tinkled a warning, and Suraya Patel came from the back of the shop, smiling. She was a dark, petite woman, wearing a beautiful gold-trimmed sari, her eyes ringed with kohl.

'Just having my breakfast,' she said cheerfully. 'What can I do for you, Miss Whittaker? Have you come to buy that handsome boy of yours some new bathing shorts?'

'Not today,' Grace replied. 'I wanted to talk to you about something . . . Is Raj here?'

'Raj!' his wife called.

Raj Patel came out and clasped Grace's hand, smiling. Although not yet thirty, his hairline was receding rapidly and his traditional loose white shirt hid an expanding waistline, a testimony to Suraya's good cooking. Soon he's going to look exactly like his father, Grace thought, amused.

'Money Isn't Everything'

'Good morning, Raj,' Grace said. 'I'll get to business straight away. Have you been approached by a man called Richard Hugo to sell your property?'

The husband and wife looked at each other silently.

'Yes,' Suraya blurted out. 'He's offered us a lot of money, but Raj doesn't want to sell.'

Grace looked enquiringly at Raj, who frowned at his wife.

'I have no intention of selling,' he said quietly. 'This is a family business. My grandfather started it and I will pass it on to Adeep when he is old enough. Like my father did to me.'

'Raj! Adeep is five years old!' Suraya exploded. 'And I'm sure he won't want to run a clothes shop when he is older. Already he is loving his computer. He will do something better than staying in this dreary old shop!'

She bit her lip and looked appealingly at Grace.

'Miss Whittaker, don't you agree that selling this place would be a good opportunity for us? But Raj is so stubborn he won't even discuss it sensibly. Even though we received a letter from Mr Hugo yesterday offering us a little more!'

'Money isn't everything, Suraya.'

Grace could tell her question had disturbed a nest of wasps in the Patel family, but although she sympathised briefly with Suraya, she was delighted with Raj's attitude.

'Raj, I have to admit I'm very pleased that you feel that way,' she told him. 'Mr Hugo has approached me, too. He won't take no for an answer and he's made my life a misery.'

'You, too? I can't think why he would want to buy both these properties,' Raj said. 'I got the impression he wanted to run a clothes shop like this one, just modernise it somewhat.'

Grace snorted.

'A clothes shop? Far from it. Mr Hugo has far grander plans. He wants to pull down the buildings and put up a hotel.'

'But these two together would be too small for a hotel, surely?'

The thought struck Grace immediately.

'What if he's offered to buy Alf Thompson's next door as well? And the Venters' next to him? With four buildings he could build a fair-sized hotel, I should think.'

'Let's go and ask him,' Raj said firmly. He lifted the wooden counter.

'Suraya, please look after things for a while.'

Suraya watched silently as they left.

'Your wife doesn't seem all that happy in the shop,' Grace commented.

'She hasn't thought about it properly,' Raj said curtly. 'She should not have discussed her feelings with you. I will speak to her.'

'Oh, no!' Grace cried, distressed. 'I quite understand. Suraya's a young woman and men's clothes probably don't interest her. She could be right, though, about your son wanting to do something else when he grows up. There are so many wonderful things they can do with their lives and children these days don't have the same sense of tradition as they used to.'

Raj nodded thoughtfully.

'I believe your niece has returned and is helping you in your shop, isn't she? You see, she knows her duty — it's a family business!'

'She's a partner now,' Grace explained. 'But she couldn't wait to leave when she was a teenager. She's made a lot of changes now. My old shop is quite different these days, thanks to Mo.'

'I have noticed.' Raj was quiet. 'Perhaps we could make a few changes in our shop, too.'

'You should speak to your wife. I'm sure she will have lots of good ideas,' Grace replied diplomatically.

She opened the door and entered the second-hand book shop, followed diffidently by Raj.

The dimly lit room was lined from floor to ceiling with reading matter: old books, paperbacks and magazines. Some shelves were marked *Westerns* or *Thrillers*, but it was mostly a lucky dip of books of every age and condition. Grace loved this place and often found some treasures hiding in the shelves. She'd picked up a first edition of 'The Memoirs Of Sherlock Holmes' printed in 1894 and was pretty sure it might be very valuable one day. But the gold-embossed tooled cover was so beautiful that she knew she'd never part with it.

'Ah, Miss Whittaker! Mr Patel! On the hunt for a good book, or do I sense some other purpose behind your visit?'

Alf Thompson was a small man with a walrus moustache and twinkling eyes hidden by shaggy grey eyebrows. In both summer and winter he wore a pin-striped waistcoat and bow tie and was, in Grace's opinion, the perfect bookshop owner. He allowed visitors to browse and left them alone unless they asked for assistance.

'Indeed, we do have a purpose, Alf,' Grace said firmly. 'Raj and I would like to know if you have been approached by a young man called Richard Hugo.'

Alf frowned.

'Hugo? Well, yes, I have. Fellow from Johannesburg. He was in here last week,' he replied.

'Well, what did you tell him? We know he must have made you an offer for your property,' Grace said. 'He's tried it with both of us.'

'I told him I'd think about it,' Alf said quietly. 'I'm not getting any younger, you know, Grace.'

Grace was shocked.

'How can you even *consider* selling, Alf? You've been here for forty years. You're a Simonstown institution! We can't do without you!'

'Maybe. But I have a devil of a time getting up that ladder to reach the top shelves these days. My knees are packing in and my back hurts.' He smiled ruefully. 'It's no fun getting old, is it, Grace?'

'I wouldn't know,' Grace replied tartly. Alf had plenty of years in him yet, but she'd always suspected that men could be real hypochondriacs. 'What on earth are you going to do with yourself?'

'I don't know,' Alf said. 'Retire, I suppose. That's what people do when they reach my age, isn't it?'

Grace rolled her eyes at her old friend.

'Don't be daft — you'll have to do *something*. You can't just sit about with your arms folded. Do you have any hobbies?'

'None,' Alf admitted. 'Books have a way of taking over your time; buying them, cleaning them, reading them. I guess I'm the original bookworm.' He smiled at his own joke but Grace pounced.

'You see! Books are your life and you'd be miserable if that was taken away.'

'Perhaps. But I've always envied those people who can do as they please. I'm tied to my shop the whole day.'

Battle Lines

Raj cleared his throat. 'Mr Thompson, if I may make a suggestion?' he began. 'Why not open your shop for half days? You could take some time off but still run your business. You would be sadly missed here.'

'I suppose it would be nice to have a lie-in sometimes,' Alf agreed.

Grace could tell that Alf was coming round to the idea.

'Alf, you simply cannot let that upstart fellow buy up this lovely row of buildings and turn them into a hotel. These developers have the money to buy whatever they want and we can't let them get away with ruining our beautiful main road! I will not allow it to happen!' Grace said excitably.

Alf laughed.

'Grace Whittaker! I'd hate to be on the wrong side of you in a battle!'

She smiled sweetly.

'So, you'll tell him no, then? Refuse his offer?' she asked and he nodded in reply.

'I don't dare accept, do I? Heaven knows what you'd do to me!' Alf chuckled. 'But you're right. I wouldn't like to see any of these shops pulled down — they all have such an interesting history.'

Grace was still smiling as she left the bookshop and headed for the health shop. Disappointingly, the sign on the health shop door read Closed. Back in ten minutes.

'I'll come back later,' Grace said. 'It's essential that none of us signs that wretched man's offer.'

'Absolutely,' Raj agreed. 'All for one and one for all!'

Large Amount Of Money

Grace knew that ten minutes could well mean an hour with the Venter sisters, so she left it until mid-afternoon to call round again.

She had always liked the two Venter women. Both of them were tall and bony, with fly-away greyish-blonde hair and a habit of ending each other's sentences. They'd started the health shop some years ago, after Betsy's husband died and she'd come to have a holiday with her younger, widowed sister, Adele.

While she'd been visiting, they'd both suffered a bout of flu and Betsy had been horrified that nowhere in Simonstown could she buy a herbal remedy called echinacea, her favourite cure-all for everything.

There and then, the sisters had decided to open a health shop. Betsy sold her house up the coast, moved in permanently with Adele and used the money to purchase the building. Ten years later they were still the only health shop for miles around and very well known.

The door pinged as Grace walked in, but only Betsy Venter was in, kneeling on the floor and restocking the shelves of mung beans and sunflower seeds in front of the till.

'Afternoon, Betsy,' Grace said.

Betsy straightened up with a stifled groan when she saw her and knocked a small basket from the counter, sending cards scattering across the floor.

'Oh, my poor knees.' She smiled apologetically. 'These days they let me know when it's going to rain. I'm not getting any younger!'

'Join the club,' Grace replied. 'But I find some of your arnica tablets very helpful. Have you tried those yourself? Here, let me help you.'

Together the two women retrieved the contents of the basket.

'I wish Adele wouldn't keep that thing up there,' Betsy fussed. 'I'm going to put it under the counter. It gets in the way, and it's only business cards from salesmen.'

'So I see,' Grace murmured, spotting Richard Hugo's card amongst the others. 'So you've met our Mr Hugo, have you?'

'No, but Adele has. I think she's quite smitten with him! She says he's a very charming young man. He's made an appointment to see both of us on Friday, as a matter of fact.'

Hmm, Grace thought. That big warm smile and those boyish good looks don't cut any ice with me!

'Did he tell you why he wanted to speak to you both?' Grace asked.

Betsy frowned.

'Well, Adele thinks that perhaps he wants to buy a share in our business. He seemed most impressed with everything, she said. Why else would he want to speak to both of us together?'

'To ask you to sell your property to him,' Grace informed her. 'He hopes you'll jump at the opportunity.'

'Really? Well, he's sadly mistaken.'

Betsy shook her head. 'We both enjoy running this shop. Why should we sell?'

'Well,' Grace began, 'perhaps he's hoping you'll be tempted by the very large amount of money he's going to offer you. He wants to knock the building down to build a big hotel.'

Betsy was astonished.

'Surely not here on the main road? They'd never allow it.'

Grace suddenly had an alarming thought. What if Richard Hugo made them such a good offer that the Venter sisters were tempted, after all? Neither of them was young any more. Betsy's first impulse was to refuse, but what if they discussed it later and they changed their minds?

She wasn't exactly sure how well the health shop did. Whenever she called, it wasn't exactly overcrowded with customers, but the two women drove expensive cars and closed their shop for a month every year to take holidays together overseas.

The Perfect Answer

'My goodness. I wonder why he thinks we should want his money? Although, of course, I can't speak for Adele, but I have quite enough for my own needs!' Betsy said. 'My late husband left me very well provided for. And since we started this shop together, we've had such fun.'

'There'd be an outcry from all your customers if you ever closed up,' Grace said sincerely. 'I often wonder how we managed before you came. You've made everyone more aware of healthy living and so many people I know swear by your homeopathic remedies.'

'I'm glad to hear that,' Betsy said. 'He won't get very far with us. Besides, isn't there a preservation order on all the buildings in the street? When we wanted to put up our sign we had to get permission from the Historical Society and they asked us to make it smaller than we intended.'

Grace shook her head.

'Ah, but Mr Hugo thinks his money will talk,' she said.

Just then, Adele Venter breezed into the shop, smiling, her arms full of packages.

'Good afternoon, Grace! How nice to see you. Betsy, I've left a little box of ginseng and those capsules of olive leaf extract on the seat of the car. Could you — '

'Give you a hand to bring them in? Of course,' Betsy said obligingly.

'We were just discussing the fact that Mr Hugo is planning to buy up this whole block of shops to build a hotel,' Grace told Adele. 'Betsy seemed pretty sure that you wouldn't want to sell to him.'

Adele looked nonplussed.

'Sell to him? He's planning to build a hotel?' she repeated. 'I thought he was just interested in becoming a partner in our business. But selling to him outright? Yes, I would certainly consider his offer.'

Grace was stunned. She'd been so

sure that she'd have the support of all three shop owners that she looked at Adele in shocked disbelief.

'To tell the truth, Grace,' she continued before Grace could say anything, 'I'd be very happy if he wants to buy it. That would be the perfect answer to everything.'

Grace couldn't think of anything to say.

Mountain View

This afternoon was the second time Rick had driven out to Mont Liberte, taking Patsy with him. He didn't explain the reason for his visit, but when they arrived he parked the car under the oak trees.

'I've just got to drop some papers off for Andre,' he said. 'Wait here, I won't be a minute.'

Patsy lay back and looked up at the leaves, turning russet in the autumn weather. A grey squirrel peered down at her inquisitively, then chattered away up the trunk. I wonder why Rick's always in such a hurry, she thought. I'd love to go for a walk or something before we roar off back to town.

He returned a few minutes later with a cool box.

'Andre wasn't at home,' he said briefly. 'But shall we take a look at the view from the top of the mountain before we go back?'

'Lovely,' Patsy said. 'I don't have to rush back for anything.'

Driving up the bumpy farm road with Rick, she looked about her in delight. They were almost at the top of the mountain behind the farm and the view below stretched for miles, across a neat patchwork of green vineyards to the mountains on the other side of the valley.

Early Warning

'What are all those little red flowers along the edge of the rows?' she asked.

'Roses,' Rick explained. 'We plant them because roses get the same diseases as grapevines. So if the rosebush shows signs of downy mildew or fungal infection, then we know to spray all the vines immediately. A sort of early warning system.'

'Like a canary down a mine?' Patsy asked and Rick nodded. 'That's why there are so many beautiful roses in the house!'

'Maria loves arranging flowers,' he said, bringing the car to a halt in the shade of a tree. 'You both seemed to hit it off pretty well. I heard her mention Andre. Did she say anything about him?'

'Well, yes . . . ' Patsy admitted, relieved that he had broached the subject of his brother. 'Maria thinks he might be ill. She says he hardly eats a thing and spends a lot of time doing odd exercises and standing on his head. She says he's doing yoga.'

Rick nodded.

'He told me that he'd started going

to classes. That's his latest craze and that's probably why he's lost so much weight and doesn't eat much. He's always been interested in weird stuff, like acupuncture. Reflexology. Looking into someone's eyes and telling them what's wrong with them. Crazy.'

'That's called iridology,' Patsy said. 'It's not weird or crazy, you know. And reflexology really works. My mum had terrible headaches at one time and the reflexologist massaged a certain point on the soles of her feet and it actually helped enormously.'

'Really?' Rick looked doubtful. 'It sounds too daft for me.'

Patsy grinned.

'You're so hard-headed and practical! There's a lot that's good in alternative medicine. You should keep an open mind. There might be more to Andre than you know. He sounds interesting.'

'You think so? I don't suppose I'll ever understand Andre. He and I have always been on different paths, ever since we were small.'

Patsy was sympathetic.

'Have you talked to him lately?' she asked him. 'I mean, other than about the farm?'

Rick shook his head. He got out of the car and came round to open her door.

'That's enough about my brother. Would you like a glass of wine?'

'What?' She giggled. 'You've brought wine with you?'

'And some of Maria's biscuits. And a rug,' he added.

He spread out the rug in the shade and brought out a frosted bottle and two glasses from a cool box on the back seat.

Patsy watched while he poured it and leaned against the tree, looking back towards the farmhouse far below. Rich farm smells rose up from the lands around them and somewhere in the valley cattle called plaintively.

'This is perfect,' she said, happily clinking glasses with him. 'Beats Maria's lemonade, I think.'

'Cold white wine is just right for this time of day. It's great up here, isn't it? It used to be my favourite place to come.' The sun was setting and cool shadows started to creep up from the valley. 'Andre and I used to ride all over these mountains, bareback. Sometimes at twilight, if you sit still, you can see little buck grazing amongst the rocks.'

'This must have been a wonderful place to be a child,' Patsy said dreamily, remembering the small garden back in Witham with a view of the neighbours' washing-line. 'A river all of your own, and the beautiful trees . . . Weren't you lucky?'

'I was.' His voice was soft. 'When I was a kid I thought I'd live here for ever and imagined I'd marry and carry on with my life right here.'

'That sounds like pretty strong roots. I thought you said you didn't care about them?' she teased.

Tradition

'Things change. No point in wanting what you can't have,' he said shortly.

'The farm is Andre's now.'

'But Maria told me he's lost interest in farming,' Patsy said.

Rick shook his head.

'He's never had any interest in it,' he told her. 'It's not his fault that he's the way he is, I suppose. But he's the wrong person to run Mont Liberte and he'll be the first to admit it. From an early age, Andre made it very clear to my father that he wanted nothing to do with the farm.'

'So what happened? Shouldn't you be running it, then?' Patsy was confused.

'Of course I should be,' he growled. 'I was helping to tie up the vines and spray the grapes before I was twelve. I loved everything to do with viticulture. Andre would be in his room reading and I'd be in the little laboratory at the back of the winery with my dad, testing the wine for acid content. If it wasn't for that ridiculous Hugo will . . .'

He picked a piece of grass and chewed it moodily before continuing.

'Traditionally, the eldest son inherits

337

the farm. That's the way it has been for three hundred years. We Hugos are big on tradition.' He smiled weakly. 'But as we grew older, my father realised that Andre wouldn't be happy running the farm and in my final year of school he told us both that he intended changing his will. Andre seemed quite happy about that — he admitted he'd been dreading taking charge one day.'

'Well, then,' Patsy said, puzzled. 'What was the problem?'

'Are you sure you want to know all this history?' he said lightly.

Patsy helped herself to one of Maria's cinnamon cookies.

'Of course I am. So, your father was going to change his will?' she prompted.

Rick took a deep breath.

'Well, there was the fire, and my father was badly affected,' he began. 'When he tried to save the winery, the smoke damaged his lungs so badly he never recovered. He died about two weeks later and never had the chance to do anything about it.'

An Impossible Dream

His voice was so bleak that without thinking Patsy took his hand in hers.

'But, surely, if Andre knew your dad meant you to have it . . . He wasn't interested in running the farm, anyway.'

'It's complicated,' he explained. 'Andre's five years older than I am, and I think his friends persuaded him that, by rights, the place was his. Which it was, technically. But I knew he had no idea how to run the place; he'd never taken any interest. I could see Andre didn't want me hanging around pointing out his mistakes.'

'So what did you do?' Patsy asked, interested.

'I decided right then that if I couldn't run the farm, then I'd do something completely different with my life, and I studied Economics and Business Science instead.'

'And then you went to Johannesburg, about as far away from the valley as you could get,' Patsy murmured.

'You can get used to anything,' he said briefly. 'I found myself enjoying the buzz, after a while. But I need to come down to the Cape and sail at least once a month to keep me sane!'

He turned to her.

'So now you know, Miss Henderson. The sad story of the younger Hugo son . . . ' His voice was mocking, but she could see the pain in his eyes.

'Who left home and found the streets of Johannesburg were paved with gold,' she finished. 'But look on the bright side. Andre's not happy, but you have a great life. You love wheeling and dealing and you're very successful at it. You've got loads of friends, a lovely big house in Johannesburg and a beautiful boat down here.'

'But he's got the farm,' Rick said crisply. 'I sometimes think — oh, well, you're right. Wheel and deal, that's what I do.'

Patsy became aware that she was still holding his hand. She pulled away sharply, the mood broken, but he took

340

her hand in his and lifted it, kissing it gently.

'The rant's over. Thanks for listening, Patsy. You're good at that.' He kept hold of her hand and looked down at her with a little smile. 'You're the best thing that's happened to me in a long time, did you know that?'

'Am I?' she croaked, her heart pounding.

He bent and kissed her lips, gently at first, then with more passion, his arms pulling her tightly to him. There was a singing in her ears and it seemed for ever until they drew apart and gazed at each other.

'You are, indeed. Come on, it's time we were getting back.'

Dry-mouthed and shaken, she sat next to him silently as he navigated the rough track back down to the farm without looking at her. Every fibre of her being was aware of his closeness in the bucket seats of the little sports car. Patsy couldn't believe what had just happened, and all the way down she relived the kiss. Ever since their day together driving around the Peninsula, she'd tried not to fantasise too much about Rick, because she thought anything more than working on his boat was an impossible dream. She could hardly believe that he'd been thinking about her, too.

That afternoon he'd shown her a side of himself she'd never suspected, a younger, boyish Rick with unfulfilled dreams that lived just below the surface of the confident, assured, high-flying businessman. A tender Rick with a gentle side, one she much preferred to the arrogant, impatient man she'd first met on the yacht. She turned to him with a smile of pure happiness.

'This has been a lovely afternoon, hasn't it?'

'Yeah, well, we're going to hit the traffic now. Everyone will be coming back from work so the freeway will be busy.'

He reached the tarred road and spun the wheels, heading back on to the road towards Cape Town. It was as though their kiss had never happened.

'By the way,' he said abruptly, 'speaking of buying and selling, I haven't forgotten about your aunt's shop. I'll be going to speak to her again next week when I come down for the regatta.'

'Must you?' Patsy asked in dismay. 'I'd thought you'd given up on the idea. She really doesn't want to sell to you, or anyone else.'

'I'm sure I can change her mind in the end. If she thinks about it, she'll see the sensible thing for all of you would be to sell to me.'

'My aunt isn't someone who changes her mind very easily,' she said crisply. 'And your silly family motto about never giving up just made her all the more determined not to sell to you.'

'She'll find she can't stand in the way of progress,' he said. 'Come on, Patsy, surely you can see it would be better for her to sell?'

Patsy's heart sank. Rick the property developer was back in charge.

'I think we should have a little exhibition,' Maureen said, unpacking a consignment of brilliant turquoise hand-blown glasses from a local studio and holding them up to the light in admiration. 'Priscilla is bringing us ten gorgeous bowls next week. I had coffee with her yesterday and she showed them to me. They'll need two shelves all to themselves, at least.'

'And we have those beautiful bead necklaces from Swaziland and those woven mohair wall hangings from Botswana arriving this afternoon. It would be fun to invite a few people around after work. Offer them some sherry and let them see everything before the public does.'

'And the newspaper,' Mellie chimed in. 'Invite their photographer and we'd get some free publicity.'

'Aunt Grace, what do you think?' Maureen asked.

Grace had been oddly silent since her

absence from the shop the day before, and Maureen still had no idea where she had been.

'That might be nice,' her aunt said vaguely. 'Although I expect we'd have no trouble selling the things in the ordinary way.'

Maureen was puzzled by her lack of interest. Usually Grace embraced all new ideas with enthusiasm, and this colourless response was very unlike her. She was struck by an icy thought. What if Aunt Grace had been to the doctor and received some bad news she didn't want to share?

The more she thought about it, the more likely it became. Aunt Grace was never ill, and she hadn't let a rotten cold the month before prevent her from coming down to the shop every day. So if she *had* felt bad enough to see the doctor, it must be for something serious.

'Feel like a cuppa, Aunt Grace?' she asked. 'Patsy can finish unpacking the glass and we could go and sit outside.

Mellie can bring us a tray and you can put your feet up for a while.'

'I don't need a rest,' Grace retorted. 'But a cup of tea might be nice. And a slice of that pecan nut tart, if you have one, Mellie.'

They sat in the shade of a big green and white striped umbrella and Mellie brought the tray. Maureen waited until she'd gone before speaking.

'Aunt Grace, is anything wrong? With you, I mean? What did the doctor say?'

Grace frowned, confused.

'The doctor? What on earth are you talking about?'

'I thought you'd — ' Maureen was confused. 'Yesterday, when you were all dressed up, I thought you might have gone to see Doctor Lazarus. And you've been so quiet today, I thought you might be worried about something he said.'

Grace threw back her head and laughed.

'Whatever gave you that idea? No, I didn't see the doctor. I went to have a word with our neighbours about Richard Hugo and his hotel idea. I came away a little depressed.'

Lack Of Communication

She reported back briefly on her visit to the Patels, Alf Thompson and the Venter sisters.

'They'd all agreed not to sell,' she finished. 'After speaking to Betsy I was certain Adele would agree, too. Then we could all get together and act as one — unity is strength, as they say! But if Adele wants to sell up as she said, there's nothing I can do about it.'

'It's odd that her sister doesn't know how she feels,' Maureen commmented slowly. 'You say Adele claimed it would be the perfect answer to everything. So she's obviously got a big problem that Betsy is unaware of. Any idea what it might be?'

Grace shrugged.

'None,' she said. 'Perhaps she has

financial problems of her own that she hasn't discussed with her sister?'

'I don't think that's the case.' Maureen shook her head. 'Betsy told Mrs Phillips at the library that Adele insists that they close the shop next month and go to Greece for a fortnight. But Adele would hardly insist on going overseas if she was short of money.'

'Well, whatever it is, she's thrown a spanner in the works of my nice little idea.' Grace sighed. 'Not that I will ever give in to that Hugo man, but it would be nice to feel we were united against him.'

'So, what was your little idea?' Maureen queried.

'Nothing much,' Grace said. 'Anyway, it won't work without all of the shops doing the same thing.'

And more than that she would not say.

Maureen wondered about Adele's eagerness to sell up their business, so at lunchtime she took a walk up the street to the health shop. She found Adele on her own, doing a crossword puzzle behind the till.

'Hello, Maureen, my dear,' she said, putting it aside. 'Come for your seed bread?'

Maureen had forgotten she was supposed to collect their daily loaf, but she took it, then lingered, not sure how to broach the subject. In the end, she jumped right in.

'Adele,' she began, 'is there any special reason you're so keen to sell up? I've always thought you and Betsy were so happy running this little shop.'

'So Grace told you what I said. Well, of course we're happy. We both love it. But it's Betsy I'm thinking of, you see.' She lowered her voice to a whisper. 'She's nearly ten years older than I am, you know. I've often thought this shop might be getting too much for her. She has a touch of arthritis and she really should be retired, not running a shop! I have this guilty feeling that she's only keeping going because I enjoy it so much.'

'Oh, Adele, I'm absolutely sure that's not the case!' Maureen said, immensely relieved. 'She told my aunt yesterday how much she loves the shop and what a sense of purpose it gives her.'

'Did she really say that? Of course, every time I ask her, she tells me the same, but one never knows. She's such a selfless soul.'

'I think perhaps you're both guilty of that,' Maureen murmured with a smile.

'But I don't want her to work herself into the ground. If we sold up, we'd have the time to do a world trip, and go first-class into the bargain. I know how much Betsy loves to travel,' Adele said.

Maureen had to bite her lip to stop herself from laughing. Aunt Grace would be delighted to learn that Adele's wish to sell was just the result of a serious lack of communication between the Venter sisters! She had a feeling that another visit from her aunt would have Adele on board with the rest of them and she'd be able to go ahead with her idea. Whatever it was.

* ★ *

That evening Patsy was on kitchen duty.

'I'm making fish cakes and they won't stay nice if we have to wait for Jack,' she said. 'I'll put his in the oven to keep them warm.'

Jack had texted from the boat to say he'd be working late and that Dan would give him a lift home when they were done.

'Make enough for Dan, as well, then,' Maureen said. 'I expect he'll stay for a bite.' She couldn't help noticing how pretty her daughter was looking lately. Glowing. She was pretty sure of the reason, but Patsy hadn't discussed anything about her day out at Fransch Hoek earlier in the week, and Maureen knew she'd have to wait to be told!

The three women had nearly finished their meal when they heard the bang of a car door outside and the thump of boots on the front steps.

'Hi, Mum,' Jack called. 'What's for

supper? I'm starving. I'll just go and wash up.'

'I should hope so!' Maureen commented, getting up to greet Dan. But there was no-one in the hall. That's odd, she thought, I was so sure he'd come in.

'So, how was your day?' she asked when Jack was washed, changed and seated at the table, wolfing down fish cakes and mashed potato.

'Great. One of our clients caught a forty-kilo black marlin. He fought it for over an hour and when he reeled it in he was so excited he nearly fell over the side. Now he wants it stuffed and mounted.'

'A waste of good fish,' Aunt Grace said. 'I always say you should only take from the sea what you need for your plate.'

'Don't let Dan hear you say that, Aunt Grace.' Jack grinned. 'Those guys pay top dollar to go out with him!'

Maureen turned to her son.

'So, where's Dan? I thought he might

come up with you tonight,' she said.

'He was going to, but — ' Jack looked discomfited. 'You know that woman with red hair? Ella? She often comes down to the harbour to chat with Dan and tonight she invited him to supper at her house. Said she wouldn't take no for an answer. She's bought a cottage in Kalk Bay right above the beach and she wants him to look at some plans for alterations that she has.'

'Of course. He mentioned she'd bought a house,' Maureen said, disappointed. 'She often asks him for advice.'

'I think he's tired of it,' Jack added. 'He never looks pleased to see her, Mum, when she rushes up to say hello.'

'Really?' Maureen felt immensely cheered. Grace patted her hand.

'Dan's such a kind-hearted fellow, Mo. He's just doing Ella a favour. I'm sure he'd rather be having supper with us,' she said.

'We should have told him I was making fish cakes, Mum, then he would have turned her down flat!' Patsy joked.

'Well, what about this exhibition of yours, then? Are we definitely going to go ahead with it?'

'I thought it was an excellent idea,' Grace said at once. 'Let's do it. We can invite the newspaper to send someone from their arts page. And maybe we could get someone from the Historical Society to stand up and say a few words?'

'The Historical Society?' Maureen asked with a frown. 'Wouldn't someone from the art world be more suitable?'

'I think that Henry Morton from the library would make an excellent speech,' Grace explained. 'He's been a leading light in the Historical Society for years and I know he's delighted that we've made such a success of the shop.'

'Well, if you think so . . . '

'I do,' Grace said. 'It would all tie in very nicely with the plan I have to stop that Richard Hugo in his tracks, once and for all. I'll tell you about it when I've spoken to the others.' She looked over her glasses at Patsy. 'And Patsy, promise me you won't mention a word of this to that man.'

Taking Sides

Mention what, exactly? Patsy had no idea, but it sounded as if Aunt Grace meant business. Oh, dear.

'Of course I won't,' she said shortly. 'It's got nothing to do with me. But — '

'But what?' Grace asked.

'But he's very determined to buy it,' Patsy said. 'He talked about it last weekend and he's not going to change his mind, Aunt Grace.'

'And neither am I,' came Grace's reply. 'But you're starting to sound as though you think we should give in.'

Grace's stare made Patsy feel uneasy.

'No, of course I don't. But . . . well, he's right in a way, isn't he? We could easily find premises somewhere else and still run the shop, and at the same time have lots of extra cash. We could use it to do all the repairs to your house. Take a holiday. And have something to put away for when you retire.'

'Patsy!' Maureen was astounded. 'You're talking exactly like Richard Hugo now!'

She looked in astonishment at her daughter and then at her aunt. Both of them were glaring at each other.

'You were quite correct, Patsy,' Grace said coldly. 'It's got nothing to do with you.'

With a sinking feeling, Maureen realised that one of these days she was going to have to take sides with either her daughter or her aunt. There would be no middle ground for any of them. That wretched man — why couldn't he leave them alone?

9

Mysterious

The uneasy atmosphere between Grace and Patsy didn't last long, and the following day Grace announced she'd be away from the shop all morning as she had 'things to do'.

'Would you open up the shop, please, Mo?' she asked. 'I'll be in as soon as I can, but I need to make some phone calls and see some people.'

'That sounds very mysterious, Aunt Grace. What's going on?' Mo teased.

'It's just an idea I have,' Grace said. 'If it works, you'll soon know all about it!'

Patsy went down the hill with Maureen, leaving Grace to make her phone calls in private.

'I wonder what she's up to?' Patsy mused. 'I hope that she and Rick won't come to blows over this whole thing, Mum. Last night I didn't mean I was on his side — I'm not, really. But when he talks about what he thinks Aunt Grace should do, he seems to make such good sense.'

'The man's got a golden tongue,' Maureen said. 'I know it's difficult for you to take sides, but what you and Rick need to remember is that Aunt Grace and I are partners now. I don't want to sell, either, so he's not just dealing with an elderly person he hopes to wear down by sheer persistence. He's got to deal with me, too.'

'You're right,' Patsy agreed. 'He's got no chance with the two of you. It's odd, Mum, when we were at the farm I got the feeling that he wasn't all that happy doing what he does. He'd rather be growing grapes and making wine. Although, because he's so competitive, he'd probably end up making the best wine in the country!'

Maureen nodded.

'Some men are like that,' she said.

'Whatever they do, they want to do it better than anyone else.'

'That's not a bad trait,' Patsy said defensively. 'Rick likes to win, that's all.'

'I'm sure he has lots of good traits.' Maureen smiled. 'You just concentrate on those and leave Aunt Grace and me to deal with his bad ones. Like stubbornly refusing to take no for an answer!'

Mellie was already waiting outside the shop when they arrived, laden with boxes of goodies for the coffee shop from her grandmother.

'Hi, Mellie, you're early,' Patsy said, taking a deep sniff of the tantalising smells from the boxes. 'Oh, luckily I hardly had any breakfast! I've just got room for one of Rugaya's cinnamon pastries!'

'They're still warm. I'll make coffee for us all,' Mellie said. She busied herself with switching on the coffee machine and unpacking the cakes and pastries Rugaya had made. 'We really need to order more of everything, Mrs

Henderson. Yesterday I was sold out by early afternoon.'

'You're the coffee shop boss!' Maureen said cheerfully. 'If you think you can sell more, ask your gran to make more.'

Mellie smiled. Maureen could tell she was quietly pleased at being given so much responsibility. Although she was young, she had a good head on her shoulders and had earned Maureen's trust.

'We've got to get on with arranging this exhibition,' Maureen said. 'Patsy, could you work out a nice design for the invitations? There's a print shop on the main road that could run off as many as we want. We need a list of people we want to invite . . . and ask Rugaya about making some snacks. I hope things aren't too hectic in the shop today.'

'If we invite all the local people who supply us, that would be thirty already,' Patsy said. 'The baskets, the rugs, that glassmaker fellow. And the bead workers and the woodcarver.'

'And people from the shops around us. A list!' Maureen said. 'We are going to need to make a list.'

'You and your lists,' Patsy said affectionately. 'You do that and I'll see to the shop. Remember to put the interior designers at the top, as they're the big spenders we want to impress.'

Maureen opened her telephone book and got busy.

Just before lunch, Grace appeared, followed by Raj and his wife, Suraya, Alf Thompson and lastly, the Venter sisters. Maureen had to pause for a minute to think who they were. All were wearing what appeared to be fancy dress.

'Aunt Grace! What on earth — '

'Is he here yet? The lad from the newspaper with his camera?'

Grace was dressed in a long dark blue dress, with leg of mutton sleeves and an enormous flowered hat, and she looked flushed and excited.

'They promised to send someone at midday,' she added.

'Isn't this fun?' Betsy Venter was wearing a long yellow dress sprigged with rose buds, and wore white stockings and dainty white satin slippers. Her younger sister was dressed identically but in green.

'You all look as if you've stepped out of history!' Patsy exclaimed. 'What are you supposed to be?'

'Don't you recognise us?' Alf Thompson asked solemnly. 'We are the original owners of these shops from 1860.'

'We've arranged a little write up in the weekly paper, Mo,' Grace explained. 'Alf has written such an interesting bit about the history of all our shops.'

Alf nodded.

'Thought we'd get some publicity so that when the Johannesburg fellow comes sniffing round again, he'd see how impossible it would be to convince us to sell to him,' he said.

Maureen and Patsy were listening intently.

'So I asked the paper to come and take a photo and I told him we'd dress up for the occasion,' Grace continued. 'I think the editor was quite excited about it. He says if the picture looks good, he'll put us on the front page!'

'Mr Patel, you look amazing,' Maureen said truthfully.

All Worked Out

Raj was dressed in magnificent oriental robes, with gold embroidered slippers and a scarlet turban with a peacock feather waving in front. Mrs Patel glittered majestically in a gold and blue sari with a pearl-encrusted head covering.

'We do not look genuinely ancient Indian, I think,' Raj said regretfully. 'But this is the best the Drama Society could do for us.'

'You both look wonderful,' Patsy assured them in admiration. 'What's the article about, Alf?'

'I found this old book documenting how each shop traded from the time it started two hundred years ago,' he said. 'And — '

'And you'll never guess what our shop was!' Betsy giggled. 'A grog shop! For the sailors.'

'And there were women,' Adele added apologetically. 'For the sailors, too. I'm afraid our little corner had a very bad reputation!'

Both sisters looked guiltily delighted at the dubious past of their little shop.

'Well, you've certainly improved things!' Maureen smiled. 'And Mr Patel?'

'Our shop has been a tailoring establishment ever since it was built,' he said proudly. 'For two hundred years people have been sewing there.'

'That's incredible,' Patsy said. 'An unbroken line of tailors! How wonderful. And, Alf, what was yours?'

'A ships' chandler,' he replied. 'It was a storeroom for provisioning the ships that called in the harbour. Then it became a tea-house.'

'And Whittaker's started life as a

candle-maker's shop,' Grace said, smiling. 'We thought readers would be interested in what Alf's written. Of course, he has cleverly tied it in with the fact that none of us intends to sell!'

'We're heading off Mr Hugo before he can get started!' Betsy said gleefully.

'What a good idea, Aunt Grace,' Maureen said in admiration. 'You've got it all worked out.'

Grace gestured towards Alf.

'Alf did all the writing,' she said modestly.

'Excuse me . . . ' A young man with a camera around his neck stood hesitantly in the doorway. 'I'm looking for Miss Whittaker?'

'You've found her,' Grace said 'We'd like you to take a photo outside in the street, if you will, to show the shop front.'

They all trooped out behind him and Maureen watched as he arranged them in a pleasing group. Adele Venter produced a lace-trimmed parasol and held it up coquettishly and Alf stuck his thumbs into his scarlet braces and grinned hugely.

The others watched through the window as the photographer tried them in different poses and passers-by stopped to watch in fascination.

'Whatever is going on outside?' one customer asked, intrigued.

'I guess you'll have to read the paper next week to find out,' Patsy replied.

It sounded as though this publicity move of her great-aunt's would at least give Rick pause for thought. And she hoped she wouldn't have to be the one to tell him about it.

A Special Occasion

It was the evening of the Whittakers' exhibition and Maureen was so exhausted after one of the busiest days she could remember, she would happily have gone home and put her feet up with a nice cup of tea.

Instead, after serving no fewer than

seven bus-loads of tourists determined to buy almost everything they saw, she had to pack away the usual goods on display and bring out the things they'd kept back for the exhibition.

Then she had to run home and make herself look good for the invited guests, leaving Patsy and Mellie to arrange the last-minute details.

'You go off for half an hour, Mum,' Patsy said. 'This is a special occasion and you need to sparkle!'

'We'll be fine, Mrs Henderson,' Mellie agreed. 'You're the one who has to talk to the interior designers!'

So, after hurrying home, Maureen showered, changed into her blue dress, clipped on her sparkly earrings and dabbed on some perfume in record time. Then she headed back to the shop at as brisk a trot as her high heels would allow. She'd given Jack a special invitation for Dan and she hoped he'd put in an appearance.

When Maureen opened the shop door again, she looked around in wonder.

'This looks really beautiful. Thank you, girls!'

Creative

Patsy and Mellie had arranged the special pieces to their best advantage. Hand-made glass, colourful new mohair wall hangings, enormous beaded animals, some little watercolour paintings from a local artist and two shelves of Priscilla's ceramic bowls were now grouped together. A metre-high woodcarving of a rhinoceros had pride of place in the centre of the floor.

Stemmed glasses, opened bottles of wine and plates of Rugaya's spicy nibbles were strategically placed amongst the pieces, and in every corner elegant scented candles cast a soft glow on everything.

'These candles are an inspired touch,' Maureen admired. 'I can't believe the transformation in half an hour!'

'That was Mellie, Mum. She's very creative,' Patsy told her. 'You're looking smashing. Where's Aunt Grace?'

'Coming soon. I think Henry Morton from the library is giving her a lift and they're picking up Rugaya, too.'

The bell of the door tinkled and Graham Ivy, an interior designer, walked in. He was one of Maureen's favourite customers. Besides buying a lot of their bowls and rugs, he was tall and good-looking, with long fair hair that flopped lazily over his forehead.

'Evening, ladies! Maureen, you are looking beautiful tonight! Oh, what have we here?' He picked up a glass of wine and wandered over to study Priscilla's big platters. 'These are something new. The glaze is so unusual.'

All at once the shop started to fill up with people and within minutes there was a loud buzz as the guests examined the goods on display and chatted. Mellie and Patsy mingled with plates of snacks and made sure the glasses were topped up. Maureen did her best to have a word with everyone who was there and slowly relaxed when she realised things were going well.

Rugaya and Grace made a grand entrance with Henry Morton, who was dressed in a three-piece suit with a carnation in his buttonhole that Maureen recognised from their front garden. The three of them seemed to know everyone in the room. That comes with living here for seventy years, Maureen thought, watching them smile and chat to the guests as old friends.

Thinking of friends, where was Dan? Her son had come in some time before and was helping Mellie hand round the snacks. Jack and Mellie — they make a sweet couple, she thought, and she's such a good influence on him.

'Hello there, Maureen! Long time no see!'

She turned round and there was Ella on Dan's arm. She was looking gorgeous in a sleek black dress, her hair piled in a froth of curls held with a glittering diamante band, and her wide smile embraced Maureen and Dan.

'Isn't Danny boy a sweetie? He told me he was coming to your exhibition so I absolutely insisted he bring me! I'm not gate-crashing, am I? But I've wanted to see your little shop for ages.'

'No, not at all. I'm very glad you could come.' Maureen tried to keep the stiffness from her voice and glanced at Dan.

He winked broadly and disengaged his arm from Ella's.

'I'll get you a glass of wine, shall I?' he said. 'And for you, Mo, my love?'

Maureen nodded, feeling warmed all over by his endearment. She turned to Ella with more confidence.

'Dan tells me you've bought a house at Kalk Bay?'

'Yes,' Ella replied, her eyes following Dan's progress as he fetched the wine. 'It's on the slopes of the mountain. Glorious views. Dan's been such a great help.'

'Yes, I know. He told me.' Well, strictly speaking, Jack had.

'I can't believe how much there is to

do when one moves into a new house! Choosing the furniture and the curtains. Even the right colour of paint can be a problem. It's quite exhausting.'

Suddenly, Maureen had a flash of inspiration.

'Ella, maybe you could use some professional help? There's a lovely man here you simply must meet. An interior designer. Come on.' She steered Ella across the crowded room to Graham Ivy who was deep in conversation with Priscilla about her new glazes.

'Graham, I'd like you to meet a friend of mine. This is Ella.' Maureen noticed that Ella was giving Graham her thousand-watt smile.

Graham was entranced. He took her hand in his and raised it gallantly to his lips.

'Delighted, Ella,' he murmured. 'Are you also in the trade?'

'Not at all. Actually, I need some expert advice. I've bought a little house and I'd be grateful for a bit of help . . . '

'Then I'm your man,' Graham said.

'Shall we go outside where it's a bit quieter and we can talk properly?'

The two of them made for the tables in the courtyard and Priscilla and Maureen grinned at each other.

'The old charmer,' Priscilla said comfortably. 'I hope your friend realises that asking Graham's advice means she'll be writing out some pretty hefty cheques before she's done!'

'I think she can afford it,' Maureen said. 'Oh, here's my wine. Thanks, Dan.'

'Good evening, Priscilla.' Dan smiled, putting his arm around Maureen. 'Are these your bowls? Very pretty.'

'Pretty?' Priscilla raised her eyebrows. 'I hope not. You can buy pretty bowls in the supermarket. These are — '

'Collectible works of art!' Maureen finished. 'They're gorgeous, Priscilla, your best yet. I'm sure Graham will want to buy a couple.'

'He's already chosen three. Have you any red stickers? For what you sell tonight?'

Maureen's heart sank. She'd completely forgotten that people would want to buy!

'Of course, I'll get them,' she muttered and went to find Mellie who was deep in conversation with Jack.

'Mellie, we need red stickers!' she whispered. 'Have you any good ideas?'

Surprisingly, it was Jack who solved the problem.

'How about using those white pricing stickers of yours, Mum and we'll scribble over them with a red felt tip pen?'

'Jack, my boy, you're a genius!'

Speech

Maureen waited while the two of them coloured several stickers, then went back to Priscilla who stuck them on the platters that Graham had selected. This seemed to trigger an avalanche of sales to the other guests and for the next half-hour Maureen and Mellie were taking money and attaching stickers.

Then Henry Morton tapped a glass to get everyone's attention.

'Speech time,' Jack muttered. 'Boring!'

Henry cleared his throat before beginning.

'I'm very glad to be here tonight to welcome you all,' he said. 'Whittaker's building has been part of the history of our town ever since I can remember. It started out two hundred years ago as the premises of a candle-maker and has changed hands many times since then.

'During the war years, Grace Whittaker's mother opened the shop as a general dealer, and many of our older residents will remember that she sold everything from a needle to an anchor, as she claimed. Today we see it revitalised as a modern retailer supplying arts and crafts, as well as serving the most delicious coffee and home-baked products. I believe these are the work of Rugaya Daniels. Am I right, Rugaya?'

Maureen and Rugaya exchanged smiles.

'Grace Whittaker and her niece Maureen are to be congratulated for breathing new life into this old building and ensuring that the tradition of serving the public continues in the heart of Simonstown. The old world charm of so many of our country's small villages has been ruined by so-called progress and greedy developers, and we owe these ladies, and the owners of the buildings along this stretch of road, a hearty vote of thanks for preserving the heritage of our town.'

Grace smiled at him proudly. She's obviously told him about the offer Rick made, Patsy thought. I wish he could be here tonight to listen to this. He'd see why pulling these buildings down would be impossible.

'The exhibition this evening is a showcase of the very best in South African crafts and on behalf of all of you, I'd like to wish Grace and Maureen every success for the future of this worthy endeavour.'

There was loud applause and a few

'hear, hears' from everyone. Then the guests continued to stand around with glasses of wine and the level of conversation rose considerably.

An Old Hand

Dan manoeuvred Maureen into a quieter corner. 'I'd say this evening is a big success, love,' he said, looking around. 'Thanks to all of your hard work. Sorry about Ella. She wouldn't take no for an answer.'

'It's fine, really. I've got her talking to an interior designer so she's quite happy.'

'If he stops her from asking my advice about every blessed thing, I'll be grateful,' Dan said. 'I haven't the first idea about home decorating, but she seems to think I'm some sort of expert on pretty little knick-knacks!'

He looked so offended that Maureen had to laugh.

'Not you!' she comforted. 'Fishing,

maybe, but not knick-knacks.'

'I can tell you who is becoming quite the fishing expert — Jack,' he said. 'I'm really pleased, Mo, he's taken to the job like an old hand. He's interested in everything and has a flair for working with motors. The clients like him, too. He's able to get on with them all, even the ones who haven't a word of English!'

'I'm so pleased!' Maureen felt a glow of pride. 'Thanks for giving him a chance, Dan. I knew he wouldn't let you down.'

Dan smiled at her.

'He's your son, isn't he? You've raised two great kids, Mo. You must be very proud of them both.'

'I am,' she replied, returning his smile. 'Jack was always a bit of a worry, as you know, but I think giving him this responsibility was the best thing you could have done. It was the vote of confidence he needed.' She took his hand in hers. 'You're a pretty good rôle model for him, you know. Something he's never really had before.'

'You think so?' Dan looked mischievously at her. 'Maybe it's time we made this rôle model thing more permanent?'

'What do you — ' Maureen was interrupted by Ella.

'Ah! There you are!' she said, breezing up behind them, followed by Graham. 'Did I see a camera flashing? Is that the social reporter?'

Dan pulled a face.

'I hope not,' he said.

'Don't be such an old stick! It would be fun to have our picture in the paper,' Ella insisted.

She made as if to link her arm through Dan's, but he stepped back with a smile, his arm still around Maureen.

'I don't want to crack the camera,' he said firmly.

Ella put her hand possessively on Graham's arm.

'Tell him to take one of us, Graham. Seeing as you're going to be my interior decorator, we should get some publicity for you.'

'Graham hardly needs the publicity, Ella,' Maureen said quietly. 'He's very well known already.'

'Of course,' Graham agreed gravely. 'But let's ask him, anyway.'

Ella posed prettily for the cameraman, who snapped a few shots before turning to Maureen and Dan.

'Just hold that smile!' he said, clicking away cheerfully. 'I already have a good shot of your aunt, Mrs Henderson. So, what's the caption? Maureen Henderson and — '

'And her fiancé, Dan Clayton,' Dan said firmly.

What? Had Dan gone mad?

'What?' Ella exclaimed, her voice rising to an indignant squeak. 'You old rascal! And you never said a word! Oh, my, what a surprise!' Her expression told everyone listening that it wasn't a very pleasant one, but that she was going to try to make the best of it.

'I suppose congratulations are in order then!' She gave Dan a brief peck and proffered her cheek to Maureen, who stood frozen with surprise.

'I think it's wonderful that you're going to try marriage again after your last attempt, Dan. What's your magic charm, Maureen? How ever did you manage to drag this old sea-dog to the altar?' Without waiting for a reply, Ella burbled on.

'Of course, I'll never forget how surprised I was when my late husband Neville proposed to me! On the top of Table Mountain under a full moon! It was just so romantic. He produced this absolutely enormous diamond — you remember my ring, don't you, Danny? He always told me the sparkle in my eyes was brighter than any diamond . . . '

She looked rather pointedly at Maureen's left hand, bare of any jewellery.

'Ah, well. I wish you both the best of luck. Come on, Graham, let's see if we can find a nice woven mat for my front hallway. I thought something in shades of turquoise and blue . . . '

Dan tightened his grip around Maureen's shoulders and waited until they were alone. Then he turned to look at her, a look of such love in his eyes that she melted.

'Sorry, that just popped out. I couldn't help it.' He smiled a little guiltily. 'I know this isn't the most romantic place, or the best time, but we are, aren't we? Going to get married?'

'Of course,' she said softly, her arm tight around his waist. 'But only on one condition . . . '

'What's that?'

'That you ask me again, somewhere more romantic. Somewhere when we're on our own.'

'That's a promise,' he said. 'Although I can't guarantee the top of a mountain or a full moon!'

They smiled at each other in complete understanding. Maureen felt such a surge of happiness that she was surprised that everyone didn't see a light shining from inside her.

'How about a walk on the beach tomorrow after work?'

'It's a date,' she said softly.

History

'It's lovely up here, isn't it, Jack? Aren't you glad you came?'

Mellie and Jack were standing on top of the mountain above Simonstown looking over the wide bay, the mountains in the distance a hazy blue and the rooftops of the town far below. A small band of white clouds on the horizon heralded a change in the weather but, for the moment, it was hot with the sweet smell of veldt flowers all around.

In front of them was the grave of Just Nuisance, the headstone proclaiming: *Great Dane Just Nuisance, Able Seaman RN*, HMS Afrikander *1940–1944*.

'All those steps!' Jack grumbled. 'Why couldn't they have buried Just Nuisance like any other dog?'

'Silly. He was too famous for that!' Mellie replied. 'Do you know, when they buried him over a hundred sailors came up here? They gave him full Naval honours and wrapped his body in the White Ensign. All the men were in tears. Don't you think he must have been a very special dog?'

'I suppose so,' Jack said. 'My great-aunt's got that photo of herself with him, but I don't know much about his story. It was all during the war, wasn't it? Before my time!'

'Just Nuisance is a part of our history,' Mellie said firmly. 'I'll lend you a book about him. Have you read that other book I gave you yet? The one about the boats from here going down to the Antarctic.'

'Not yet,' Jack admitted guiltily. 'When I get home from work I'm so bombed out I don't feel like reading. But I will, I promise.'

A Marriage Arrangement

Mellie seemed to have taken it upon herself to improve Jack's mind and make sure he knew a bit about the history of this country. He didn't mind at all. In fact, he loved it when she told

384

him things he didn't know. She had
made him realise that there were a lot
of subjects that could be interesting,
things he'd ignored at school. She was
unlike any other girl he'd ever known
and, in his opinion, by far the most
beautiful, with her expressive, delicate
features and long dark hair.

'It's great that you've got that job,
Jack. Dan told your mum he's really
pleased with you.'

'Did he?' Jack felt cheered by this
approval. 'And you, Mellie? Are you
pleased with me?'

'Me? Don't be silly; what I think of
you doesn't count!'

'Of course it does,' Jack said quietly.
'There's no-one whose opinion I value
more, Mel.' He swallowed hard. 'You're
the one who inspired me to get a proper
job in the first place.'

'I'm glad it worked out, Jack.' Mellie
smiled.

Jack took a deep breath.

'So, I was just thinking, maybe if I
had a good job, you might consider . . . '

'Consider what?' She turned to him in genuine surprise.

'Being my girlfriend,' he mumbled, his face turning red.

Since he'd arrived in South Africa, he'd never even looked at another girl, and he knew Mellie enjoyed his company, too. They'd been to films together, and taken long walks across the mountains, and discussed everything under the sun, but somehow she still kept him at a friendly distance. He'd never even held her hand. He hoped she wouldn't laugh at him and that this declaration would move things forward a little.

There was a long silence.

'That's not possible, Jack,' she replied quietly. 'I like you a lot, but I can't be your girlfriend. My brother wouldn't allow it and neither would my granny.'

'*Allow* it? Your *brother*? We're not living in the Dark Ages!' Jack was stunned.

But Mellie continued.

'It wouldn't be right, you see. I'm sort of . . . engaged.'

Jack stared at her, open-mouthed.

'Engaged to be married?'

Mellie nodded.

'To a man in Mumbai. He knows my family; in fact, he works with my uncle there. Because my father has died, my uncle and my granny arranged it when I was fourteen,' she explained.

'An arranged marriage? Do you love him?' Jack was shocked.

'I've never met him. When I've finished studying for my degree he will come over here and we will marry. He has written me letters. He sounds very nice,' she added.

'But you said you liked me!'

'Of course I do,' Mellie told him. 'But just as a friend.'

'I don't want just to be your friend!' Jack picked up a stone and threw it savagely down the mountain in frustration. In his worst nightmare he'd imagined Mellie turning him down because he wasn't smart enough to go to university, or because he wasn't good-looking or something. Not because she was engaged to a total stranger on another continent.

One look at her resolute expression told him there was no point in arguing.

'Come on,' she said cheerfully, getting up and reaching for his hand. 'It's not the end of the world. I'll still be your friend, even if you don't want to be mine. Let's go down another route along the path by the waterfall.'

They walked down in silence, but as they reached the bottom Jack blurted out, 'Of course I want to be friends. Sorry, Mellie, I just didn't know about this other arrangement.'

'How could you? I haven't talked about it. I knew everyone in the shop would find it difficult to understand.'

Difficult? It was impossible! Jack felt a thick black cloud of misery envelop him, and he could hardly find the words to say goodbye to Mellie. He watched her walk off to catch the bus, her hair swinging jauntily from side to side, and then plodded slowly up the hill to the house, feeling as though he was saying goodbye to every chance of happiness he'd ever had.

He opened the front door, glad that there was no-one else home. As he made for his own room to lick his wounds, the phone rang.

It was Dan.

'Jack? I'm glad I caught you, lad. I know we agreed we'd have two days off, but I've just been contacted by two German fellows who want three days out at sea and they're willing to pay top dollar to catch a marlin. Can you meet me at the boat in half an hour?'

'Sure, Dan,' Jack replied.

The last thing he wanted to do was to go out to sea to laugh and joke with clients fishing for marlin, drinking gallons of beer and having a good time. He just wanted to be by himself and be miserable.

But he knew he couldn't let Dan down.

As he left the house with his bag over his shoulder, he noticed the dark clouds banking up and felt a sudden chill in the air. He turned back for an extra sweater.

★ ★ ★

Dear Warren,
How are you and Rita? I hope you are both well. We have been so busy with everything here, my feet have hardly touched the ground. Sorry I haven't been in contact before, but I'm sure Patsy has been keeping you up to date with the family doings.

Maureen wondered if Patsy had told her dad about Rick and how her yacht-owner employer had turned out to be the same man trying to buy Aunt Grace's shop. She sighed. Patsy probably still had difficult choices to make. Rick hadn't been back, claiming business pressures in Johannesburg, but he wouldn't give up without a fight. Secretly, she didn't think a glowing newspaper article would do the trick, although Aunt Grace was convinced it would.

I have some big news. Dan Clayton and I are to be married. I knew Dan when I was at school here years ago and these days he is the skipper and owner of the deep-sea fishing boat who employs Jack.

She would have liked to tell him more about Dan. About his gentle, considerate manner and the way he made everyone feel special when he talked to them. About his kindness to Jack and his love of the sea. About how he'd proposed a second time at sunset on the beach the day after the exhibition and about the flood of happiness she felt every time she looked at him.

Just reliving that moment made her glow.

Perfect

As he'd promised, she and Dan had been all alone, except for three interested penguins that waddled across and stood watching, their heads cocked to one side. As Dan went down on his knee on the sand, they made throaty little grunts of approval and Maureen was helpless with giggles by the time he produced a small velvet box.

'Mo, my darling, will you marry me? Please?' He had been smiling broadly, but she'd noticed a small flicker of nervousness in his expression.

'Yes, Dan, I will,' she'd replied solemnly, not wanting to spoil the moment by laughing.

He had watched her face as she opened the tiny box with trembling hands.

'I hope you like antique jewellery. I thought, seeing as you're surrounded by beautiful modern pieces all day, that this might be something different,' he'd said uncertainly.

It was an exquisite sapphire surrounded by tiny seed pearls and diamond chips in an ornate gold setting. He slipped it on her finger and they looked at it together as the blue gem sparkled in the rays of the setting sun.

'It's perfect,' she breathed, her eyes filled with tears. 'I've never seen a more beautiful ring, Dan!'

'I'm glad you like it,' he said before continuing hesitantly. 'You know I'm not a wealthy man, Mo. And going off to sea all the time — it's quite a rough life. Uncertain, too. Are you OK with that?'

'Of course I am,' she assured him. 'Just remember you'll have a wife waiting for you now, so no silly risks at sea!'

'I never take risks,' he said soberly. 'And my house . . . well, you've seen it and it's not exactly a dream house filled with modern conveniences, I know.'

'Dan!' She laughed. 'Are you trying to put me off the whole idea of marrying you? Because you won't succeed!'

'Good,' he said. 'I just want you to be sure you know what you're getting.'

'I know,' she teased. 'I love you, Dan.'

'I love you, too.'

They kissed, gently at first, then with more passion, a long, lingering embrace that left her breathless.

'You know what I'd like to do? Go out on your boat one day,' she'd said as they walked barefoot back along the darkening sands. 'And see what you and Jack get up to.'

'The first nice day in summer, the three of us can take a trip around the Point. We'll teach you how to catch marlin. Or a tuna. Hey . . . ' he'd said with mock concern. 'I hope you have a lot of good recipes for fish. You're going to be eating quite a lot of it in future, once you're Mrs Clayton.'

But Maureen guessed that Warren wouldn't be interested in all these details!

Both Patsy and Jack like him a lot and he has been a very good influence on Jack, who has become quite a responsible citizen since working with him.

A distant Memory

I hope Warren doesn't take that as criticism, she thought, pausing. He was never a good influence on Jack, but I know he did his best. He might have been a hopeless husband, but he's always loved both our children and would do anything for them.

So this means I have made the decision to stay here permanently, Warren, and I would like to sell my house. I'm hoping you could handle this for me? Perhaps my present tenant would like to buy it? The same goes for my furniture and everything I have left behind. There is nothing that is so precious to me that I want to ship it out here at great expense. Dan has a house full of furniture in Simonstown anyway, and we don't need duplicates of anything.

Although, to tell the truth, 'functional' was the kindest way to describe the furnishings in Dan's old house. It was quite obvious that no woman lived there and the man that did didn't notice his surroundings. The curtains were faded, the fittings in the kitchen were unchanged since the house had been built more than fifty years before, and the lumpy easy chairs needed recovering. The only thing to commend was the magnificent view across the bay from the verandah.

'I know it looks a bit sad,' Dan said comfortably, when he'd shown her around. 'But you can have fun changing things as much as you like. Just as long as you don't ask my opinion on everything!'

Maureen couldn't wait.

Patsy seems very happy with her job on board the yacht. She'll soon have to make up her mind whether she intends to go to college back in the UK or not. I hope she will. I don't like the idea of her not having a good qualification, even though she considers this her dream job. It might not last. On the other hand, she might decide to do a catering course in Cape Town.

I'm pretty sure Jack will be staying and working here for the foreseeable future. He is talking of studying mechanics at the technical college here, but you know what Jack's like, his plans could change tomorrow!

Now why did I say that, she thought. Jack really has become much more responsible and serious about his work lately. It's all Dan's influence, of course, although maybe Mellie has something to do with it, too. She deleted the last part of that sentence, substituting:

and has fallen for Mellie, the young girl who runs our coffee shop. She has been a steadying influence. Long may this last!

Dan and I haven't set a date yet, but I will let you know when we do. I *hope you'll both be happy for me and wish us well.*

Regards, Maureen.

How did one address one's ex-husband? With love? Yours sincerely? She and Warren had shared so much together for so long, but looking back across the six thousand miles between them, all of that part of her life seemed to have happened to someone else. When she thought of him, he paled into a distant memory compared with the solid presence of Dan.

She leaned back in her chair and pressed *Send*. Really, she was so lucky. Patsy and Jack were doing well, the shop was successful and she'd never felt more blessed. Everything in her life was perfect.

As she left the internet café, she heard the distant rumble of thunder and started hurrying for home. The sky was dark with storm clouds and an icy wind blew off the sea, signalling a change in the weather. She'd been warned about the sudden storms that swept across the bay at this time of year and she was glad that Dan and Jack were not scheduled to go to sea for the next couple of days.

10

In A Whirl

It was Friday, Patsy's morning off from
the shop, and she'd been expecting to
receive her usual e-mailed instructions
to provision the boat for the weekend.
But when she opened her mail at the
internet café, there was only a brief
note from her father. She was surprised,
because Warren wasn't comfortable
with writing and preferred to phone
every now and then to hear her news.

> *My dear Patsy,*
> *Your mum wrote and told us her*
> *good news and of course we are very*
> *pleased for her. She mentioned that*
> *you might decide to stay on there*
> *and do a catering course at a local*
> *college, but I hope that you will con-*
> *sider all of your options very carefully.*

A qualification from the college here would be recognised anywhere in the world, should you wish to travel again, but the standards might not be as high at a college in Cape Town. Rather selfishly, I am hoping you'll choose to come home soon and study here. There is always a room waiting for you at our house, now that your mother is selling hers, and Rita and I would love to have you back.

As for our Jack, I don't suppose he'll enjoy being a fisherman for very long, so tell him that any time he wants to, I can arrange a job with our company as a trainee salesman for plastics.

Dad.

Oh, dear. Her father obviously wanted her to come home, but Patsy felt no pull to return to Witham. She had made some enquiries and discovered that Cape Town college offered an excellent two-year course in catering and she'd more or less made up her mind to register for it. But there was no rush; she could happily continue as she was for another year, helping out at the shop and working on *Sea Freedom* at the weekends.

When she remembered her life before coming to South Africa, it all seemed very tame and she couldn't picture herself catching the bus to college every day. Besides, there was more to keep her here than just enjoying the life she was leading. Rick was here. But this wasn't something she was prepared to admit to anyone else.

Perhaps I can persuade Dad and Rita to come out here for a holiday instead, she thought. I'll speak to Mum.

As she walked back to the house, she pulled up the hood of her waterproof jacket and bent against the wind. It had started to rain heavily that morning and the weather still looked bad, with fierce gusts tossing the palm trees and black clouds massing on the horizon. Patsy doubted if Rick would want to sail in these conditions and wondered if she should phone his office to see if he was cancelling his weekend flight down to the Cape.

The house was empty; her mother and Aunt Grace were down at the shop and Jack had unexpectedly gone off with Dan on the *Mermaid* the day before. Surely no-one would stay out at sea in this awful weather? He'd probably come bursting through the door at any minute, ravenous as usual.

She sat idly, sipping coffee and making a list of what to buy to feed the crew if Rick decided he wanted to sail after all. Patsy was pretty certain that, while he was here this time, he intended to meet with all four shop owners and pressure them into finally selling to him. Would he do this before the sailing trip, or after?

If he spoke to them before the sailing trip, Aunt Grace would certainly show him the article in the paper that was due out that morning, featuring everyone dressed up and Alf's story about the historic value of the row of shops. The two of them would probably exchange strong words again and Rick would be in a horrible mood.

But if he intended to see them after

sailing, she didn't think she'd be able to stay silent about the fact that all the owners intended to make a mass rejection of his offer.

The shrill of the phone interrupted her thoughts and she jumped up to answer it.

'Patsy? Rick here.'

'Oh, hi.' She wished she could stop these ridiculous little flutters of pleasure every time she heard his voice. The memory of his kiss still sent shivers down her, but since that visit to the farm they hadn't spoken.

'I wonder if you could do me a favour and go down to the boat. I think I might have left a file there the last time we sailed. It's bright orange and marked *Pegasus Properties*. If you find it, can you let me know?'

'Of course. I'll go down right away. Shall I phone you back in Johannesburg?' she asked.

'No, I'm not in my office,' he replied. 'I'll call you in an hour to see if you've found it.'

'OK, I'm on my way.'

Glad of something to do, she picked up the keys of the yacht, shrugged on her jacket and walked briskly down to the harbour, her head down against the strong north wind that tore at her clothes, but smiling with the sheer exhilaration of the wild weather.

The yachts at their moorings were heaving up and down in the choppy water and there was an orchestra of ropes pulling and straining, metal stays clanging against masts and the creak of protesting hulls.

As she neared *Sea Freedom*, Patsy was alarmed to see that the hatch cover was pushed back. That could only mean one thing. Someone must have broken the lock and still be down below, or had left in a hurry without bothering to close it. There had been a spate of petty thefts from the yachts lately, ropes cut and stolen, aluminium fittings wrenched off to be sold as scrap. The week before, security men in the harbour had caught two youngsters red-handed and handed them over to the police, but it appeared there were others with the same idea.

She stopped dead, wondering whether to approach the boat or to find the security men and ask them to board *Sea Freedom* for her. Then, suddenly angry, she picked up an iron bar lying on the quay and stormed towards it, jumped lightly on board and stood above the open hatchway with her arm raised.

'Come out of there,' she yelled above the wind. 'What do you think you're up to?'

'Hang on!' Rick's head appeared above the deck. 'Goodness me, woman, put that down!'

'Oh, it's you!' She let the iron bar drop, feeling extremely foolish. 'But you can't be here! Ten minutes ago you were in Johannesburg.'

'Nope. You only thought I was.' He smiled. 'The wonders of mobile phones. Come on inside. It's too cold and wet out here and I want to talk to you in private.'

Rick's expression wasn't giving anything away. He simply turned and went down to the cabin. Her thoughts were in a whirl. Asking her to fetch something from the boat had obviously been a trick to get her down here, but what did he want to talk to her about?

It could only be that he'd talked to Aunt Grace and seen the article in the paper. He's furious with her and my whole family, myself included, she thought. He probably wants nothing more to do with me.

With a sinking heart and a cold, sick feeling in her stomach, she followed him numbly down the stairway, grabbing firmly on to the railings to prevent herself falling forward as the boat tossed at anchor.

Front Page News!

On her way to work that morning, Mellie bought a copy of the paper. When she saw the headlines she bought two more and hurried on, stuffing the papers under her jacket to protect them from the rain.

She burst into the shop, grinning triumphantly.

'Miss Whittaker! You're all on the front page!'

Everyone crowded round to read it.

We're Here To Stay! trumpeted the headline above a four-column-wide photograph of all the shop owners. Adele and Betsy Venter were posed saucily, drawing up their frilly dresses to reveal their white-stockinged knees. Alf stood next to them, beaming behind his walrus moustache, and Grace smiled graciously from under her wide, feathered hat. Only Raj and his wife were serious and unsmiling, but looking impressive in their ornate robes.

'Let's see what it says.' Maureen read out loud.

'*Disquieting rumours of major changes along the Historic Mile of Simonstown have been firmly quashed by these long-term bastions of our retail establishments . . .*'

'That sounds good,' Grace interjected. 'Then it names you all and goes on . . .

All four shops can trace a record of unbroken trading for the past two hundred years, and although they have been approached by a developer to sell, they have firmly resisted his offers.'

'That'll tell Mr Hugo!' Grace said with satisfaction.

' . . . 'The rich heritage these handsome old buildings represent far outweighs any financial inducement this man might offer,' says Alf Thomson, owner of Twice Upon A Time, the well-known second-hand bookshop. 'Can you imagine a nasty glass and chrome hotel edifice standing in place of these charming structures?''

'Grace Whittaker,' Grace took over reading in a firm voice,

'who with her niece, Maureen Henderson, operates the recently revamped shop her mother opened in the early

1940s, says, 'It is very satisfying to think that three generations of our family have been working here. We have no intention of moving — Whittaker's is here to stay!''

'Miss Whittaker, that's wonderful.' Mellie smiled. 'Such good publicity for our shop.'

'For all of us.' Grace smiled. 'What an excellent picture, too. We should buy a copy from the paper and frame it for the shop.'

'Turn to the social pages,' Maureen said. 'Let's see what photos they've used of the exhibition. The photographer took so many, I hope he used at least one.'

She needn't have worried. The whole of page five was devoted to people who had attended the exhibition. Besides pictures of some people she didn't recognise, there were shots of herself and Dan, Grace and Henry Morton with Priscilla, and Ella with Graham, the interior designer. The ceramics and

410

rugs formed colourful backgrounds and across the top of the page ran the headline

A Night To Remember At Whittaker's Exciting Exhibition Of Local Arts And Crafts.

'Goodness,' Maureen breathed. 'We couldn't have hoped for better coverage.'

Right in the centre was a delightful shot of Jack, Mellie and Patsy carrying plates of snacks and roaring at a joke Jack had just made.

'This is a lovely picture of the three of you,' Maureen said fondly. 'We should buy a print of this, too. I'm sure your gran would like a copy, Mellie. And I'm sure Jack would as well.'

Then she remembered that Jack was still out at sea with Dan and the cloud of worry that had hovered over her ever since she'd gone home the previous evening returned.

How on earth could they still be out

at sea in this weather? This morning she'd awoken to find a thick mist hiding the horizon and the water grey and choppy with sheets of rain driving over the town.

Dan had phoned her the afternoon before, telling her that two German clients had insisted on a trip, but only on the understanding that if the wind turned to rain they'd return to shore.

She knew he'd never take any careless chances and could only imagine that something had gone wrong. Something mechanical? Or perhaps somewhere on the ocean they'd hit a freak wave and turned over? No, she wouldn't allow herself to think that sort of thing.

Stay positive, she told herself. There's nothing you can do about it from here. You'll just have to wait for news.

Change Of Heart

'Morning, all!' Alf Thompson opened the door and shook his umbrella vigorously before coming in. 'Nice weather for ducks, isn't it? Have you read the paper? Oh, I see you have. Have you had a call from Mr Hugo yet?'

'No,' Maureen replied. 'Actually, our phone isn't working. I couldn't get a dial tone this morning, so maybe he was trying to get through.'

'Ah, that'll be the storm,' Alf said. 'Often happens when it's wet. Well, our young Mr Hugo phoned to tell me he's no longer interested in making an offer on my property. So I expect he'll be calling you with the same message.'

'Well!' Grace said in deep satisfaction. 'I knew he'd give up in the end. All of us united against him would be enough to put anyone off. I expect he saw the newspaper.'

'How could he, Aunt Grace? He's up in Johannesburg,' Maureen said. 'I must admit I'm amazed. He didn't strike me as a man who'd back off from a fight, and the last thing he said to you was that he would never give up.'

'Oh, yes. That stupid family motto,' Grace said crossly. 'I suppose good sense must finally have prevailed.'

'Finances might have had something to do with it,' Alf put in. 'He probably did his sums and came to the conclusion that knocking all this block down and building a hotel wouldn't be such a profitable idea after all.'

'I'm sure Patsy will know the reason,' Mellie said suddenly. 'She's good friends with him.'

'I know she is, but she doesn't tell me anything,' Maureen said.

It was true. Lately Patsy had been returning from sailing with a happy smile which Maureen recognised as a sign of being in love, but she hadn't said anything. She'd mentioned casually that Rick had taken her on drives out to the country to visit his family farm in Fransch Hoek, but she told her mother no details. Just that it was beautiful, and the farmhouse was very old and they'd had a lovely day out.

Maureen would have liked to know

more, but she didn't want to pry. She had no doubt that Patsy would tell her in her own good time.

'You never told me anything, either,' Aunt Grace observed with a smile. 'If it hadn't been for the bush telegraph around here I would never have known you were going out with that red-haired boy — what was his name? — George?'

'George Wellings!' Maureen said. 'But I didn't go out with him officially, we just used to meet at the disco! I thought he was wonderful!'

The doorbell tinkled and a lone customer walked in out of the rain, putting an end to her reminiscences.

* * *

'I don't suppose we'll get any takers for coffee today, Mellie,' Maureen observed later in the morning. The courtyard was awash and the chairs and tables full of puddles. 'We really must think about using upstairs during winter. We could just carry everything up and build a counter along one side for the coffee machine and the snacks. I'll ask Jack to help us move everything. What do you think?'

'That's a good idea,' Mellie said. 'And you've been talking of hanging pictures up there, too. How about some woven rugs and asking the art club to show their pictures? They could put prices on and we could sell them, if anyone asked.'

'They'd welcome the exposure,' Maureen said. 'Paintings would brighten up the walls, even if they weren't very good! I'll get Jack busy over the weekend.'

Mellie looked nervously at Maureen.

'Mrs Henderson, I just wanted to ask — is Jack all right?' Mellie had been fairly quiet all morning.

'Why shouldn't he be, Mellie? I'm sure he's fine. I haven't seen him today, though, as he went off unexpectedly with Dan yesterday afternoon on a fishing trip.'

'And they're not back yet? In this weather?' Mellie looked worried.

'I'm hoping they are, actually,' Maureen admitted.

'I hope so, too.' Mellie peered out at the sheets of rain. 'I'm very fond of Jack, you know, Mrs Henderson. As a friend.'

'I know you are, Mellie. And he thinks the world of you. You've been such a good influence on him.' Maureen hugged the younger girl. 'I couldn't have wished for a better friend for Jack.'

'That's just the problem. I really am just a friend, but Jack wanted to get more serious about everything and when I told him I didn't, he was very upset.'

Sympathetic

Oh, my poor boy! Maureen felt an overwhelming wave of sympathy for her son. She remembered the total misery of her broken romance with George Wellings, when she'd thought she'd never even look at another boy. And she'd been so sure that Jack and Mellie were serious about each other, and been so pleased about it!

'I'm sorry to hear that, Mellie,' she said carefully. 'But he's still lucky to have you as a friend. I'm sure he'll understand and get over it soon.'

But she knew she'd have to treat Jack with a lot of consideration for the next few days and understand any moodiness.

Maureen started to worry all over again. She wished Dan would phone and let her know they were all right. Maybe he had tried, but the shop phone was out of order. Of course, that must be it!

'Aunt Grace,' she said suddenly. 'Do you think I should call the harbour master at Kalk Bay and just check that Dan's back? I could pop next door and use Alf's phone.'

'Do that, if it will set your mind at rest, love,' Grace said. 'Mellie and I will hold the fort. It's not exactly busy today.'

'Use my phone? Of course,' Alf said. 'It's back here.'

'I'll try Dan's mobile first,' she said.

But all she got was a disembodied voice telling her the number was not available at present.

Darn it! That meant Dan had either switched it off, or they were too far out to sea for the server to connect.

She ran her finger down the listings in the phone book and dialled the number of the harbour master. It rang and rang and she was about to give up when a voice said gruffly, 'Yes? Kalk Bay Harbour.'

'Oh, good. Could you tell me if Dan Clayton and his party have arrived back yet? On *Mermaid*?'

'*Mermaid*? No, she's not berthed. No sign of her this morning.'

Maureen swallowed.

'So they're still out in this storm?'

'Must be. I haven't heard from Dan, but that could be the weather. Where were they heading?'

'I don't know,' Maureen admitted. 'They took some clients late yesterday afternoon looking for marlin.'

'They've probably gone round Cape Point, then. He could have headed right out to sea to try to outrun the weather, or he could have gone round the Point and taken shelter in Hout Bay. I'm surprised he hasn't made contact. Why don't you phone the harbour there before we get alarmed?'

Maureen put down the phone with a sinking heart.

'No luck?' Alf's sympathetic face almost brought tears to her eyes. 'Still not back?'

'No. He suggested I try Hout Bay, in case they've gone round the Point and anchored there.'

Hout Bay was right around the mountains on the other side of the Peninsula. It was a lively little fishing harbour, usually abuzz with pleasure boats loaded with tourists.

'Nothing moving in or out today,' the harbour master said when she phoned. 'We've got a forty-knot gale blowing here. No *Mermaid* sighted. Perhaps you should consider alerting the National Sea Rescue people?'

Bad News

'Coffee?' Rick had the kettle boiling and two mugs waiting.

'There are no biscuits, I'm afraid,' Patsy told him.

'Not to worry. Let's sit down.'

Patsy sat opposite him at the long, shiny table in the main cabin. She swallowed, waiting for him to say something.

'Patsy, you know I think you've been doing a great job as housekeeper.'

Here it comes, she thought wretchedly. He's firing me.

'And as cook. Your meals are the best,' he went on.

'Thanks,' she muttered.

'But I've got some bad news. I'm afraid your job has come to an end.'

'Oh,' she whispered in a small voice, unable to meet his eyes.

'I'm putting *Sea Freedom* up for sale.'

'What?' Her head jerked upwards. This was the last thing she'd expected to hear. 'You're selling this beautiful boat? But you love it!'

'That's true. I do.' He pulled a face. 'But I need to raise a large amount of capital in a hurry, and this is the only way I can think of doing it. It's a pretty valuable boat.'

Oh, dear. He's still so sure he's going to buy the shops and build a hotel, she thought, biting her lip. He's going to sacrifice his beloved boat and then find they won't sell.

'Rick, it's not going to happen,' she said quietly. 'Have you seen today's paper? They're all united against you. They'll never sell — not one of them.'

'What on earth are you talking about?'

'My aunt Grace, of course. And the bookshop man, and the tailor and the health shop ladies. They've all decided to refuse your offer, no matter how much you offer them. So you won't have to sell your boat after all!'

'Oh?' he said casually. 'I've given up that whole idea, Patsy. No point in making everyone unhappy about it.'

Seeing Sense

Patsy felt her jaw drop. She could hardly believe what she had just heard. After all the anxiety his persistent offer had caused everyone, especially her great-aunt and mother!

'When did you decide this?' she asked, puzzled. 'I mean, I'm delighted and I'm sure Aunt Grace and my mum will be, too, but what made you change your mind?'

'A number of things. You, mainly.'

'Me?' Patsy was confused.

'The last time we went to the farm, you made me see sense,' he explained. 'You told me I loved wheeling and dealing. That made me feel as though all I had going for me in your eyes was being a sharp businessman. I didn't like the image.'

'But I didn't mean that at all! Being a clever businessman isn't something to be ashamed of! I think it's great. I think you're great.'

She hadn't intended that to slip out.

'Do you, Patsy?' He looked at her with an odd expression, then seemed to change the subject completely.

'What do you want to do with your life, Patsy? I mean, this part-time job on the boat had to come to an end eventually. You must have known it would. But you weren't going to make looking after three hungry men your career, were you? Do you intend to stay in Simonstown and help your family in the shop? Or do you think you'll return to England?'

'I don't know. I always meant to study catering when I'd finished travelling. We have a college quite near my old house in Witham and my dad wants me to go back and do the course there. But I've decided to stay here in South Africa,' she replied.

'Very sensible.' He grinned.

'I'm not even sure if I want to do catering any more,' Patsy added.

'Well, you're a great cook, but maybe you should stretch yourself. Study something you're not already good at, expand your horizons.'

Patsy nodded.

'Maybe I could do marketing. Or a business course. Mellie's been telling me about the degree she intends to do and it sounds pretty interesting.'

'Or maybe you could study wine-making?'

'Me?'

'Just joking.' Rick had a funny little grin, but he couldn't have been serious, could he?

'I haven't been thinking about my future. I've just been drifting along happily, I suppose.' She looked him in the eye.

'How old are you, Patsy? Twenty?'

'I'll be twenty-one in December. What does that have to do with anything?'

He leaned across the polished table and took her hand in his.

'Because I'm twenty-nine. Sometimes I feel like an old man compared with you. You're just starting out in life and here I am coming to the end of one stage of mine, and starting another.'

'Another stage of your life? Has this got something to do with selling your boat? Are you emigrating to America or something?' she asked.

Patsy suddenly felt as if a black hole had opened in front of her. If she didn't see Rick again, all the meaning and colour would go out of her life. She realised that recently she'd just been marking time through the week, waiting for the weekends to sail with him and the crew, going for drives out to the farm and just talking to him!

It had been ages since she'd wanted to join her old mates at the Yacht Club, but instead had been content to stay at home and wait for the weekends and Rick's arrival in Simonstown.

'Emigrating? No way. No, I'm buying Mont Liberte from Andre. I'm going to take over the farm completely.' He looked at her quizzically. 'So, what do you think?'

Patsy was astounded.

'I think that's wonderful! Fantastic! Oh, Rick, that's what you wanted all along, isn't it? How did you persuade Andre to sell to you?'

'It was quite easy in the end. I've never told him I'd like to buy it, but when you told me about his interest in yoga and so on, I mentioned that I'd had a look at a few books on yoga because I knew he was keen on it. And then he started to talk about it and about his whole life, actually.'

'I'm glad,' Patsy said carefully. 'You two have never really talked, have you?'

Rick shook his head.

'That's what he said, too. But once he heard I'd been interested enough to read up on yoga, there was no stopping him. To tell the truth . . . ' He grinned. 'I wouldn't have bothered, except you told me there was more to all this New Age stuff than I thought. So I decided I'd better check it out.'

'Anyway,' he continued, 'Andre came out with this incredible story that what he really wanted to do was go into partnership with a woman who wanted to get in touch with their inner spiritual being . . . ' he pulled a face ' . . . whatever that means! He called it a holistic healing centre and rattled on about yoga and crystal therapy. Apparently she wants to buy a huge old house on the slopes of the mountain above Gordon's Bay, because the healing vibrations from the sea add to the power of . . . some nonsense or other!'

Another Stage

Patsy couldn't help laughing. 'You'll never believe there's anything in this, will you?' she said. 'I've heard of wellness centres like that. A lot of perfectly sane but stressed people check in for a week or so and feel wonderful afterwards. It's better than a holiday, or so I've heard.'

'Well, that's what Andre wants to do, run one of those places. He might even have thought of turning the farm into a retreat, but luckily his lady friend Deirdre has her own ideas and feels they need to be near the sea.'

'So, once he'd told you all of this, did he offer to sell you the farm?' Patsy asked.

Rick shook his head.

'Not at first. He wished he could get rid of Mont Liberte, but he thought that as the Hugo will was entailed, he couldn't break it by selling to anyone else. But when I pointed out that it would stay in the family if I bought it, he saw the light and thought it was a brilliant idea.'

'It is,' Patsy said warmly.

'He's not exactly giving it away, though. He's had it valued by an appraiser and I'm paying the full market value. That's why I need to sell *Sea Freedom*.'

'And now you'll be able to rebuild the winery and make your own wine on the estate again!' Patsy said excitedly.

'That's the plan. My father made a very successful Merlot, as well as a Cabernet that won prizes at the local wine show, and the vines are all still there.' His eyes sparkled with enthusiasm. 'I'll have a go at bottling Chardonnay, too. Those vines that Andre planted are maturing well and they'll give us a harvest this summer.'

Patsy smiled.

'You're right. You really are entering another stage in your life.'

'The thing is, Patsy — I love you.'

He was still holding her hand, gripping so tightly it was almost painful. She looked into the deep warm brown of his eyes and thought she might drown in them. She was suddenly aware of the loud creaking protests of the boat straining at the moorings, and above the howling of the wind she could hardly hear his next words.

'I wanted to ask you to marry me and come to live on the farm. Be a part of my life for ever.'

Patsy's heart was pounding so hard she thought it might burst out of her chest. Was this a proposal?

'But I haven't any right to ask you,' he continued in a low voice. 'It isn't fair to you for me to expect you to come and bury yourself on a farm miles from anywhere. You're so young, and I'm older than you are. You should go off to college and study something like your parents want you to. Discover what you really want out of life before you settle down.'

She was silent. Then she stood up and walked round to his side of the table.

'Rick,' she said, smiling. 'Just because you're older than me doesn't mean that you can tell me what to do! I've met you and I know what I want out of life. I want to be your wife.'

He stood up and took her in his arms, pulling her towards him.

'That's what I hoped you'd say,' he muttered.

At first he peppered her neck with sweet, soft little kisses, and then his mouth found hers. A wonderful, unfamiliar fire started to build in her body, leaving Patsy breathless and clinging to him, when suddenly the boat rocked sharply in the water. Rick staggered slightly, falling backwards on to the bench and pulling Patsy on to his lap, the moment broken.

'So,' he said, tenderly smoothing the hair from her forehead and gazing at her face as if he wanted to imprint it on his mind for ever. 'Was that a yes?'

She smiled and snuggled against his chest.

'If that was a proposal, then yes!'

Rick smiled.

'It was! But I mean that about waiting, Patsy, my darling. There's nothing I'd like more than to sweep you up and take you back to the farm as my bride . . . '

'On your white horse?' she teased.

'But I don't think we ought to get married for a year or two. I'll be very busy on the farm and you'll always regret not finishing your education and . . . '

She kissed him.

'Are you backing out of this whole thing already?'

'Of course not. It's just that we should be sensible about things.'

'I can see we'll have to discuss this,' she said softly. 'Your family motto might be 'We never give up', but I've got a better one. *Carpe Diem*! Seize the day!'

'That could work for both of us, I guess,' Rick murmured, kissing her again.

Don't Give Up

When Patsy and Rick ran up the steps to the front door, hand in hand and brimming with news, they were met with an ominous silence within the house.

'Mum?' Patsy called, bursting into the living-room. 'We've got something to tell you!'

'Hello, darling. Patsy, it's Jack and Dan. They're missing!'

Maureen's voice was choked with misery, her face rigid with unshed tears. Aunt Grace sat crumpled in her chair, looking smaller and older than usual with a handkerchief pressed to her mouth. She hardly looked up when they came in.

Mellie came through from the kitchen, bearing a tray with tea.

'We shut the shop,' she explained to Patsy quietly. 'We're just waiting for news.'

'Missing at sea?' Rick took charge. 'Have you phoned the National Sea Rescue people?'

'Yes,' Maureen whispered. 'They said they couldn't do a thing in this weather. They can't launch a rescue boat and they can't get a helicopter into the air until the storm dies down.'

'But they said they'd alert any shipping for fifty kilometres off shore to keep a lookout, didn't they?' Mellie encouraged. 'The man told your mum that Dan's boat could have lost power and drifted miles out, driven by the storm.'

'It's blowing one heck of a north-westerly,' Rick said. 'But that shouldn't be a problem for a boat like Dan's. So, if he's in trouble, he could have lost his steering. Or his motor might have seized up. Either way, he could have been blown round the Point. Has no-one had any radio contact with Dan? He has to have a VHF radio on board.'

Maureen shrugged.

'He has, but no-one's heard from him. Not the harbour master or any other boat out at sea, as far as we know,' she replied.

'Those radios often don't work in bad weather, or if he's behind a mountain he may not be able to transmit a clear signal. Have you called Cape Town Radio? They monitor all shipping calls and they might have picked up something from him.'

'The Sea Rescue man said he'd

phone them and then let me know if
there was any news.'

'Consider The Facts'

Patsy sat down on the arm of
Maureen's chair and put her arm
around her mother.

'They'll be all right, Mum, I'm sure
of it,' she comforted, feeling sick with
anxiety herself.

'But what if they've hit a rock or
something and sunk? Or capsized and
they're clinging to the boat ... '
Maureen's voice wavered and she bit
her lip, determined not to cry.

'Mrs Henderson, just consider the
facts.' Rick's voice was calm and
authoritative and Maureen looked up,
watching his face as he spoke. 'Dan's a
very experienced sailor, isn't he? He
might have got caught in bad weather
and decided to motor further away
from the coast to ride out the storm.
He could be fine, but just not able to

make contact for some reason.'

'And if they are in trouble, he has life jackets and a rubber life raft on board. If anything had happened he would have got everyone into that and they're likely to be quite safe, even if they are cold and wet.'

Patsy hugged her mother.

'Have some tea, Mum,' she said helplessly. The thought of her little brother in trouble, struggling in the icy water, was more than she could bear. And Dan. What would her mother do if Dan . . . ?

The phone rang in the hall and Patsy leapt up to answer it. They all listened to her replies.

'Yes? Yes? Really? Is that good or bad? Oh . . . well, thanks for letting us know.'

'What?' Maureen asked. 'Who was that?'

'It was Alan, the Sea Rescue guy. He says they've just been told that a distress flare was sighted off the Point early this morning. A fishing boat spotted it but couldn't report it because their radio was broken. They've just come back to Hout Bay and told the harbour master there.'

'That must have been Dan,' Grace said. 'Richard's right, Mo, Dan's an excellent sailor and he'll get the boat back with everyone safe. For all we know, they're drinking cocoa and playing cards, just waiting for the storm to pass so they can get back.'

But her voice sounded hollow.

'If only there was something we could do,' Maureen said. 'It's terrible feeling so helpless.' She got up and walked to the window. 'If only this wind would stop. I can't see where the sea ends and the sky begins.'

Rick looked thoughtful.

'I wonder if I'd have any luck raising Dan,' he said suddenly. 'I have an SSB radio on board for emergencies. It's much stronger than the usual VHF. Dan's battery might be getting low, in which case his broadcast would be very weak, but it's worth a try.'

'Could you?' Maureen swung round,

hope blazing. 'Oh, Richard, please do! Can we go down now? If we could just hear something — a voice — '

'I'll stay with Miss Whittaker,' Mellie said. 'Someone needs to be here if the Sea Rescue people ring with some news.'

'Here's my mobile number,' Rick said, scribbling it on a piece of paper. 'Mellie, if they phone here, let me know at once. I'll call you if we pick up anything from the radio.'

Maureen shrugged on her mackintosh and grabbed an umbrella from the stand in the hall. The three of them hurried downhill through the driving rain to the harbour, with the umbrella turned inside out almost immediately.

The quay was swept with rain and completely deserted of life, with just the prows of the yachts tossing in the huge swells.

'Careful, Mrs Henderson,' Rick said, helping her on board as *Sea Freedom* surged up and down at her moorings. 'Don't slip.'

He unlocked the hatch and they clambered downstairs to the warmth and shelter of the huge cabin.

'Goodness,' Maureen said, looking around at the panelling. 'Isn't this beautiful? I've often wondered what it looked like inside.'

'Show your mum around, if you like, Patsy, while I get the radio going,' Rick said.

Maureen peered hastily into the cabins and admired the bathroom, but Patsy could tell that her mind wasn't on the guided tour.

'Can you hear anything?' she asked anxiously when they came back to the main cabin.

'Don't Give Up'

Rick had ignored his usual VHF radio and had pulled out a smaller piece of equipment. He was adjusting the radio dials, frowning.

'There's a lot of static,' he said. 'This

storm makes the reception really bad. I doubt I'll pick up anything, even with this.'

He leaned into the microphone grille and spoke slowly and clearly.

'*Sea Freedom* to *Mermaid*. Do you copy? Over.'

Nothing.

'There could be a lot of reasons he's not answering,' Rick said. 'He could be in a dead area where there isn't reception. His battery could be flat. His radio could be wet . . . anything.'

'Keep trying. Please, Rick.'

'I will, Mrs Henderson, of course. If anything can hear them, it will be this powerful SSB radio. Why don't you make us all a cup of coffee, Patsy? Or maybe something a bit stronger. There's some sherry in the cupboard.'

Patsy poured them all a warming glass of sweet sherry. It was strange to think that only an hour before Rick had proposed to her in this very cabin and she hadn't even mentioned it to her mother. But the news could wait; all anyone could think about was Jack and Dan and the fate of all on board *Mermaid*.

Rick kept repeating his call, over and over, but after thirty minutes of trying there was still no reply.

'It's not working, I'm afraid. This radio is extra powerful but I'm not getting a thing . . . '

He stood up and made to switch off the radio.

'Just try once more, Rick. Don't give up,' Maureen appealed, her face drawn and white.

'One more time. OK. *Sea Freedom* to *Mermaid*. Do you copy? Over.'

And out of the static and crackling suddenly there came a faint voice as if it was being transmitted from the moon.

'*Mermaid* to *Sea Freedom*.'

It was Dan.

11

Relief

Dan's voice! He was alive!

Almost in tears, Maureen grabbed the small microphone from Rick and babbled brokenly.

'Are you all right? Is Jack all right?'

'Hang on,' Rick said. 'I have to switch this to 'send'.' He flipped a little silver toggle on the radio and she repeated what she had said.

From far away Dan's voice surged and faded.

' . . . fine . . . lost power . . . broken . . . ' Then nothing but crackling static.

Rick took the microphone and tried to make contact again, but that was the last of the communication.

'Well, at least we know he's alive and the boat is upright. What we don't know is his position,' Rick said. 'But we can more or less work it out once we know the wind strengths and the currents. The Sea Rescue guys are on the ball with things like this.'

'What a relief just to hear his voice,' Patsy said shakily, wiping her eyes.

'Oh, Rick, thank you for not giving up!' Maureen said, hugging him. 'Just hearing his voice has given me faith that he'll be found.'

'I'm sure they will. But there's nothing we can do here now,' he replied. 'Let's go back.'

Reunited

The three of them battled their way back to the house, almost bent double against the icy wind. Patsy felt the warmth of Rick's arm around her and remembered that they hadn't told anyone their news. But that would have to wait for a better moment. Right now all that mattered was finding Dan's boat and getting everyone on board back safely to harbour.

Grace and Mellie were waiting anxiously.

'That Sea Rescue man, Alan, phoned again. He said the wind force is predicted to drop within a couple of hours and they'll get a helicopter into the air just as soon as it's safe,' Grace said. 'I've heated some soup. I'm sure we could all do with something hot for lunch.'

'Good idea,' Rick said. 'I'll get back to Alan and tell him we've made contact of a sort.'

The afternoon dragged past. Maureen brought out a board game, but no-one could concentrate. Alan had said he'd call just as soon as he had news, and when the phone rang, Maureen jumped up to answer.

It was Alf Thompson, asking if there had been any word.

'Nothing yet, Alf, but we've managed to speak to Dan briefly on the radio, so at least we know they're out there somewhere,' she said quickly. 'We're just waiting for a call from the rescue people, actually.'

'Won't keep you, then,' Alf said. 'Just called to let you know that the Venter sisters said to tell you that everyone on the boat is in their prayers, lass. Mine, too.'

'Thanks, Alf,' she whispered.

Maureen took a deep, trembling breath.

'I'll make us some tea,' she called from the kitchen. Alf's kind voice had almost undone her and she needed time to compose herself.

The wind dropped gradually all afternoon and by four o'clock the rain had stopped.

'Surely they must have taken off by now?' Grace muttered, standing at the window and scanning the sky. 'I wish I could see a helicopter in the air.'

'You probably won't see it, Miss Whittaker, as it would leave from the air base and go straight out to sea, over the mountain without crossing the bay,' Rick said.

'So, do you think they'll do one of those rescues where they winch people up in the air to the helicopter?' Mellie asked.

'It would depend on the state of the boat, and everyone on board,' Rick said. 'Leaving the boat would mean abandoning it completely and I can't see Dan wanting to do that, unless the *Mermaid* was very badly damaged. I think they'd just fix the position and tell the Sea Rescue boat exactly where they are. They'll probably get towed in.'

★ ★ ★

Rick was right. Just after ten the next morning, the phone rang and it was Dan.

'We're back,' he said. 'We're all OK, but Jack would appreciate some dry clothes, if you happen to be passing this way?'

'Dan! Oh, thank heavens! We'll be there in ten minutes.'

Maureen scooped up dry sweaters and trousers for both of them from

Jack's cupboard and they all piled into Rick's car. He'd spent the night in Jack's room, saying he couldn't leave until he knew they were safe, and they were grateful for the speed at which he drove to the harbour.

Mermaid was tied up in her usual berth, with Dan talking to a group of men on the quay.

'Mo!' He strode over to Maureen and held her tight in a wordless embrace.

'Bet you thought we'd disappeared, didn't you?' His clothes felt thoroughly damp, but he didn't seem to notice.

'Something like that,' she said, trying to smile.

'Don't cry, Mum, we're fine.' Jack patted her shoulder awkwardly. 'Look, we're all here. Kurt, Klaus, this is my mum.'

Hero

Behind Jack were two men, staggering under the weight of an enormous silver fish that they carried between them. They were both grinning from ear to ear. Maureen couldn't believe it.

'We had quite an adventure, *ja?*' Klaus grinned. 'But all OK now. So, where's the camera, Master Jack?'

'I'll get it, hang on.'

Jack disappeared into the cabin and came back with a little digital camera.

'I must have my picture,' Kurt said. 'Otherwise people won't believe I caught this monster.'

'It certainly is a big fish,' Maureen said politely.

A photograph? How could everyone behave so casually when they'd all nearly perished at sea?

'Tuna. Sixty kilos, at least,' Kurt said proudly. 'Is what I came to South Africa for. And all the excitement we had was just thrown in for extra pleasure, *ja?*'

Maureen was pretty sure the man was putting on a brave front, already rehearsing his version of their terrible ordeal to tell his friends back home in Germany.

There was a hook and tackle in place next to the harbour master's office for game fishermen to pose with their catch, and Dan hooked the massive fish and winched it up. The two men stood on either side while Jack took several shots. Maureen noticed he was trembling with cold.

'I brought some dry clothes, Jack. I think you should change as soon as you can,' she said anxiously. 'And for you, Dan.'

'Ah, no, first we must have a photo of this young man with us,' Klaus said. 'The hero of the hour, as they say, yes?'

'Not really,' Jack said, blushing, but he went and stood next to them while Dan took their picture.

'What was that all about?' she whispered.

'Tell you later,' Dan replied. 'What we both need is a long hot bath and some hot food. In that order!'

He shook hands with the men from the Sea Rescue, saw his clients into a taxi back to their hotel and let out a deep breath.

'Glad to be back in one piece,' he said. 'Let's get home.'

Overboard

Dan was a man of few words and Maureen was sure he would have preferred to leave it there, but, of course, he wasn't allowed to. Not with all of them sitting around Aunt Grace's kitchen table, demanding all the details and hanging on to their every word.

'Remember I said we'd return to harbour if the wind picked up?' Dan said. 'Well, for the first couple of hours it was fine. Fresh, but fine. I reckoned on at least one full day out and those two were keen to catch themselves a big one.'

Jack continued the story.

'And it was OK. They'd caught that flipping thing and Dan had said we'd call it a day, but we were right on the Whittle Reef and an enormous freak wave came up out of nowhere and washed right over us,' he said. 'Kurt had just come up on deck and forgotten to close the hatch cover, so the wave went right into the cabin and wet everything.'

'Including the radio,' Dan went on. 'As I discovered when I tried to call up a weather forecast. That was disaster number one. I could see the barometer dropping like crazy and I knew we had to get back fast. Then disaster number two was the rope.'

'Any more soup, Auntie Grace?' Jack had finished his second bowl of bean and bacon soup and still looked hungry. 'This is great stuff, thanks. Anyway, just as we turned, the engine seemed to lose power. Dan was revving the engine and we weren't moving at all. I looked overboard and found we were trailing a long piece of rope, which had got caught in the prop.'

'I had that once before, with a huge strand of kelp,' Dan said. 'But seaweed was easier to get rid of. In the end, Jack had to go overboard and cut the prop free.'

'Jack? Went overboard? Wasn't that terribly dangerous?' Maureen looked at Dan in horror.

'Not really, Mum. Dan roped me very securely. It was freezing, though. And the swells were enormous, so it took ages to get all the rope away.'

Dan put his hand on Maureen's shoulder.

'He was quite safe, Mo, I promise,' he said. 'I wouldn't have let him, otherwise. He did a darned good job. The trouble was, of course, that I had to stop the motor while he cut the rope, and it wouldn't start again.'

'What a nightmare,' Rick put in.

Dan nodded.

'I've never been out in seas like that in my life. The swells must have been twenty feet high and we were just tossed about like a cork.'

'And those two German fellows were crazy.' Jack laughed. 'They didn't seem to realise that this wasn't normal. They loved it. Kept saying it was a big thrill and better than hunting for lion!'

'They loved it at first, you mean,' Dan corrected him. 'But when all the power went and there were no lights, they stopped telling me what fun they were having!'

Maureen was aghast.

'All your power? How did that happen?' she asked.

'It was my fault,' Jack said abruptly. 'If I'd remembered to collect that extra battery last week . . .'

'None of that, lad,' Dan said. 'It was no-one's fault but my own.' He turned to Rick, explaining. 'I kept trying to start the motor, and it wouldn't catch. So we got the cover off and I found the fuel line was cracked. Diesel was slopping about everywhere in the engine hole.'

'We patched that up,' Jack said. 'But it still wouldn't start.'

'I tried for nearly an hour. I was getting a bit desperate, as you can imagine, and then eventually the battery gave out.'

'And there wasn't a spare,' Jack said miserably. 'My fault.'

'Jack, the buck stops with me,' Dan said. 'I should have checked it was on board. Anyway, with the motor not running, it couldn't charge the auxiliary battery, either. I knew we had to conserve what little we had to use the radio, if we could only get it working again. So we had no lights, no GPS — nothing.'

'And Dan spent ages taking the radio apart and drying each piece,' Jack said.

'You must have felt so helpless,' Maureen said, her hand in Dan's.

'Visibility was practically nil,' Dan continued. 'The rain was coming in squalls and I reckon the wind was blowing at least forty knots out there. Northerly, so we were being driven further and further away from the coast.'

'Then we saw a tiny light through the mist,' Jack interrupted. 'We thought it was a trawler or a fishing boat, so Dan sent up three flares and we hoped they'd come over, or at least alert the Sea Rescue.'

'They saw one,' Maureen told him. 'But their radio wasn't working so they could only report it when they arrived back later.'

'Dan was amazing, Mum,' Jack said. 'He got Kurt and Klaus singing all their old drinking songs, and he taught them 'Ten Green Bottles'.'

'We were frantic,' Patsy said. 'Then Rick said he'd try on the radio on his yacht, and he tried for over half an hour and was just about to give up . . . '

'And then we heard your voice!' Maureen said, wiping her eyes again. 'I'm sorry, Dan, but we were all so worried.'

'Believe me, so was I,' Dan said grimly. 'Fishing boats disappear without a trace all the time, and little bits of wood wash up weeks later. We were extremely lucky.'

'Well, thank heavens for the National Sea Rescue,' Aunt Grace said firmly. 'Do you know, they run entirely on donations? From now on, we'll have one of their collection boxes on our shop counter. More soup, Dan?'

An Invitation

Patsy couldn't believe she'd been engaged for more than a day and hadn't told anyone about it. But with Dan and Jack being lost at sea on the very day Rick had proposed, and all the drama afterwards, the right moment had never presented itself.

Rick had to return to Johannesburg that evening and she wanted him to be with her when they announced their wonderful news together.

'I'll be flying back next weekend,' Rick whispered as they clung together, saying goodbye in the street outside the house. 'How about we invite everyone out to Mont Liberte for the weekend and tell them then?'

'That would be lovely. Mum's always wanted to see the farm. But I'm not going to say a word about anything until then, even if it kills me!'

'I don't mind if you do,' Rick said. 'I mean, it's not a secret or anything. I'm so bursting with happiness I want to let everyone know!'

He stepped back from their embrace and shouted at the moon.

'Woo hoo! Patsy Henderson and Rick Hugo are getting married!'

'Oh, you idiot!' She laughed. 'Ssh! I want to announce it properly. Now's not the time.'

'I see that cat is very happy for us,' Rick said, nodding at a black cat staring at them from the wall opposite. 'OK, my lips are sealed until next weekend. We'll have a party at the farm and I'll phone Maria and let her know to make the rooms ready and cook something. She'll be thrilled.'

Patsy waved until his car was out of sight, then ran back up the steps to the house, hugging her news to herself.

'Rick's gone off, then?' Maureen asked. 'Weren't we lucky he was here, and had such a powerful radio? By the way, did he mention anything to you about buying Whittaker's? Alf says he's not going to make an offer on his shop any longer.'

'Oh, that?' Patsy said casually. 'He's given up the idea completely. Said Auntie Grace was too much for him! I expect he's got other plans and I'm sure he'll tell us one of these days.' She bit her lip. 'He's going to move down to Fransch Hoek and run the farm full time, Mum. I think he's giving up the whole property development thing.'

'Oh, my goodness,' Maureen said. 'Does that mean you'll see more of him? Or less? What about your job on the boat?'

Patsy shrugged.

'I don't know. It's all up in the air,' she said. 'I'm off to bed, Mum, goodnight.'

It was very, very difficult not to tell her mother her news! And difficult not to grin like a Cheshire cat.

Something's happened between those

459

two, Maureen thought. I suppose I'll be told one of these days.

George Wellings

The following week seemed busier than ever. Instead of taking a few days off, as Maureen was sure they would, Jack and Dan had gone down to the harbour first thing the next morning to assess the damage to *Mermaid*.

'Luckily, it's mostly just sea water,' Dan said, calling in for a quick sandwich lunch in the upstairs coffee room. 'I'm going to have to buy new cushions for the main cabin, I think. I'll have the motor completely overhauled and get the fuel line properly fixed.'

'So, no clients for a while?' she asked. 'I'm so glad. It's too cold to be out in this weather.'

'No, we'll be going out the first good day we can,' Dan replied. 'The forecast is for sun next week and I have a booking for Wednesday.'

'Oh.'

He caught the tone of her voice.

'Mo, if you're worrying about Jack, don't. He was fine — really good in a tight spot. He kept a cool head and never once did anything to indicate to those two clients what a bad situation we were in.'

'Perhaps he didn't know himself,' Maureen said quietly. 'Anyway, it's not only Jack. I worry about you, as well. No matter how good your boat is, when things go wrong like that, you're powerless against the sea.'

'That was the first and last time I've ever been caught in that sort of storm. I was stupid to allow those German tourists to persuade me to take them out, especially when I could see the weather was changing. From now on, if I see a cloud in the sky, we won't go out!'

She grinned.

'OK, good! Then I won't have to worry!' she said.

'Let's change the subject,' Dan said.

'When and where are we going to get married? Have you had any thoughts about that?'

Maureen shook her head.

'When isn't a problem. As soon as we can! But where?'

Dan thought for a moment, then smiled slowly.

'I can think of somewhere pretty special. And I know someone who will conduct the service to bless us. Do you remember a guy called George Wellings?'

George!

'Yes, I do,' Maureen said. 'Red hair? Glasses? Michael Jackson fan? He was the year ahead of me in school.'

'That's the one. Well, he's a minister now, and I know that he would be willing to marry us where I have in mind!'

'He sounds perfect,' Maureen said, wondering if George still moon-walked. 'But you're not thinking we should get married at sea, are you? There wouldn't be room for everyone on your boat, and besides, Aunt Grace might get seasick.'

'Absolutely not on the boat,' Dan promised. 'You'll love what I have in mind, but I don't want to tell you until I've arranged it. I wouldn't want you to be disappointed if, for some reason, it's not possible.'

And Maureen had to be content with that!

★ ★ ★

'Mo, dear, I don't think I'll be coming down to the shop today,' Aunt Grace said, settling a pile of old newspapers on the dining-room table. 'I want to write my first column for the newspaper and I need to be really careful with the research. I don't want any inaccuracies, or Henry Morton will spot them at once!'

'Aunt Grace, this is so exciting,' Patsy said. 'A weekly column! Wasn't that wonderful of the editor to ask you? But how are you ever going to think of something to write each week?'

'Oh, very easily,' Grace replied. 'The history of Simonstown is full of interesting anecdotes. It's always been quite an important little harbour because of the Naval base. For instance, did you know the Royal Navy had to feed Napoleon Bonaparte when he was a prisoner on St Helena? All his food came from here and he demanded forty kilos of meat and thirty bottles of red Constantia wine every month! Even though he was a Frenchman, he recognised our wine was superior!'

'Well, they were made by the Huguenots who made wine in France, so of course they were good,' Patsy said. 'Rick told me.'

'Ah, yes, Rick!' Aunt Grace said. 'And when are we seeing that young man again?'

Now that Richard the property developer was no more, Aunt Grace was quite prepared to like Rick, the polite young man who had been so helpful.

'Actually, Auntie, Rick has invited the

whole family out to his farm for the weekend, and Dan, too, of course. I was hoping we could go straight after lunch on Saturday, once the shop's closed?'

'Really? How nice of him. I'll look forward to seeing it — it's listed as one of the oldest homesteads in the Fransch Hoek valley. So, is he not racing this weekend?'

Patsy shook her head.

'No. I don't think there's a regatta planned, anyway . . . '

'If he gets tired of that boat, you'll be out of a job, won't you?' Aunt Grace smiled. 'But you can always keep busy in the shop. You're planning to go to college after Christmas, aren't you?'

'I haven't actually applied yet, but I'll do that next week.'

Oh, dear. She was getting herself more and more tied up in knots! She wished Saturday would hurry up and arrive so that all their plans could be discussed. Though she still had to convince Rick that she didn't want to study for two years before they married.

She was quite sure she would never change her mind about him, and anyway, how would she use her catering skills if she was to be a farmer's wife?

There was so much to consider and she wished that she could discuss her plans with her mother. After the weekend everything would be easier.

'We're Engaged!'

Driving out to the farm with Dan was a leisurely experience. Unlike Rick, he drove for enjoyment and stopped so they could get out and enjoy the view of the valley from the top of the mountain pass.

'Imagine living here,' Maureen breathed, gazing down at the distant farms with their neat rows of vines and, all around, the soaring ring of blue-grey mountains. 'It all looks so peaceful and green. Which one is Mont Liberte, Patsy?'

'It's at the far end of the valley. You can't see it from here,' Patsy said, impatient to get on. 'Come on, Dan, we can look at the scenery another time. Rick's expecting us for tea.'

She couldn't have wished for a better day to show her family her future home. For the first time this week the rain had stopped, and as they drove up the long, oak-lined drive to the farmhouse, the sun broke through and seemed to illuminate the gracious old place against the backdrop of trees.

Rick heard Dan's car brake to a halt and came outside.

He shook hands with them and then took Patsy's hand in his.

'Have you told your mother yet?' he whispered, while the others were walking to the house.

'No. I've been wanting to so badly, but we'd agreed to wait.'

'Not any more,' Rick said. 'Let's tell them right now. Then I can kiss you properly!'

He waited until everyone was inside, seated on big, comfortable easy chairs around a crackling log fire in the enormous sitting-room.

'This is a beautifully proportioned room!' Aunt Grace looked around her approvingly. 'Has that armoire been in your family for a long time, Richard?'

Patsy noticed for the first time how old the handsome, highly polished cupboards and tables were. A copper bowl of spiky pink proteas stood on a brass-bound kist, and there was an unusual triangular cupboard attached to the wall.

'Yes,' Rick replied. 'That kist came out with the original Hugo family in the 1600s. The rest of it is pretty ancient, too.'

'Ancient? These antiques are wonderful! And that armoire is a collector's piece,' Aunt Grace said. 'Yellow wood and stinkwood, if I'm not mistaken. Magnificent! My goodness, you're surrounded by history, young man!'

'I suppose I am,' Rick said. 'But I grew up with all this stuff, so I don't notice it that much.' He clearly didn't want to waste time talking about the furniture. He moved closer to Patsy and put his arm around her, grinning hugely.

'Patsy and I have something to tell you.'

I knew it, Maureen thought, catching Patsy's eye. They're engaged!

'It's hard to believe, but Patsy has done me the honour of agreeing to marry me. We're engaged! If that's all right with you, Mrs Henderson?' He looked suddenly nervous and a lot younger.

Maureen got up and kissed them both, a lump in her throat. The two of them were so obviously in love, unable to stop looking into each other's eyes.

'I'm very happy for you both! Darling, that's lovely!' She hugged Patsy hard.

'Oh, Mum, it was so difficult not to tell you,' she whispered. 'But I wanted to wait and have the two of us together before we announced it.'

'Of course you did. I understand,' Maureen said. 'And it's not such a big surprise to me, after all. I suspected something was up!'

'Well, I certainly didn't,' Aunt Grace said, beaming broadly. 'Congratulations, both of you. Goodness, Patsy, you'll be living amongst all this history! When do you intend to marry?'

'Well, at first we were thinking of a long engagement,' Rick said, holding fast on to Patsy's hand. 'Maybe waiting for a year or two.'

'Then we decided not to,' Patsy said firmly. 'I don't have to study. I can be far more useful here on the farm while Rick gets the winery going again.'

'Well, that's something we're going to discuss,' Rick added. 'The studying bit, I mean. But let's have a cup of tea. Maria is dying to meet you all.'

As if on cue, Maria came in, her brown face split by a huge smile. She was bearing a tray set with an ornate silver teapot and delicate china cups.

'Oh, Miss Patsy! I am so happy for you! And for Mr Richard! Very nice that you will be married!'

She put down the tray and gave Patsy

a resounding kiss.

'I told Maria, I'm afraid,' Rick admitted. 'I had to tell someone!'

'Very good news for us,' Maria said. 'Now we have a wife here again. Soon we have children, too. Much better!'

'I'm glad you approve, Maria.' Patsy laughed. 'I'm not sure about the children, though, not for a while. You'll have to teach me a lot. How to grow all those vegetables and how to make that wonderful bread of yours . . . '

'And these,' Jack said, eyeing a silver dish piled with cinnamon cookies. 'These look great!'

'I give you some to take home,' Maria said at once. 'Ah, I like a boy that likes to eat.'

'Then you'll love my little brother,' Patsy told her. 'Shall I pour the tea?'

Afterwards, Richard showed them to their rooms, which were all furnished with antique pieces and old Persian carpets. Maria had placed a bowl of flowers in every room and laid a fire in each against the evening chill.

'Isn't this gorgeous?' Maureen said. 'It's like stepping back in time. To think you'll be the mistress of this house, darling. It's like a dream come true.'

'I hope I can live up to all of it,' Patsy said. 'I guess Maria will show me the ropes. And it *is* like a dream.' She looked at her mother closely. 'Are you sure you're OK with me and Rick, really? I know you said that he and I move in different circles, but he's changed. He's completely out of the rat-race in Johannesburg and he's going to be running the farm full time.'

'Of course I'm fine, I really am,' Maureen said. 'I liked him the first day I met him, remember? I'm sorry that you don't want to go to college, though. You know how important I've always said it is to get a proper qualification. I suppose you can't live here in Fransch Hoek and study in Cape Town, though. It's a two-hour drive.'

★ ★ ★

While it was still light, Patsy and Rick wandered across to inspect the burnt-out winery, while the others admired Maria's vegetable garden. Rick already had plans drawn up to rebuild and Patsy thought he wanted to show her, but as soon as they were away from the house, he drew her to him and kissed her soundly. They broke apart, breathless and joyful.

'That's something I've been wanting to do all week,' he said softly. 'I still can't believe we're engaged. Oh, by the way — ' He produced a small box. 'Here's something to make it official. I hope it fits.'

An Heirloom

Patsy opened the box. Inside was an old-fashioned ring set with a small diamond and garnets.

'Oh, Rick, this is perfect!'

He slipped it on her finger and together they examined the sparkly band. He kissed her palm.

'It was my grandmother's,' he said. 'And it looks just right on you. Now this . . . ' He produced another small box. 'This is the official Hugo diamond. Handed down to the mistress of Mont Liberte! It's ridiculously big, but it's yours. I just thought it wouldn't be practical to wear if you're going to work in the garden and so on.'

Inside was a diamond so big that Patsy would have thought it was fake if he hadn't told her it was an heirloom.

'Oh, my goodness! I could never wear this!' she cried, amazed by the sheer beauty of the ring.

A big car swept to a halt and parked under the trees.

'Yo!' came Greg's shout. 'Where's the party, my man?' He unwound his long frame from behind the steering wheel, followed by Linda and Martin.

'Party?' Patsy said, confused.

'Congratulations, Patsy!' Linda kissed her gleefully. 'I was thrilled to hear your news.'

There was a flurry of kisses and congratulations and laughter.

'We couldn't miss your engagement bash!' Martin said.

'We're having an engagement bash?' Patsy turned to Rick. 'I thought it was just my family?'

'Maria insisted,' Rick said. 'She loves a celebration. She's been cooking all day so I hope you're all set for a good old-fashioned dinner party! But I'm sure you're all dying of thirst after your drive. Come inside for a cool drink.'

'Here's another car,' Patsy said. 'Oh, it's Andre!'

Rick's brother was accompanied by a sweet, smiling woman dressed in a long, flowing kaftan, with several layers of floating chiffon billowing about. Long crystal earrings dangled below a wiry mop of grey hair tied back with a loop of amber beads.

'You must be Deirdre,' Rick said. 'I'm glad you managed to persuade this crazy brother of mine to come.' He clapped Andre on the shoulder. 'All that hard work getting your new place ready must be doing you good. You're looking very fit.'

'Oh, he is,' Deirdre said at once. 'We've both been detoxifying for a week! How nice to meet you and Patsy. You two must come and visit us when our wellness centre is up and running. Take the time to cleanse the poisons and attune your bodies to your inner selves. That will be our wedding present to you, won't it, Andre?'

'If they'd like to,' Andre said. 'Rick might take some persuading, though.'

'We can talk about it,' Rick said with a straight face. 'Come inside and meet Patsy's family.'

Maria had laid the long dinner table with a white linen cloth, set with silverware and tall silver candlesticks. The long, gold velvet curtains were drawn and a pine-scented fire burned in the grate beneath a marble mantelpiece. From the walls, several gilt-framed Hugo ancestors looked down rather disapprovingly. Patsy had never been in this room. It felt rather daunting, a bit like dining in a museum.

'Sorry it's so gloomy,' Rick said. 'We usually use the breakfast room for meals, but this is the only table that will seat eleven people.'

'It's perfectly beautiful,' Maureen said.

'Patsy's not going to know us once she's living here,' Dan murmured. 'Just the furniture in this room is worth a fortune.'

'Patsy won't let it turn her head,' Maureen said with certainty. 'She'll never change. And think of all the bottles of wine we'll get, once we're Hugo in-laws and Rick is making wine again!'

A Toast

While Rick poured the wine in cut-glass long stemmed glasses, Maria served a delicious creamy butternut soup with home-made bread.

'Everything tonight came from our

garden,' she whispered to Patsy. 'Mr Andre, he don't like to eat meat, so tonight, Mr Rick tell me to serve only vegetables.'

Patsy was touched that Rick had taken Andre's tastes into consideration. He'd softened his attitude to his older brother so much that she was sure they'd become better friends in time.

'Before we start, I'd like to offer a toast,' Rick said, standing up and clinking his glass for silence. 'To Miss Whittaker, who showed me what a determined woman can do. And to Mrs Henderson, who produced such a wonderful daughter. And to Patsy, my fiancée. Three generations of feisty women with whom I will be proud and honoured to be connected in the future.'

Glasses were drained amidst cheers and everyone relaxed.

'Now that was a very nice toast, thank you,' Grace said. 'Richard, my boy, has anyone ever written the history of this house?'

'Not as far as I know,' he replied. 'I'm sure there's lots of old papers and so on in the attic, but no-one's ever put them all together.'

Grace's eyes gleamed.

'I wonder if you'd allow me to take a look at them?' she said. 'I'd love to try my hand at recording the story of how it came to be built and everyone who lived here, down the years.'

'Would you really? I'd appreciate that very much,' Rick said. 'I can't think of anyone better to do it.'

'So are you getting more interested in history?' Patsy murmured mischievously. 'I thought all this old stuff was so boring?'

'Not if it's *our* old stuff,' he said indignantly. 'Our children need to grow up with a sense of their family roots. Like I did.'

Roots. The ones Rick thought his brother had snatched away from him ten years before. It sounded as though he intended to put down roots in Mont Liberte as fast and as deep as possible!

One course followed another: a mushroom quiche and salad, then tiny sweetcorn and hazelnut fritters, fried battered slices of aubergine, baby potatoes tossed in garlic butter and crisp cauliflower florettes in a cheese sauce with fresh asparagus.

Conversation ebbed and flowed around the table, with gales of laughter from Martin and Greg.

'We're celebrating, too. Did Rick tell you?' Greg asked, pouring some more champagne. 'Martin and I have bought *Sea Freedom* between us. We couldn't have let that boat fall into the wrong hands!'

'That's wonderful.' Patsy beamed. 'That means we can still go sailing, then!'

'Ah, but Rick won't be captain,' Martin said solemnly. 'Greg and I will take it in turns to boss everyone else. The first time he comes, we'll put him on kitchen duty, I reckon.'

'No, that's my job!' Patsy said indignantly.

'Speaking of kitchens . . . ' Just at that moment there was a lull in the conversation and everyone heard what Rick said next.

'I had an idea that you might like to try, Patsy. Instead of doing that catering course, why not study under a French master chef right here in Fransch Hoek?'

'How could I do that?' Patsy looked up. She couldn't help her gaze returning every so often to her dear little ring, flashing in the light of the candles.

'There are some excellent restaurants here in the valley and one of them is L'Auberge Etienne. The man who runs it is Etienne le Roux and he's a legend here. He used to own a little restaurant in France that earned two Michelin stars. People used to make a point of coming to his place from miles away. Then he moved out here about five years ago and opened his restaurant. You have to book two months ahead to get a table, he's so popular.'

'He probably wouldn't let someone

like me into his kitchen, let alone teach me!' Patsy said.

Rick had a twinkle in his eye.

'I'm pretty sure he will. I spoke to him this week and it just so happens that he's looking for someone,' Rick said, smiling. 'What they call a cassis chef. A dogsbody. But you'd be at the feet of the master and you'd learn. Most qualified chefs would kill to win a place with him.'

'Why should he choose me, then?'

'I took him sailing lots of times last year,' Rick admitted. 'He loved it and kept inviting me to eat in his restaurant for nothing. I never have, so perhaps he feels he owes me a favour.'

'Wow.' Patsy considered this. 'That could work out beautifully. I don't mind starting at the bottom. I'm a fast learner.'

Maureen was immediately enthusiastic.

'Then, once you've been there a year or two, you could open your own little restaurant right here, like those other wine farms have done.' She grinned. 'And serve the wines that Rick is going to make! Oh, this will be wonderful! What a good idea!'

As Maria brought in a sinfully rich chocolate mousse with a silver bowl of thick cream, Maureen reflected that everything seemed to be falling into place for Patsy. Tonight was a celebration of a whole new life for her, living in this grand old home in the valley, and a lovely fiancé who was actively encouraging her career.

And the next celebration would be her own, hers and Dan's. But where would that be?

On Top Of The World

'On top of Table Mountain,' Dan said. 'It's all fixed, if you approve. George is game for it. How would you feel about getting married on top of the world?'

'On top of the mountain? But we'd all be hot and sweaty by the time we climbed up there! And how on earth would Aunt Grace make it to the top? Or Rugaya? There's no road!'

'You daft girl,' Dan said. 'We'd go up by cable, of course. In great style. We will arrive at the top looking as elegant as when we set off.'

'Oh, I forgot about the cable car! That's a great idea, then. You are clever!'

The more she thought about it, the more Maureen loved the idea. And Patsy and Jack were thrilled.

'That'll be dead cool, Mum!' Jack said. 'At last I'll get to the top of that mountain and by cable car, too! Excellent!'

'Where will you and Dan have your reception afterwards? Would we all come back here to the house?' Patsy asked.

'No, Dan's booked a special section of the little stone restaurant at the top,' Maureen said happily. 'We don't have to do a thing except tell them the number of guests!'

Inspirational Setting

Meeting George Wellings again had been quite a revelation. Who would have thought the look-alike Michael Jackson one-gloved wonder could change so much? He was now quite tubby, with a friendly twinkle behind thick lenses, and he had become a successful writer of self-help books when he was not ministering to his flock.

'It will be a charming ceremony,' he'd said. 'I think the top of Table Mountain will be a most inspirational setting for the start of your life together.'

Even though she didn't have to think about the catering, Maureen was surprised by how much she had to think about before the wedding. To start with, who would she invite? Dan had already given her a list of eight friends he wanted to include.

'I'd really like to ask all of our suppliers,' she said. 'Some of them have become real friends. But we simply can't afford to pay for so many people to go up on the cable car, and the lunch afterwards isn't cheap, either. We want to keep the whole thing small and intimate.'

'Why not just invite Priscilla?' Aunt Grace suggested. 'She's also a friend of Dan's so she qualifies as a family friend as well as a supplier. And you'll have to invite Ella, too, won't you?'

'Dan had her on his list and she's coming with Graham Ivy, who's now her official interior designer! I believe he and Ella are quite an item these days. Then there's Rugaya and Mellie, and of course I must invite the Venter sisters, and Alf and Raj and his wife Suraya.'

'And Rick?' Patsy asked.

'Of course, but he counts as family. I thought of inviting Henry, too, Aunt Grace. We've known him for ever.'

'That would be nice. And did Dan think of Rafe — Rugaya's grandson who used to crew for him?'

'Yes, he's on the list. Now what will I wear? And what will you wear, Aunt Grace? Patsy?'

'I think we'll all have to go shopping!'

Patsy said gleefully.

'I won't, will I?' Jack said in horror. 'We're going up a mountain, right? I won't have to wear a suit or anything, will I?'

'No, smart casual will do,' Maureen assured him. 'Wear your nice blue shirt. I know that Dan's just wearing sports slacks and a jacket. I'm not sure if he even possesses a tie!'

Surprise Guests

A successful trip to the shops in Cape Town resulted in an elegant purple dress for Maureen with a matching jacket, a gorgeous pink flowing maxi dress for Patsy, and a pair of stockings for Aunt Grace, who insisted that she didn't need anything new, thank you very much.

'I have three good outfits in my wardrobe already, and I'll wear the grey silk,' she said firmly. 'No point in throwing money away. Oh, there's the phone. Get it, will you, Patsy? My feet are killing me. Three hours of shopping is two hours too many!'

Patsy was away for quite a while, and when she came back she was flushed with excitement.

'Add another two names to your list, Mum — Dad and Rita are coming!'

'What?'

'They were planning to come for a holiday some time, anyway,' Patsy said. 'So they've timed it for the wedding. And Dad can meet Rick and see the farm.'

'Oh, that's great!'

Maureen was surprised at how quickly she came to terms with the idea of her ex-husband attending her wedding. And Dan, when she told him, took it in his stride.

The night before the wedding, she and Dan had finished dinner at a little restaurant on Jubilee Square, and were walking slowly back to the car, hand in hand.

'I'm so glad Jack's taken your advice

and has applied for college,' she said. 'You've been such a good influence on him, Dan.'

'Well, he's a bright boy and I'll be sorry to lose him. But he can't stay crewing for me for the rest of his life,' Dan said comfortably. 'He can work for me at the weekends, though, and earn some pocket money.'

'At least he knows exactly what he wants to do with himself,' she said. 'Marine mechanics. I remember when he said he didn't fancy getting his hands dirty!'

'Ah, well, I put him right on that score,' Dan said. 'He can gut a marlin without pulling a face, too! The lad's come on well!'

They stopped next to the life-size statue of Just Nuisance.

'You know what they say about this statue, don't you?' Dan asked. 'You have to pat his nose for luck.'

The tip of the dog's nose gleamed brightly in the moonlight, but Maureen ran her hand over the smooth bronze coat instead and smiled.

'I don't need any more luck,' she said contentedly. 'Tomorrow I'll be Mrs Clayton. What more could I possibly ask for?'

He pulled her to him and they kissed.

'Next time I see you will be on top of the mountain,' he said softly. 'It wouldn't do for me to see you before the ceremony. George and I will go up half an hour earlier.'

'You've organised everything!' she said. 'Are you sure you haven't done this before?'

'Quite sure. But the only thing I can't organise is the weather,' he said ruefully. 'Getting married in a downpour isn't part of the plan.'

Surely it wouldn't be wet? The wide sky above was studded with brilliant stars and the nearly full moon bathed the whole cobbled square in light and was reflected on the calm water of the bay.

'It won't rain,' she said with certainty.

Special Occasion

Spring was notoriously unpredictable in Cape Town, but when the wedding party met on the mountain at the lower cable station the next morning, the sun was shining and, miraculously, there was almost no wind. Warren stepped forward from the group and greeted Maureen with an affectionate kiss.

'I'm glad we could be here,' he said. 'Rita and I both wish you all the best and lots of happiness. The kids seem pretty taken with Dan. I look forward to meeting him.'

'Thanks, Warren.' She smiled, pleased that it felt perfectly all right that Warren and Rita had come.

She looked around at everyone dressed in their wedding finery. Raj and Suraya Patel were splendid in colourful robes and Aunt Grace had brightened her grey silk with a corsage of red rosebuds provided by Dan for her and Patsy. Maureen was carrying a small bouquet of Blushing Bride proteas, delicate waxy pink blooms that Rugaya had picked from her own garden.

Tourists queuing for the ride smiled in delight at them, guessing it was a special occasion.

'Follow The Balloons!'

As the cable car rose swiftly into the air, Patsy and Jack stood at one of the open windows, gazing in wonder as the landscape below them widened as they rose higher and higher. The mottled carpet of the city was spread below them, flanked by the mountains of Lion's Head and Devil's Peak. Beyond, Robben Island nestled in a ring of blue sea.

'Look at those guys, Mum.' Jack pointed to some rock climbers scaling the sheer wall of rock just below the crest of the mountain. They looked like insects but waved vigorously as the cable car zoomed effortlessly past them. 'That's what I'd like to do one day.'

'Just don't tell me about it before you do or I'll worry myself sick,' Maureen replied. She was already worrying about where they'd find Dan and George. They'd made no arrangements and the top of the mountain looked bigger and bigger the closer they got.

All too soon the exhilarating ride was over, the door clanged open and they alighted at the upper cable station, where groups of tourists stood looking through the telescopes provided or took pictures of themselves against the weird rock formations. Jack wanted to stop and look at the view.

'Come on, silly, we'll have plenty of time for that afterwards.' Patsy pulled him back from the fenced-off edge. 'We need to find Dan. This is a wedding, remember?'

'Where to now, Mo?' Aunt Grace was arm in arm with Henry Morton, who had dressed for the occasion in a dark three-piece suit with a grey trilby and a gold tie pin in his club tie. No nonsense with smart casual for Mr Morton!

'Follow the balloons!' Jack said. 'Dan told me he'd mark the way.'

This man really had thought out every little detail!

They walked slowly along the path, small red balloons leading away from the buzz of the cable station, past veldt bushes bursting with yellow flowers. An aromatic smell wafted across on the breeze and high above, a pair of eagles circled and swooped in the wind. Maureen took a deep, pleasurable breath, wishing she could remember everything about this day for ever.

Dan and George were standing in the veldt a way off on the path, in a little hollow next to a big, brown sandstone rock. Someone, she suspected Dan, had placed an enormous bunch of dark pink proteas in a pot below. He turned and smiled when he saw the party approaching, giving her a little salute of relief.

'Come on, Mum.' Jack hooked her arm in his. 'My pleasure. Dan says it's my job to give you away.'

Perfect

She smiled up in surprise at her tall, handsome son, feeling suddenly choked and she hoped she wouldn't spoil everything by crying. The others walked forward and arranged themselves in a semi circle in front of the rock, and she and Jack picked their way carefully over small, blue wild flowers towards Dan and George.

Whoever would have imagined that I would marry again, to a man as wonderful as Dan — and in the veldt top of a mountain, she thought, wondering. And how lucky I am to be surrounded by everyone who is important in my life.

As George cleared his throat to begin the ceremony, she was sharply aware of the sound of the breeze rustling the bushes and small, invisible birds chirping nearby. She suddenly remembered a line she'd seen long ago in a poem: 'One is nearer God's heart in a garden than anywhere else on earth.'

Surely this mountain was God's own garden? Maureen took Dan's hand, warm against her own, marvelling at how absolutely right this moment felt.

He turned and looked at her, his eyes crinkling in a loving smile, and she knew this was the perfect place to marry the man she loved the most in all the world.

THE END

FALSE PRETENCES

Phyllis Humphrey

When Ginger Maddox, a San Francisco stock-broker, meets handsome Neil Cameron, she becomes attracted to him. But then mysterious things begin to happen, involving Neil's aunts. After a romantic weekend with Neil, Ginger overhears a telephone conversation confirming her growing suspicions that he's involved in illegal trading. She's devastated, fearing that this could end their relationship. But it's the elderly aunts who help show the young people that love will find a way.